# GRAVE SIGHT

Also by Charlaine Harris from Gollancz:

*Dead As A Doornail*

# GRAVE SIGHT

Charlaine Harris

The right of Charlaine Harris to be identified as the
author of this work has been asserted by her in accordance
with the Copyright, Designs and Patents Act 1988.

First published in Great Britain in 2007 by Gollancz
An imprint of the Orion Publishing Group
Orion House, 5 Upper St Martin's Lane, London WC2H 9EA
An Hachette Livre UK Company

This edition published in Great Britain in 2007 by Gollancz

13 15 17 19 20 18 16 14 12

A CIP catalogue record for this book is
available from the British Library

ISBN 978 0 57507 9 236

Printed and bound in the UK by
CPI Mackays, Chatham ME5 8TD

The Orion Publishing Group's policy is to use papers that
are natural, renewable and recyclable products and made
from wood grown in sustainable forests. The logging and
manufacturing processes are expected to conform to the
environmental regulations of the country of origin.

www.orionbooks.co.uk

# grave sight

THE silent witnesses lie everywhere, passing from one form of matter to another, gradually becoming unrecognizable to their nearest and dearest. Their bodies are rolled into gullies, shut in the trunks of abandoned cars, harnessed to cement blocks and thrown down to the bottom of lakes. Those more hastily discarded are tossed on the side of the highway—so that life, having swerved away, can swiftly pass them by without pausing to look.

Sometimes I dream I am an eagle. I soar above them, noting their remains, bearing testimony to their disposal. I spy the man who went hunting with his enemy—there, under that tree, in that thicket. I spot the bones of the waitress who served the wrong man—there, under the collapsed roof of an old shack. I detect the final destination of the teenage boy who drank too much in the wrong company—a shallow grave in the piney woods. Often, their spirits hover, clinging to the mortal remnants that housed them. Their spirits do not become angels. They were not believers during life, why should they be angels now? Even average people, people you think of as "good," can be foolish or venal or jealous.

My sister Cameron lies somewhere among them. In some drainage pipe or under some foundation folded into the rusted trunk of an abandoned car or strewn across a forest floor, Cameron molders. Perhaps her spirit is clinging to what is left of her body, as she waits to be discovered, as she waits for her story to be told.

Perhaps that's all they desire, all of the silent witnesses.

# One

~~~~~~

THE sheriff didn't want me there. That made me wonder who'd initiated the process of finding me and asking me to come to Sarne. It had to be one of the civilians standing awkwardly in his office—all of them well dressed and well fed, obviously people used to shedding authority all around them. I looked from one to the other. The sheriff, Harvey Branscom, had a lined, red face with a bisecting white mustache and close-cropped white hair. He was at least in his mid fifties, maybe older. Dressed in a tight khaki uniform, Branscom was sitting in the swivel chair behind the desk. He looked disgusted. The man standing to Branscom's right was younger by at least ten years, and darker, and much thinner, and his narrow face was clean-shaven. His name was Paul Edwards, and he was a lawyer.

The woman with whom he was arguing, a woman somewhat younger with expensively dyed blonde hair, was Sybil

Teague. She was a widow, and my brother's research had shown that she had inherited a great deal of the town of Sarne. Beside her was another man, Terence Vale, who had a round face scantily topped with thin no-color hair, wire-rimmed glasses, and one of those stick-on nametags. He'd come from a City Council open house, he'd said when he bustled in. His stick-on tag read, "Hi! I'm TERRY, the MAYOR."

Since Mayor Vale and Sheriff Branscom were so put out by my presence, I figured I'd been summoned by Edwards or Teague. I swiveled my gaze from one to the other. Teague, I decided. I crossed my legs and slumped down in the uncomfortable chair. I swung my free foot, watching the toe of my black leather loafer get closer and closer to the front of the sheriff's desk. They were shooting accusations back and forth, like I wasn't in the room. I wondered if Tolliver could hear them from the waiting room.

"You all want to hash this out while we go back to the hotel?" I asked, cutting through the arguments.

They all stopped and looked at me.

"I think we brought you here under the wrong impression," Branscom said. His voice sounded as though he were trying to be courteous, but his face looked like he wanted me the hell away. His hands were clenched on the top of his desk.

"And that wrong impression was . . . ?" I rubbed my eyes. I'd come directly from another site, and I was tired.

"Terry here misled us somewhat as to your credentials."

"Okay, you all decide, while I get me some sleep," I said, abruptly giving up. I pulled myself to my feet, feeling as old as the hills, or at least far older than my actual age of twenty-four. "There's another job waiting for me in Ashdown. I'd just as soon leave here early in the morning. You'll owe us travel money, at the least. We drove here from Tulsa. Ask my brother how much that'll be."

Without waiting for anyone to speak, I left Harvey Branscom's office and went down a corridor and through a door into the reception area. I ignored the dispatcher behind the desk, though she was looking at me curiously. No doubt she'd been aiming the same curiosity at Tolliver until I'd redirected her attention.

Tolliver tossed down the aged magazine he'd been riffling through. He pushed himself up from the fake-leather chair. Tolliver's twenty-seven. His mustache has a reddish cast; otherwise, his hair is as black as mine.

"Ready?" he asked. He could tell I was exasperated. He looked down at me, his eyebrows raised questioningly. Tolliver's at least four inches above my five foot seven. I shook my head, to tell him I'd fill him in later. He held open the glass door for me. We went out into the chilly night. I felt the cold in my bones. The seat on the Malibu was adjusted for my legs, since I'd driven last, so I slid back behind the wheel.

The police department was on one side of the town square, facing the courthouse, which stood in the center. The courthouse was a massive building erected during the twenties, the kind of edifice that would feature marble and high vaulted ceilings; impossible to heat or cool to modern standards, but impressive nonetheless. The grounds around the old building were beautifully kept, even now that all the foliage was dying back. There were still tourists parked in the premium town square parking spots. This time of year, Sarne's visitors were middle-aged to old white people, with rubber-soled shoes and windbreakers. They walked slowly and carefully, and curbs required negotiation. They tended to drive exactly the same way.

We had to navigate around the square twice before I could get in the correct lane to go east to the motel. I had a feeling that all roads in Sarne led to the square. The stores on the square and those immediately off of it were the dressed-up part of the town, the part primed for public consumption. Even the streetlights were picturesque—curving lines of metal painted a dull green and decorated with curlicues and leaves. The sidewalks were smooth and wheelchair accessible, and there were plenty of garbage bins carefully disguised to look like cute little houses. All the storefronts on the square had been remodeled to coordinate, and they all had wooden facades with "old-timey" signs in antique lettering: Aunt Hattie's Ice Cream Parlor, Jeb's Sit-a-Spell, Jn. Banks Dry Goods and General Store, Ozark Annie's Candy. There was a heavy wooden bench outside each one. Through the bright store windows, I caught a glimpse of one or two of the shopkeepers; they were all in costume, wearing turn-of-the-century clothing.

It was past five o'clock when we finally left the square. In late October, on an overcast day, the sky was almost completely dark.

Sarne was an ugly place once you left the tourist-oriented area centered around the courthouse. Businesses like Mountain Karl's Kountry Krafts gave way to more pedestrian necessities, like First National Bank and Reynolds Appliances. The further away I drove from the square on these side streets, the more frequently I noticed occasional empty storefronts, one or two with shattered windows. The traffic was nearly nonexistent. This was the private part of Sarne, for locals. Tourist season would be over, the mayor had told me, when the leaves fell; Sarne was about to roll up its carpets—and its hospitality—for the winter months.

I was irritated with our wasted time and mileage. But I hadn't given up hope yet, and when I felt the unmistakable pull at a four-way stop five blocks east of the square, I was almost happy. It came from my left, about six yards away.

"Recent?" Tolliver asked, seeing my head jerk. I always look, even if there's no way I'll see a thing with my physical eyes.

"Very." We weren't passing a cemetery, and I wasn't getting the feel of a newly embalmed corpse, which might indicate a funeral home. This impression was too fresh, the pull too strong.

They want to be found, you know.

Instead of going straight, which would've gotten us to the motel, I turned left, following the mental "scent." I pulled over into the parking lot of a small gas station. My head jerked again as I listened to the voice calling to me from the overgrown lot on the other side of the street. I say "scent" and "voice," but what draws me is not really something as clear-cut as those words indicate.

About three yards into the lot was the facade of a building. From what I could read of the scorched and dangling sign, this was the former site of Evercleen Laundromat. Judging by the state of the remains of the building, Evercleen had burned halfway to the ground some years before.

"In the ruin, over there," I told Tolliver.

"Want me to check?"

"Nah. I'll call Branscom when I get in the room." We gave each other brief smiles. There's nothing like a concrete example to establish my bona fides. Tolliver gave me an approving nod.

I put the car into drive again. This time we reached our motel and checked into our respective rooms with no interruption. We need a break from each other after being together all day; that's the reason for the separate rooms. I don't think either of us is excessively modest.

My room was like all the others I've slept in over the past few years. The bedspread was green and quilted and slick, and the picture above the bed was a bridge somewhere in Europe, looked like. Other than those little identifiers, I could have been in any cheap motel room, anywhere in America. At least it smelled clean. I pulled out my makeup-and-medicine bag and put it in the little bathroom. Then I went and sat on the bed, leaning over to peer at the dial-out instructions on the ancient telephone. After I'd looked up the right number in the little area phone book, I called the law enforcement building and asked for the sheriff. Branscom's voice came on in less than a minute, and he was clearly less than happy to talk to me a second time. He started in again on how I'd been misrepresented—as if I'd had anything to do with that—and I interrupted him.

"I thought you'd like to know that a dead man named something like Chess, or Chester, is in the burned laundromat on Florida Street, about five blocks off the square."

"What?" There was a long moment of silence while Harvey Branscom let that soak in. "Darryl Chesswood? He's at home in his daughter's house. They added on a room for him last year when he began to forget where he lived. How dare you say such a thing?" He sounded honestly, righteously, offended.

"That's what I do," I said, and laid the receiver gently on its cradle.

The town of Sarne had just gotten a freebie.

I lay back on the slippery green bedspread and crossed my hands over my ribs. I didn't need to be a psychic to predict what would happen now. The sheriff would call Chesswood's daughter. She would go to check on her dad, and she'd find he was gone. The sheriff would probably go to the site himself, since he'd be embarrassed to send a deputy on such an errand. He'd find Darryl Chesswood's body.

The old man had died of natural causes—a cerebral hemorrhage, I thought.

It was always refreshing to find someone who hadn't been murdered.

THE next morning, when Tolliver and I entered the coffee shop (Kountry Good Eats) that was conveniently by the motel, the whole group was there, ensconced in a little private room. The doors to the room were open, so they couldn't miss our entrance. The dirty plates on the table in front of them, the two empty chairs, and the pot of coffee all indicated we were anticipated. Tolliver nudged me, and we exchanged looks.

I was glad I'd already put on my makeup. Usually, I don't bother until I've had my coffee.

It would have been too coy to pick another table, so I led the way to the open doors of the meeting room, the newspaper I'd bought from a vending machine tucked under my arm. The cramped room was almost filled with a big round table. Sarne's movers and shakers sat around that table, staring at us. I tried to remember if I'd combed my hair that morning. Tolliver would've told me if I'd looked really bedheaded, I told myself. I keep my hair short. It has lots of body, and it's curly, so if I let it grow, I have a black bush to deal with. Tolliver is lucky; his is straight, and he lets it grow until he can tie it back. Then he'll get tired of it and whack it off. Right now, it was short.

"Sheriff," I said, nodding. "Mr. Edwards, Ms. Teague, Mr. Vale. How are you all this morning?" Tolliver held out my chair and I sat. This was an extra, for-show courtesy. He figures the more honor he shows me publicly, the more the public will feel I'm entitled to. Sometimes it works that way.

The waitress had filled my coffee cup and taken my first swallow before the sheriff spoke. I tore my gaze away from my paper, still folded by my plate. I really, really like to read the paper while I drink my coffee.

"He was there," Harvey Branscom said heavily. The man's face was ten years older than it'd been the night before, and there was white stubble on his cheeks.

"Mr. Chesswood, you mean." I ordered the fruit plate and some yogurt from a waitress who seemed to think that was a strange choice. Tolliver got French toast and bacon and a flirtatious look. He's hell on waitresses.

"Yeah," the sheriff said. "Mr. Chesswood. Darryl Chesswood. He was a good friend of my father's." He said this with a heavy emphasis, as if the fact that I'd told him where the old man's body was had laid the responsibility for the death at my door.

"Sorry for your loss," Tolliver said, as a matter of form. I nodded. After that, I let the silence expand. With a gesture, Tolliver offered to refill my coffee cup, but I raised my hand to show him how steady it was today. I took another deep sip gratefully, and I topped the cup off. I touched Tolliver's mug to ask if he was ready for more, but he shook his head.

Under the furtive scrutiny of all those eyes, I wasn't able to open the newspaper I had folded in front of me. I had to wait on these yahoos to make up their minds to something they'd already agreed to do. I'd felt optimistic when I'd seen them waiting for us, but that optimism was rapidly deteriorating.

A lot of eye signaling was going on among the Sarnites (Sarnians?). Paul Edwards leaned forward to deliver the result of all this conferencing. He was a handsome man, and he was used to being noticed.

"How did Mr. Chesswood die?" he asked, as if it were the bonus question.

"Cerebral hemorrhage." God, these people. I looked at my paper longingly.

Edwards leaned back as though I'd socked him in the mouth. They all did some more eye signaling. My fruit arrived—sliced cantaloupe that was hard and tasteless, canned pineapple, a banana in the peel, and some grapes. Well, after all, it was fall. When Tolliver had been served his eggs and toast, we began to eat.

"We're sorry there may have been some hesitation last night," Sybil Teague said. "Especially since it seems you, ah, interpreted it as us backing out on our agreement."

"Yes, I did take it that way. Tolliver?"

"I took it that way, too," he said solemnly. Tolliver has acne-scarred cheeks and dark eyes and a deep, resonant voice. Whatever he says sounds significant.

"I just got cold feet, I guess." She tried to look charmingly apologetic, but it didn't work for me. "When Terry told me what he'd heard about you, and Harvey agreed to contact you, we had no idea what we were getting into. Hiring someone like you is not something I've ever done before."

"There is no one like Harper," Tolliver said flatly. He was looking up from his plate, meeting their eyes.

He'd thrown Sylvia Teague off her stride. She had to pause and regroup. "I am sure you're right," she said insincerely. "Now, Miss Connelly, to get back to the job we're all hoping you'll do."

"First of all," Tolliver said, patting his mustache with his napkin, "Who's paying Harper?"

They stared at him as if that were a foreign concept.

"You all are obviously the town officials, though I'm not real sure what Mr. Edwards here does. Ms. Teague, are you paying Harper privately, or is she on the town payroll?"

"I'm paying Miss Connelly," Sybil Teague said. There was a lot more starch in her voice now that money had been mentioned. "Paul's here as my lawyer. Harvey's my brother." Evidently, Terry Vale wasn't her anything. "Now, let me tell you what I want you to do." Sybil met my eyes.

I glanced back at my plate while I took the grapes off the stem. "You want me to look for a missing person," I said flatly. "Like always." They like it better when you say "missing person" rather than the more accurate "missing corpse."

"Yes, but she was a wild girl. Maybe she ran away. We're not entirely sure . . . not all of us are sure . . . that she is actually dead."

As if I hadn't heard *that* before. "Then we have a problem."

"And that is?" She was getting impatient—not used to much discussion of her agenda, I figured.

"I only find dead people."

"THEY knew that," I told Tolliver in an undertone, as we walked back to our rooms. "They *knew* that. I don't find live people. I can't."

I was getting upset, and that was dumb.

"Sure, they know," he said calmly. "Maybe they just don't want to admit she's dead. People are funny like that. It's like—if they pretend there's hope, there *is* hope."

"It's a waste of my time—hope," I said.

"I know it is," Tolliver said. "They can't help it, though."

ROUND three.

Paul Edwards, Sybil Teague's attorney, had drawn the short straw. So here he was in my room. The others, I assumed, had scattered to step back into their daily routine.

Tolliver and I had gotten settled into the two chairs at the standard cheap-motel table. I had finally begun reading the paper. Tolliver was working on a science fiction sword-and-sorcery paperback he'd found discarded in the last motel. We glanced at each other when we heard the knock at the door.

"My money's on Edwards," I said.

"Branscom," Tolliver said.

I grinned at him from behind the lawyer's back as I shut the door.

"If you would agree, after all our discussion," the lawyer

said apologetically, "I've been asked to take you to the site."
I glanced at the clock. It was now nine o'clock. They'd taken
about forty-five minutes to arrive at a consensus.

"And this is the site of . . . ?" I let my words hang in
the air.

"The probable murder of Teenie—Monteen—Hopkins.
The murder, or maybe suicide, of Dell Teague, Sybil's son."

"Am I supposed to be finding one body, or two?" Two
would cost them more.

"We know where Dell is," Edwards said, startled. "He's
in the cemetery. You just need to find Teenie."

"Are we talking woods? What kind of terrain?" Tolliver
asked practically.

"Woods. Steep terrain, in places."

Knowing we were on our way to the Ozarks, we'd
brought the right gear. I changed to my hiking boots, put
on a bright blue padded jacket, and stuck a candy bar, a
compass, a small bottle of water, and a fully charged cell
phone in my pockets. Tolliver went through the connecting
door into his own room, and when he returned he was
togged out in a similar manner. Paul Edwards watched us
with a peculiar fascination. He was interested enough to forget how handsome he was, just for a few minutes.

"I guess you do this all the time," he said.

I tightened my bootlaces to the right degree of snugness.
I double-knotted them. I grabbed a pair of gloves. "Yep," I
said. "That's what I do." I tossed a bright red knitted scarf
around my neck. I'd tuck it in properly when I got really
cold. The scarf was not only warm, but highly visible. I
glanced in the mirror. Good enough.

"Don't you find it depressing?" Edwards asked, as if he

just couldn't help himself. There was a subtle warmth in his eyes that hadn't been there before. He'd remembered he was handsome, and that I was a young woman.

I almost said, "No, I find it lucrative." But I know people find my earning method distasteful, and that would have been only partly the truth, anyway.

"It's a service I can perform for the dead," I said finally, and that was equally true.

Edwards nodded, as if I'd said something profound. He wanted all three of us to go in his Outback, but we took our own car. We always did. (This practice dates from the time a client left us in the woods nineteen miles from town, upset at my failure to find his brother's body. I'd been pretty sure the body lay somewhere to the west of the area he'd had me target, but he didn't want to pay for a longer search. It wasn't my fault his brother had lived long enough to stagger toward the stream. Anyway, it had been a long, long walk back into town.)

I let my mind go blank as we followed Edwards northwest, farther into the Ozarks. The foliage was beautiful this time of year, and that beauty drew a fair amount of tourists. The twisting, climbing road was dotted with stands for selling rocks and crystals—"genuine Ozark crafts"—and all sorts of homemade jellies and jams. All the stands touted some version of the hillbilly theme, a marketing strategy that I found incomprehensible. "We were sure ignorant and toothless and picturesque! Stop to see if we still are!"

I stared into the woods as we drove, into their chilly and brilliant depths. All along the way, I got "hits" of varying intensity.

There are dead people everywhere, of course. The older the death, the less of a buzz I get.

It's hard to describe the feeling—but of course, that's what everyone wants to know, what it feels like to sense a dead person. It's a little like hearing a bee droning inside your head, or maybe the pop of a Geiger counter—a persistent and irregular noise, increasing in strength the closer I get to the body. There's something electric about it, too; I can feel this buzzing all through my body. I guess that's not too surprising.

We passed three cemeteries (one quite small, very old) and one hidden Indian burial site, a mound or barrow that had been reshaped by time until it just resembled another rolling hill. That ancient site signaled very faintly; it was like hearing a cloud of mosquitoes, very far away.

I was tuned in to the forest and the earth by the time Paul Edwards pulled to the shoulder of the road. The woods encroached so nearly that there was hardly room to park the vehicles and still leave room for other cars to pass. I figured Tolliver had to be worried someone would come along too fast and clip the Malibu. But he didn't say anything.

"Tell me what happened," I said to the dark-haired man.

"Can't you just go look? Why do you need to know?" He was suspicious.

"If I have a little knowledge about the circumstances, I can look for her more intelligently," I said.

"Okay. Well. Last spring, Teenie came out here with Mrs. Teague's son, who was also Sheriff Branscom's nephew—Sybil and Harvey are brother and sister. Sybil's son was named Dell. Dell was Teenie's boyfriend, had been for two years, off and on. They were both seventeen. A hunter found

Dell's body. He'd been shot, or he'd shot himself. They never found Teenie."

"How was their location discovered?" Tolliver asked, pointing at the patch of ground on which we stood.

"Car parked right where we're parked now. See that half-fallen pine? Supported by two other trees? Makes a good marker to remember the spot by. Dell'd been missing less than four hours when one of the families that live out this way gave Sybil a call about the car. There were folks out searching soon after that, but like I say, it was another few hours before Dell was found. Right after that, it started raining, and it rained for hours. Wiped out the tracking scent, so the bloodhounds weren't any use."

"Why wasn't anyone looking for Teenie?"

"No one knew Teenie was with Dell. Her mom didn't realize Teenie was missing for almost twenty hours, maybe longer. She didn't know about Dell, and she delayed calling the police."

"How long ago was this?"

"Maybe six months ago."

Hmm. Something fishy, here. "How come we're just being called out now?"

"Because half the town thinks that Teenie was killed and buried by Dell, and then he committed suicide. It's making Sybil crazy. Teenie's mom's hard up. Even if she thought of calling you in, she couldn't afford you. Sybil decided to fund this, after she heard about you through Terry, who went to some mayor's conference and talked to the head honcho of some little town in the Arklatex." I glanced over at Tolliver. "El Dorado," he murmured, and I nodded after a second, remembering. Paul Edwards said, "Sybil can't stand the shame of the suspicion. She liked Teenie, no matter how wild the girl was. Sybil really assumed she'd be part of their family some day."

"No Mister Teague?" I asked. "She's a widow, right?"

"Yes, Sybil's a fairly recent widow. She's got a daughter, too, Mary Nell, who's seventeen."

"So why were Teenie and Dell out here?"

He shrugged, with a half smile. "That's a question no one ever asked; I mean, hell, seventeen, in the woods in spring . . . I guess we all thought it was a little obvious."

"But they parked up by the road." That was what was obvious, but apparently not to Paul Edwards. "Kids wanting to have sex, they're going to hide their car better than that. Small town kids know how easy it is to be caught out."

Edwards looked surprised, his lean dark face shutting down on sudden and unwelcome thoughts. "Not much traffic out on this road," he said, but without much conviction.

I put on my dark glasses. Edwards again looked at me askance. It was an overcast day. I nodded to Tolliver.

"Lay on, Macduff," Tolliver said, to Paul Edwards's confusion. Edwards's high school must have done *Julius Caesar* instead of *Macbeth*. Tolliver gestured to the woods, and Edwards, looking relieved to understand his mission, began to lead us downhill.

It was steep going. Tolliver stayed by my side, as he always did; I was abstracted, and he knew I might fall. It had happened before.

After twenty minutes of careful, slow, downhill hiking, made even trickier by the slippery leaves and pine needles blanketing the steep slope, we came to a large fallen oak piled with leaves, branches, and other detritus. It was easy to see that a heavy rainfall would sweep debris downslope, to lodge against the tree.

"This is where Dell was found," Paul Edwards said. He pointed to the downslope side of the fallen oak. I wasn't surprised it had taken two days to find Dell Teague's body, even in the spring; but I was startled at the location of the corpse. I was glad I'd put on the dark glasses.

"On that side of the log?" I asked, pointing to make sure I had it right.

"Yes," Edwards said.

"And he had a gun? It was by his body?"

"Well, no."

"But the theory was that he'd shot himself?"

"Yeah, that's what the sheriff's office said."

"Obvious problem there."

"The sheriff thought maybe the gun could've been grabbed by a hunter who didn't report what he found. Or maybe one of the guys who actually did find Dell lifted the gun. After all, guns are expensive and almost everyone here uses firearms of some kind." Edwards shrugged. "Or, if Dell shot himself on the upslope side of the log and fell over it, the gun could have slid down the hill quite a distance, gotten hidden like that."

"So the wounds—how many were there?"

"Two. One, a graze to the side of his head, was counted as a . . . sort of a first try. Then, through the eye."

"So the two wounds were counted as suicide wounds, one unsuccessful and one not, and no gun was found. And he was on the downslope side of the log."

"Yes, ma'am." The lawyer took off his hat, slapped it against his leg.

This was all wrong. Well, maybe . . . "How was he lying? What position?"

"What, you want me to show you?"

"Yes. Did you see him?"

"Yes, ma'am, I sure did. I came out to identify him. Didn't want his mom to see him like that. Sybil and I have been friends for years."

"Then just humor me by assuming the position Dell was in, okay?"

Edwards looked as if he wished he were elsewhere. He knelt on the ground, reluctance in every line of his body. He was facing the fallen tree. Putting out a hand to steady himself, he sank down to the ground. His legs were bent at the knees and he was on his right side.

Tolliver moved behind me. "This ain't right," he whispered in my ear.

I nodded agreement. "Okay, thanks," I said out loud. Paul Edwards scrambled to his feet.

"I don't see why you needed to see where Dell was, anyway," he said, trying his best not to sound accusatory. "We're looking for Teenie."

"What's her last name?" Not that it mattered for search purposes, but I'd forgotten; and it showed respect, to know the name.

"Teenie Hopkins. Monteen Hopkins."

I was still upslope of the fallen tree, and I began making my way to the right. It felt appropriate, and it was as good a way to begin as any.

"You might as well go back up to your SUV," I heard Tolliver telling our reluctant escort.

"You might need help," Edwards said.

"We do, I'll come get you."

I didn't worry about us getting lost. Tolliver's job was to prevent that, and he'd never failed me; except for once, in the desert, and I'd teased him about that for so long that he'd about gone crazy. Of course, since we'd nearly died, it was a lesson worth reinforcing.

It was best if I could walk with my eyes closed, but on this terrain that would be dangerous. The dark glasses helped, blocking out some of the color and life around me.

For the first thirty minutes of struggling across the steep slope, all I felt were the faint *pings* of ancient deaths. The world is sure full of dead people.

When I was convinced that no matter how stealthily he might be able to move, Paul Edwards could not have followed us, I paused at a rocky outcrop and took off my dark glasses. I looked at Tolliver.

"Bullshit," he said.

"No kidding."

"The gun's missing, but it's suicide? Shot twice, and it's suicide? I could swallow one of those, but not both. And anyone who's going to kill himself, he's going to sit on the log and think about it. He's not going to stand downhill of a landmark like that. Suicides go *up*." We'd had experience.

"Besides," I said, "he fell on the hand that would've been holding the gun. If by some weird chance that should have happened, I feel pretty confident that no one would be reaching under the corpse to steal the gun."

"Only someone with a cast-iron stomach."

"And through the eye! Have you ever heard of anyone shooting himself like that?"

Tolliver shook his head.

"Someone done killed that boy," he said. Some days Tolliver is more country than others.

"Damn straight," I said.

We thought about that for a minute. "But we better keep on looking for the girl," I said. Tolliver would expect me to make up my own mind about that.

He nodded. "She's out here, too," he said, a little question in his voice.

"Most likely." I cocked my head to one side while I considered. "Unless the boy was killed trying to stop someone from taking her." We started walking again, and the ground became easier going; certainly not a flat surface, but not so steep.

There are worse ways to spend a fall day than walking through the woods while the leaves are brilliant, the sun dappling the ground from time to time when the clouds shifted. I felt out with all my senses. We tracked a *ping* that, upon attaining, proved too old by a decade to be the girl. When I was standing a foot from the site, I knew the body to be that of a black male who had died of exposure. He had become naturally buried under leaves, branches, and dirt that had washed downhill over the course of the past decade. What you could see was blackened ribs with tattered cloth and bits of muscle still clinging to the bones.

I took one of the red cloth strips I keep in my jacket pocket, and Tolliver took a whippy length of wire from a supply he kept stashed in a long pocket on his pants leg. I tied a strip to one end of the wire while Tolliver ran the other end into the ground. We'd walked maybe a quarter of a mile southwest from the fallen tree, and I jotted that down.

"Hunting accident," Tolliver suggested. I nodded. I can't always pin it down exactly, but the moment of death had that feel: panic, solitude. Long-suffering. I was certain he'd fallen out of his deer stand, breaking his back. He'd lain there until the elements claimed him. There were a few pieces of wood still nailed way up in the tree. Named Bright? Mark Bright? Something like that.

Well, he wasn't part of my paycheck. This man was my second freebie for the town of Sarne. Time to earn some money.

We started off again. I began working my way to the east, but I felt uneasy. After we'd proceeded maybe sixty feet from the hunter's bones, I got a welcome, sharp buzz from the north. Uphill, which was slightly odd. But then I realized that we had to go uphill to get to the road. The closer to the road I climbed, the closer I approached the remains of Teenie Hopkins—or some young white girl. The buzzing turned into a continuous drone, and I fell to my knees in the leaves. She was there. Not all of her, but enough. Some big branches had been thrown across her for concealment, but now they were dead and dry. Teenie Hopkins had spent a long, hot summer under those branches. But she still made more of a corpse than the hunter, despite insects, animals, and a few months of weather.

Tolliver knelt by me, one arm around me.

"Bad?" he asked. Though my eyes were closed, I could feel the movements of his body as his head turned, checking in all directions. Once we'd been surprised at the dumpsite by the killer returning with another body. Talk about your irony.

This was the hard part. This was the worst part. Normally, finding a corpse simply indicated I'd been successful. The manner of its becoming a corpse did not particularly affect me. This was my job. All people had to die somehow or other. But this rotting thing in the leaves . . . she'd been running, running, breath whistling in and out, reduced from a person to a panicked organism, and then the bullet had entered her back and then another one had . . .

I fainted.

TOLLIVER was holding me in his lap. We were among the leaves—oak and gum and sassafras and maple—a ruffle of gold and brown and red. He had his back to a big old gum tree, and I was sure he was uncomfortable with all the gumballs that must be pressing into his butt.

"Come on, baby, wake up," he was telling me, and from the sound of his voice, it wasn't the first time he'd said it.

"I'm awake," I said, hating how weak my voice came out.

"Jesus, Harper. Don't do that."

"Sorry."

I leaned my face against his chest for one more minute, sighed, and reasserted myself by scrambling to my feet. I wavered back and forth for a second until I got stabilized.

"What killed her?" he asked.

"Shot in the back, twice."

He waited to see if I'd add more.

"She was running," I explained. So he would understand her terror and her desperation, in the last moments of her life.

Last minutes are hardly ever that bad.

Of course, my standard is probably different from most people's.

PAUL Edwards was waiting by his gleaming silver Outback when we emerged from the woods. His whole face was a question, but our first report should be to our client. Tolliver asked the lawyer to start back to town to assemble the committee, if that was what Ms. Teague wanted. We drove silently back to Sarne, stopping only once at a convenience store. Tolliver went in to get me a Coke, one with real sugar in it. I always crave sugar after finding a body.

"You need to drink about four of these, gain some weight," Tolliver muttered, as he often did.

I ignored him, as I always did, and drank the Coke. I felt better after ten minutes. Until I'd discovered the sugar remedy, I'd sometimes had to go to bed for a day following a successful recovery.

The same group would be gathered in the sheriff's office, and I sat in the car and stared at the glass doors for a second, reluctant to begin this segment of the job.

"You want me to wait in the lobby?"

"No, I want you to come in with me," I said, and Tolliver nodded. I paused, one hand on the car door. "They're not gonna like this," I said.

He nodded again.

This time, we were in a conference room. It was a tight fit, with Branscom, Edwards, Teague, and Vale, plus Tolliver and me.

"The map," I said to Tolliver. He spread it out. I laid

everything I wanted to say out in a line ahead of me, so I could reach my goal, which was to get out of this office and this town with a check in my hands.

"Before we get into the main subject," I said, "let me point out that we also found the body of a black male, dead about ten years, at this site." I indicated the red mark we'd made first. "He died of exposure."

The sheriff seemed to be thinking back. "That might be Marcus Allbright," he said slowly. "I was a deputy back then. His wife thought he'd run off. My God. I'll go collect what's left."

I shrugged. Nothing to do with me. "Now, for Teenie Hopkins." They all tensed, and Paul Edwards even leaned closer. "She was shot twice in the back, and her remains are right here." I touched a spot with my fingertip.

There was an audible gasp from the people seated at the table.

"You saw her?" Hi, I'm TERRY, the MAYOR asked. His eyes were wide behind his wire-rimmed glasses. Mr. Mayor was on the verge of crying.

"Saw what's left," I said, and then reflected that a nod would have been sufficient.

"You mean," the Teague woman said incredulously, "you left her out there?" Harvey Branscom gave her a look of sheer amazement.

I stared back at her with much the same expression. "It's a crime scene," I said. "And I don't do body retrieval. I leave that to qualified people. You go get her, if you don't want the sheriff to investigate." Then I took a deep breath. This was the client. "Two shots in the back, so we still don't know how it happened. If your son was shot first, then Teenie was killed by the same person. Of course, if it was your son who shot her, he then killed himself afterward. But I doubt he committed suicide."

That shut her up, at least temporarily. I had the complete and utter attention of everyone in the room. "Oh my God," whispered Sybil.

"So how do you *know*?" the sheriff asked.

"How do I find bodies in the first place? I just do. When I find 'em, I know what killed 'em. Believe me, don't believe me. It's up to you, now. You wanted me to find Teenie Hopkins, I found what's left of her. There might be a bone or two missing. Animals."

Sybil Teague was staring at me with an extraordinary expression on her face. She didn't know whether to praise me or be disgusted by me. But at least I believed her son Dell had not committed suicide. She ran her hands over her golden-brown pants suit, over and over, smoothing the front of the light jacket, then the material over her thighs.

"Call Hollis," the sheriff said into his intercom, and we sat in frozen silence until a man in a deputy's uniform came in. He was in his late twenties, sturdy and blond and blue-eyed and curious as hell about what had been going on in the sheriff's office. He gave Tolliver and me a comprehensive stare. He'd know us again. He looked pretty good in the uniform.

"Ms. Connelly," the sheriff said. "You go out with Hollis here, show him where the body is."

Hollis looked startled as he took in the sense of what was more an order than a request.

"Which one?" I asked, and his eyes widened.

"I'll go," Tolliver said. "Harper needs to rest."

"No, Ms. Connelly is the one who found her, she needs to go."

Tolliver glared at the sheriff and he glared right back. I was betting the sheriff wanted to make sure I earned every penny of my fee. I made myself stir. "I'll go," I said. I put my hand on Tolliver's arm. "It'll be okay." My fingers curled around the material of his jacket, holding on to him for a long moment. Then I let go. I jerked my head at the blond deputy. "He'll bring me right back," I said over my shoulder, because I wanted Tolliver to stay there while I was gone. He nodded, and the door closed behind me, and I lost sight of him.

The deputy led the way out to his patrol car. "My name is Hollis Boxleitner," he said, by way of introduction.

"Harper Connelly," I said.

"That your husband in there?"

"My brother. Tolliver Lang."

"Different names."

"Yeah."

"Where we goin'?"

"Drive out Highway 19, going northwest."

"Out where—"

"The boy was shot," I said.

"Killed himself," Hollis Boxleitner corrected, but with little conviction.

"Hmmph," I said contemptuously.

"How do you find them?" he asked.

"The sheriff tell you I was coming?"

"I overheard him on the phone. He thought Sybil was crazy for asking you to come. He was mad at Terry Vale for telling her what he'd heard about you."

"I got struck by lightning," I said. "When I was about fifteen."

He seemed to be groping for questions to ask. "Were you at your house?"

"Yes," I said. "Me, and Tolliver, and my sister Cameron . . . we were at home alone. My two younger half-sisters were singing in some special program. My mother actually went to the pre-school to watch." The state my mother was in by that time, it was amazing she remembered she had children. "And the storm come up, about four in the afternoon. I was in the bathroom. The sink was next to the window, and the window was open. I was standing at the sink so I could look in the mirror while I used my electric hair curler. It came in the window. Next thing I knew, I was on the floor looking up at the ceiling, and my hair was smoking, and my shoes were off my feet. Tolliver gave me CPR. Then the ambulance came."

This was babbling, for me. I decided to shut up.

Hollis Boxleitner didn't seem to have any more questions, which was wonderful and puzzling. For most people, that would just have scratched the surface of what they wanted to know. I hugged my jacket to my chest, imagining how good it would be when I could get in the bed at the motel. I would pile on the covers. I would have hot soup for supper. I closed my eyes for a few minutes. When I opened them, I felt better. We were close to the site.

I instructed the deputy to pull over when I calculated, by the pull I felt, that we were at the bit of road closest to the body. Now that I knew where she was, the body was easier to locate on my mental map. We got out for the hike downhill, a much easier one than our earlier descent to the death site of the boy. As we moved carefully downslope, Boxleitner said, "So now you find dead people for your living."

"Yep," I said. "That's what I do." I also had very bad headaches, shaky hands, and a strange spiderweb pattern on my right leg, which was weaker than my left. Though I run regularly to keep the muscles strong, making my way up and down steep slopes today had made that leg feel wobbly. I leaned against a tree as I pointed to the pile of debris that concealed what was left of Teenie Hopkins.

After he looked under the branches, Boxleitner threw up. He seemed embarrassed by that, but I thought nothing of it. You have to see that kind of thing real often to be unimpressed by the havoc time and nature can wreck on our bodies. I had a feeling small town policemen didn't see old bodies very often. And he'd probably known the girl.

"It's worst when they're in-between," I offered.

He understood what I meant, and he nodded vehemently. I started back to the patrol car, leaving him alone to collect himself and do whatever official stuff he had to do.

I was leaning against the car door when Hollis Boxleitner struggled up the slope, wiping at his mouth with the back of his hand. To mark the spot, he tied an orange strip of plastic to the tree nearest the road and the car. He gestured toward the car door, indicating I should get in, and he drove back to the town in grim silence. "Teenie Hopkins was my sister-in-law," he said as we parked.

There wasn't anything for me to say.

I let him precede me into the police station. We had only been gone forty-five minutes or so, and the crew was still assembled. The tightness in Tolliver's jaw told me that they'd been grilling him about me—maybe about my success rate—and he'd had to do some explaining. He hated that.

All the faces turned toward us, questioning: the mayor's looked only curious, the lawyer's cautious, the sheriff's angry. Tolliver was relieved. Sybil Teague was tense and miserable.

"Body's there," Hollis said briefly.

"You're sure it's Teenie?" Mrs. Teague sounded . . . somewhere between stunned and grief-stricken.

"No, ma'am," Boxleitner said. "No, ma'am, I'm not sure at all. The dentist will be able to tell us. I'll give Dr. Kerry a call. That'll be good enough for an unofficial identification. We'll have to send the remains to Little Rock."

I was sure the body was Teenie Hopkins, of course, but Sybil Teague wouldn't thank me for saying so again. In fact, she was looking at me with some distaste. It was an attitude I'd run across many times before. She'd hired me, and she would pay me a very tidy sum of money, but she didn't want to believe me. She'd actually be happy if I was wrong. And I certainly wasn't her favorite person, though I'd brought her the information for which she'd asked . . . the information she'd gone to so much trouble to bring me to Sarne to deliver.

Maybe, when I'd first started out in my business, I was able to sympathize with this perverse attitude: but I couldn't any longer. It just made me feel tired.

# Two

NO one wanted to talk to us, or needed to talk to us, any longer. In fact, the very sight of me was giving Mayor Terry Vale a serious case of the cold creepies. He was the least connected to the case, and in fact I couldn't figure out his continued presence, but the others appeared to be worried about his peace of mind, so Tolliver and I took our leave.

A series of phone calls had revealed that Teenie's dentist, Dr. Kerry, was out of town for the next four days. The body could only be identified in Little Rock. Sheriff Branscom had called the state crime lab, and they'd said as soon as they got the body they'd confirm the identification first thing, before they did their full work-up. Since the Arkansas crime lab is notoriously behind, that was a good concession. Branscom had a copy of Teenie's dental records to send down with the body.

We wouldn't get a check from Sybil until the body was

declared to be that of Teenie Hopkins, so it looked like we'd be stuck in Sarne at least twenty-four hours. Twenty-four hours with nothing to do. We spend a lot of time waiting, but it's not easy.

"The motel's got HBO," Tolliver said. "Maybe we can catch a movie we haven't seen."

But after we'd reviewed the movie list and discovered we'd already seen the ones we were at all interested in seeing, Tolliver left to pursue the waitress from the diner. Not that he spelled it out for me, but I figured.

I was too restless to read, and I'd warmed up enough to discard the crawling-into-bed plan. I've gotten into doing my fingernails and toenails, just to have a hobby. So I got out my manicure kit, and I was painting my toenails a deep, almost golden red, when Hollis Boxleitner knocked on my door.

"Can I come in?" he asked. I leaned sideways to look past him, checking to make sure he wasn't in a police car. Nope. Though he was still in his uniform, he was driving his own vehicle, an electric-blue Ford pickup.

"I guess," I said. I left the door open to the beautiful day, and the big deputy didn't protest. Hollis Boxleitner sat in one of the two chairs. I took the other one, after offering him a can of Fresca that was chilly and wet from the ice chest. He popped the tab and took a gulp. I propped my foot up on the edge of the table and continued my pedicure.

"You want to go down to the restaurant, have some chicken-fried steak?" he asked.

"No thanks." It was a little past one o'clock, so I should eat something, but I wasn't feeling too hungry.

"Not the calories, is it? You could use some more flesh on your bones."

"No, not the calories." I stroked the brush very carefully from base to end of my big toenail.

"Your brother's already down there. He's having a conversation with Janine."

I shrugged.

"What about the Sonic?" I darted a glance at him, but he only looked mildly inquiring.

"What do you want?" I asked. I don't like being maneuvered.

He looked at me, put the can of soda down. "I just want to talk to you a little bit about Monteen Hopkins. My sister-in-law. The girl you think we found today."

"I don't need to know anything else about her." It was better not to. I knew enough. I knew about her last moments on earth. That was as personal as you could get. "And I guarantee," I added, since I have professional pride, "the body we found is Monteen Hopkins."

He looked at his empty hands, big hands with golden hair on the backs. "I was afraid you'd say that," he said, falling quiet for a minute. "Come on, let's get a milk shake. I was the one who threw up at the site, and even my stomach is saying it needs something. So I know yours has got to be ready."

I looked at him for a long moment, trying to figure him out. But he was a closed door to me, since he was among the living. Finally, I nodded.

My toenails weren't quite dry, so despite the autumn bite in the air, I stepped into his truck barefoot. He seemed to find that amusing. Hollis Boxleitner was a husky man with a crooked nose, a broad face, and a smile full of gleaming white teeth, though at the moment he was far from smiling. His pale blond hair was smooth as glass.

"You always lived here in Sarne?" I asked, after we'd parked at the Sonic and he'd pressed the button to order two chocolate shakes.

"For ten years," he said. "I moved here my last two years of high school, and I stayed. I had a couple years of community college, but I commuted to class after the first year."

"Been married? Was that how Teenie was your sister-in-law?"

"Yes."

I nodded acknowledgment. "Kids?"

"No."

Maybe he'd known the marriage wouldn't last.

"My wife was Monteen's older sister," he said. "My wife is dead."

That was a shocker. I sighed. While Hollis paid for the shakes, I reflected that I was going to learn about Teenie Hopkins, whether I wanted to or not.

"I met Monteen when she was thirteen. I picked her up from outside a juke joint way out in the county, while I was on patrol. It was so obvious she was underage and had no business being there. She made a pass at me in the police car. She was totally out of hand. I met Sally when I took Monteen home to her mom's house that night." He was silent for a moment, remembering. "I liked Sally a lot, the first time I laid eyes on her. She was a regular girl, with a lot of sweetness in her. Teenie was wild as a razorback."

"So the Teagues couldn't have been that happy about their son dating her."

"You could say that. Teenie got it from her mom. At that time, Helen was drinking a lot, and not too particular about who she brought home. But Helen managed to change, finally quit drinking. When Teenie's mom settled down, Teenie did, too."

That wasn't how Sybil had tried to make it appear, at our second meeting. I filed that fact for future reference.

"How do you get hired?" he asked.

I sucked hard on the straw, thinking over the abrupt change in subject. It was a good milk shake, but it had been a mistake to get a cold drink on a brisk day when I was barefoot. I shivered.

"Lots of word of mouth. That's how I got hired here; Terry Vale heard something about me at a city government conference. Law enforcement people talk to each other, at conventions and by email. And there've been stories in a professional magazine or two."

He nodded. "I guess you couldn't advertise."

"Sometimes, we do. Hard to get the wording right."

"I can see that." He smiled reluctantly. Then he reverted to just being intense. "You just . . . feel them?"

I nodded. "I see the last moments. Like a tiny clip of a video. Can you please turn on the heater?"

"Yes, we'll ride." A minute later, we'd left Sonic and were cruising what there was of Sarne.

"How big is the police force here?" I was trying to be polite. There was an undercurrent here, and the water in it was moving faster and faster.

"Full-time, besides me? The sheriff, two other deputies right now."

"Stretched pretty thin."

"Not during this season. Now, we've just got leaf people. Come to see the colors change. They're pretty peaceable." Hollis shook his head over people taking time off from life to look at a bunch of leaves. "Summer tourist season, we take on six part-time people. Traffic control and so on."

Hollis Boxleitner's income would be small. He was a youngish man, and he seemed both capable and intelligent. What was he doing, stuck in Sarne? Okay, not my business: but I was curious.

"I inherited my parents' house here," he said, as if he were answering my unspoken question. "They got killed when a logging truck hit their car." He nodded in acknowledgment when I told him I was sorry. He didn't want to talk about their deaths, and that was a good thing. "I like the hunting and the fishing, and the people. In the summer, I get some hours in helping my brother-in-law; he's got a rafting business, rents 'em out to the tourists. I pretty much work around the clock for three months, but it helps me build up my bank account. What does your brother do, when he's not helping you?"

"He's always with me."

Hollis looked as if he were politely swallowing scorn. "That's all he does?"

"It's enough." The thought of managing by myself made me shiver.

"So, how much do you charge for your services?" he asked, his eyes on the road ahead of him.

I hoped there wasn't an implication there. I kept silent.

It took a while to make Hollis uncomfortable, longer than it took for most people.

"I want to hire you," he said, by way of explanation.

I hadn't expected that. "I charge five thousand dollars," I told him. "Payable on a positive identification of the body."

"What if the location of the body is known? You can tell the cause of death, too, right?"

"Yes. Of course I charge less if I don't have to find the body." Sometimes the family wants an independent suggestion about the cause of death.

"You ever been wrong?"

"Not that I know of." I looked out the window at the passing town. "When I can locate the body, that is. I don't always find it. Sometimes, there's just not enough information available to tell me where to search. Like the Morgenstern girl." I was referring to a case that had made headlines the year before. Tabitha Morgenstern had been grabbed off a suburban road in Nashville, and she'd never been seen since that day. "Just knowing the point where someone vanished isn't enough. She might have been dumped anywhere, in Tennessee or Mississippi or Kentucky. Not enough information. I had to tell her parents I couldn't do it."

Though the cemetery wasn't yet visible, I knew we were approaching one. I could tell by the buzzing along my skin. "How old is the cemetery?" I asked. "It's the newest one, I guess?"

He pulled over to the side of the road so abruptly I almost lost my grip on my milk shake. He glared at me, his face flushed. I'd spooked him.

"How the hell—did you and your brother drive by here earlier?"

"Nope." We were pretty far off any streets that tourists or casual visitors would take, a bit out in the countryside and away from any tourist amenities. "Just what I do."

"It's the new cemetery," Hollis said, his voice jerky. "The old one's . . ."

I turned my head from side to side, estimating. "Southwest of here. About four miles."

"Jesus, woman, you're creepy."

I shrugged. It didn't seem creepy to me.

He said, "I can give you three thousand. Will you do something for me?"

"Yes, I'll do it. Since we haven't run a credit check on you, I need the money in advance."

"You're businesslike." His tone was not admiring.

"No, I'm not. That's why Tolliver usually does this part." I finished my milk shake, making a loud slurping noise.

Hollis did a U-turn to head back to town. He went through the drive-through at the bank. The teller did her best not to act surprised when he sent his withdrawal slip over to her, and she also tried not to peer too obviously at me. I wanted to tell Hollis that if I were performing any other service, he wouldn't be sitting there all huffy; if I cleaned houses, he wouldn't be asking me to go clean his for free, right? My lips parted, but I clamped them shut. I refused to justify myself.

He thrust the money, still in its bank envelope, into my hand. I slid the envelope into my jacket pocket without comment. We drove back to the turn-off that led to the cemetery. We were parked on a gravel path winding among the tombstones, when he turned off the engine. "Come on," he said. "The grave is over here." The day had cleared up, turned bright, and I watched big sycamore leaves turn cart-wheels in the wind across the dying grass.

"Embalming mutes the effect," I warned him.

His eyes lit up. He was thinking I'd faked my results before, somehow, and that now he'd unmask me. And he'd get his money back. He had about a ton of ambiguity resting on his shoulders.

I stepped gingerly onto the nearest grave, the ground chilly under my bare feet. Since a cemetery is so full of death, I have difficulty getting a clear reading. When you add the competing emanations from the corpses to the effects of the embalming process, you have to get as close as you can. "Middle-aged white man, died of . . . a massive coronary," I said, my eyes closed. The name was Matthews, something like that.

There was a silence while Hollis read the headstone. Then Hollis growled, "Yes." He caught his breath jaggedly. "We're going to walk now. Keep your eyes shut." I felt his big hand take mine, lead me carefully to another patch of ground. I reached down deep with that inner sense that had never yet failed me. "Very old man." I shook my head. "I think he just ran down." I was led to yet another grave, this one farther away. "Woman, sixties, car accident. Named Turner, Turnage? A drunk, I think."

We went back in our original direction, and I knew by the tension in his body that this was the grave he'd been aiming for all along. When he guided me onto the grave, I knelt. This was death by violence, I knew at once. I took a deep breath and reached below me. "Oh," I said sharply. I realized dimly that because Hollis was thinking of this dead person so strongly, it was helping me to reach her. I could hear the water running in the bathtub. House was hot, window was open. Breeze coming in the high frosted window of the bathroom. Suddenly . . . "Let go!" she said, but it was as if I were the woman, and I was saying it, too. And then her/my head was under water, and we were looking up at the stippled ceiling, and we couldn't breathe, and we drowned.

"Someone had ahold of her ankles," I said, and I was all by myself in my skin, and I was alive. "Someone pulled her under."

After a long moment, I opened my eyes, looked down at the headstone in front of me. *Sally Boxleitner,* it read. *Beloved Wife of Hollis.*

"CORONER always said he couldn't figure it out. I sent her for an autopsy," the deputy said. "The results were inconclusive. She might have fainted and slipped under the water, fallen asleep in the tub or something. I couldn't understand why she couldn't save herself. But there wasn't any evidence either way."

I just watched him. Grieving people can be unpredictable.

"Vagal shock," I murmured. "Or maybe it's called vagal inhibition. People can't even struggle, if it's sudden."

"You've seen this before?" There were tears in his eyes, angry tears.

"I've seen everything."

"Someone murdered her."

"Yes."

"You can't see who."

"No. I don't see who. I see how, when I find the body. I

know it's not you. If you were the murderer, and you were right by your victim, I might be able to tell." Which I hadn't intended to say: this was exactly why I really needed Tolliver to speak for me. I began to miss him, which was ridiculous. "Can you take me back to the motel, please?"

He nodded, still lost in his own thoughts. We began to make our way between the headstones. The sun was still shining and the leaves were still fluttering across the browning lawn, but the spark had gone out of the day. I was trembling with a fine small movement as my bare feet moved through the short cool grass. On the way back to Hollis's electric-blue truck, I paused to read the name on the largest monument in the cemetery. There were at least eight graves in the plot marked *Teague*.

Good. I carefully stepped onto the one marked Dell. He was there, buried not too deeply in the rocky soil of the Ozarks. I spared a second to think that I was lucky that connecting with the embalmed dead was never as dramatic as connecting with a corpse; Hollis would never have thought to provide me with the support Tolliver did. I reached down again with that extra sense of mine, trying not to assume what I'd find when my lightning-sparked gift touched the body of Dell Teague.

*Suicide, my ass,* was my instant, and silent, reaction. Why hadn't Sybil hired me to come out here to read his grave first, instead of sending me to the woods to find Teenie? Of course this boy hadn't shot himself. Dell Teague had been murdered, just like his wild girlfriend. I opened my eyes. Hollis Boxleitner had swung around to check on what I was doing. I looked into the intent face of the deputy. "No suicide here," I said.

In the long pause that followed, I looked off to the west and saw a bank of dark clouds approaching in a hurry. The break in the weather was over. Hollis looked, too. I saw a shaft of brightness split through the distant clouds.

"Come on," Hollis said. "You just carry hard luck around with you." He shook his head.

We climbed into the truck. On the way back into Sarne, neither of us broke the silence. While he was looking at the road, I slipped his money out of my pocket and put it on the seat between us. At the motel, I scrambled out of the truck real quick, slamming the truck door behind me and unlocking my room almost in one motion. Hollis drove away without a word. I guess he had a lot to think about.

I put my ear to the wall and heard a buzz. Tolliver was home. He must have had the television on. But I waited a minute, since I'd made similar assumptions before and paid for them with my own embarrassment. It was a good thing I hesitated, because after a second I realized that Tolliver had company. I was willing to bet it was Janine, the waitress from the diner. Evidence suggested that Tolliver was much more appealing to women than I was to men. Sometimes that pissed me off. I didn't think the difference was in our looks, exactly; I thought it lay in our baggage. I sighed, feeling like sticking out my tongue or kicking the wall—something childish.

I'd imagined for a few minutes that Hollis Boxleitner was really attracted to me, but what he had wanted was what I had to offer professionally, not personally.

And there was a storm coming on.

I picked up my novel and tried to read. The darkness was thickening outside, and within ten minutes I had to turn on a lamp. From not too far off, there was a deep rumble. Thunder.

I made myself read a couple of sentences. I really, really wanted to lose awareness of the here and now. The best way for me to do that was bury myself in a book.

We keep a box of secondhand paperbacks in the backseat of the car. When each book has been read, we leave it where someone else can pick it up. If the book's in very good shape we keep it to trade. We stop at every secondhand bookstore we see to restock. I've read a lot of things I hadn't planned on reading, due to the selection at these stores. And I've read a lot of books years after they were bestsellers, which doesn't bother me a bit.

Tolliver's not quite as omnivorous as I am. He draws the line at romances (he thinks they're too predictable) and spy novels (he finds them ludicrous), but he'll read just about anything else. Westerns, mysteries, science fiction, even some non-fiction—almost any book is grist for our mill. Right now I was reading a tattered copy of Richard Preston's *The Hot Zone*. It was one of the most frightening things I'd ever read—but I'd rather be afraid of Preston's account of the origin and spread of the Ebola virus than think about the rumble of the thunder.

Before I tried to re-immerse myself in Preston's exploration of a cave in Africa, I glanced at the clock. I estimated that the waitress would leave the room next door in about an hour. Maybe by the time the storm got here, Tolliver would be alone.

With the book weighted open in front of me on the cheap table, I turned on my cordless curler and used it. Then I brushed my hair. From time to time I glanced up at the mirror. I looked okay, I thought. Not too bad. Frail and pale, though.

My brother and I didn't look anything alike, aside from the similarity in our coloring—black hair, brown eyes. Tolliver looked tough, secretive, a little forbidding. His scarred cheeks and wide, bony shoulders made him seem very male.

But it was me who frightened people.

Thunder rumbled again, much closer. Not even the Ebola virus could hold my attention now. I tried to distract myself. The sheriff would have gotten Teenie Hopkins' body out of the woods by now, and it would be on its way to Little Rock. I bet he was glad he'd gotten her out before the rain. It couldn't have taken long, since there wouldn't exactly be a crime scene to secure. Of course, even the most lax police officer would search the area. I wondered if Hollis had been part of the search. I wondered if they'd found anything. I should have asked Hollis questions while I was in his truck. Maybe he was out in the woods, right at this moment.

But what difference did it make, really? I would be gone before anyone was brought to justice. I tapped my fingernails against the table in an anxious rhythm, my feet patting along to an inaudible beat. I switched off the lamp and the light in the bathroom.

I was going to conquer this. This time, it would not get the best of me.

A boom of thunder was followed by a brilliant bolt of lightning. I jumped about a foot. Though the curler was cordless, I turned it off. I unplugged the television and went to sit on the foot of my bed, on the shiny, green, slick motel bedspread. More thunder, and another crack of lightning outside the window. I shivered, my arms crossed over my abdomen. The rain pounded down outside the motel room, drumming on the roof of our car, splashing violently against the pavement. Another lightning bolt. I made a little noise, involuntarily.

The door between the rooms opened and Tolliver came in, a towel wrapped around his waist, his hair still wet from the shower. I saw a flicker of movement in his room; the waitress, pulling on her clothes, her face angry.

He sat on the end of the bed by me, his arm around my shoulders. He didn't say a word. Neither did I. I shivered and shook until the lightning was past.

# Three

SARNE seemed like a complicated little town. I would be glad when we left it. We were supposed to show up in Ashdown within the next couple of days, and I wanted to keep the appointment. I try to be as professional as my odd calling will permit.

There were times we sat in our apartment in St. Louis for two weeks at a stretch. Then the phone would ring steadily, one call right after another. With my work schedule so unpredictable, we had to be ready to get on the road at any time. The dead could wait forever, but the living were always urgent.

The sheriff called me the next morning right before seven. Normally, I would've been out for a run, but the day after I both find a body and get through a storm is going to be a slow day. I peered at the clock before I lifted the receiver. "The body's Teenie, the lab in Little Rock said," he told me. He sounded tired, though it was early and he should just have risen from a night's sleep. "Go pick up your check at Paul Edwards's office." He hung up. He didn't say, "And never come here again," but the words were hanging in the air.

Tolliver had just come in, dressed and ready for breakfast, his favorite meal. He looked at my face as I hung up the room phone.

"Blaming the messenger," he said. "I guess it was a positive ID?"

I nodded. "I never understand that. You know, they ask me here to find the body. I find the body. Then they're pissed at me, and they give me the check like I should have done the whole thing for free."

He shrugged. "I guess we would do it for free if we could get a government grant or something."

"Oh, sure, the government just loves me." Paying taxes was excruciating—not because I minded giving the devil his due, but because accounting for my income was very difficult. I called myself a consultant. So far, I'd flown under the radar, but that would change sooner or later.

Tolliver grinned while I pulled on a T-shirt and a sweater. Since I'd planned today as a traveling day, I was wearing jeans. I don't care much about clothes, except my blue jeans. I'm particular about them. This was my favorite pair, and they were worn thin in spots.

"We'll stop by Edwards's office and get the check on our way out of town."

"We better cash it quick," I said, speaking from bitter experience.

The motel phone rang again. We looked at each other. I picked it up.

"Miss Connelly," said a woman. "Harper Connelly?"

"Yes?"

"This is Helen Hopkins. I'm Sally and Teenie's momma. Can you come talk to me?" Hollis's mother-in-law: Had he told her what I'd found at the cemetery?

I closed my eyes. I *so* didn't want to do this. But this woman was the mother of two murdered women. "Yes ma'am, I guess so."

She gave me her address and asked if I could come in a half hour. I told her it'd be an hour, but we'd be there.


IT actually took us a bit over an hour, because after we'd checked out of the motel and loaded our bags and gone into the restaurant, Janine, the waitress Tolliver had entertained the afternoon before, dragged her feet serving us. She'd glare at me, try to touch him—a performance both obvious and painful. Did she think I was forcing my brother to stay with me, dragging Tolliver all around the United States in my wake? Did she imagine that if I relaxed my grip on him, he'd stay here in Sarne and get a job at the grocery store, make her an honest woman?

Sometimes I teased him about his conquests, but this wasn't one of those times. His cheeks were flushed when we left, and he didn't say a word as we drove to Paul Edwards's downtown office. It was housed in an old home right off the town square, a home which had been painted in lime green and light blue, a whimsical combination I'm sure the original builders would have deplored. Paul Edwards was fitting into the image Sarne was trying to sell the tourists, that of a fun-house antique town with something interesting around every corner.

Tolliver said, "I'll wait in the car."

I'd assumed the lawyer would have left the check in an envelope at the reception desk, but Edwards himself came out when I told his secretary my name. He shook my hand while the parched and dyed blonde watched his every move with fascination. I could see why. Paul Edwards was a man with charm.

He ushered me back into his office.

"What can I do for you?" I asked reluctantly. I was ready to go. I sat in the leather visitor's chair, while he leaned against the edge of his huge desk.

"You're a remarkable woman," he said, shaking his head at the phenomenon of my remarkableness. I didn't know whether to laugh sardonically or blush. In the end, I raised an eyebrow, remained silent, and waited for his next move.

"In one day, you've made a tremendous difference in the lives of two of my clients."

"How would that be?"

"Helen Hopkins is grateful that her Teenie's body has been found. Now she can have closure. And Sybil Teague is so relieved that poor Dell won't be the victim of these foolish and false accusations people have been making since Teenie's disappearance."

I digested this silently, wondering what he really wanted to say to me.

"If you're going to be in Sarne for a while, I was hoping for the chance to take you out to dinner and find out more about you," Paul Edwards said. I looked at his good suit and white shirt, his gleaming shoes. His hair was groomed and well-cut, his shave had been close, and his brown eyes were glowing with sincerity.

"As a matter of fact," I said slowly, "my brother and I are leaving Sarne in an hour or so. We're just dropping by Helen Hopkins' place first, at her request. Then we're outta here."

"Oh, that's too bad," he said. "I've missed my opportunity. Maybe someday if you have business close to here, you'll give me a call?" He tucked a business card into my hand.

"Thanks," I said noncommittally, and after some more hand clasping and eye-to-eye contact, I got out the front door with the check in my hand.

I tried to tell Tolliver about the odd interview I'd just had, but I guess he was miffed at the long wait he'd had outside the lawyer's office. In fact, Tolliver was mighty quiet while he searched for the Hopkins house, which turned out to be a humble box-like building on a humble street.

Hollis Boxleitner had said some pretty bad things about his wife's mother's past, and I had formed a negative picture of Helen Hopkins. When she answered the door I was surprised to see a tidy, thin woman with wispy brown hair and popping blue eyes. She had once been pretty, in a waif-like way. Now she seemed more like a dried shell. She was wearing a flowered T-shirt and khakis, and her face was about as wide as my thin hand.

"I'm Harper Connelly," I said. "This here's my brother, Tolliver Lang."

"Helen Hopkins. God bless you for coming to meet me,"

she said rapidly. "Please come in and sit down." She gestured around the tiny living room. It was jammed with furniture and so cluttered that it took me a moment to realize the room was nonetheless extremely clean. There was a shelf mounted on the wall, full of a display of Avon carnival glass. A huge Bible was centered on the cheap coffee table. Flanking it were two starched crocheted doilies, and in the exact center of each one was a glass candlestick holding a white candle.

I knew a shrine when I saw one.

And the pictures; two brunette girls were duplicated over and over around the room. There was an age progression beginning on the north wall. Sally and Teenie were born, went to grade school, trick-or-treated, danced, graduated from grade school and junior high, went to proms, and in Sally's case, got married. This room was a panorama of the lives of two girls, both of them murdered. The last picture in the progression was a bleak shot of a white casket covered with a pall of carnations resting on a bier at the front of a church. This final picture, surely taken at Sally's funeral, had a bare spot next to it; this would be where the picture of Teenie's casket would hang. I swallowed hard.

"I been sober now for thirty-two months," Helen Hopkins said, gesturing to us to take the two armchairs squeezed together opposite the sofa, where she perched on the edge of a cushion.

"Congratulations, I'm glad to hear it," I said.

"If you've been in this town for more than ten minutes, someone will have told you something bad about me. I drank and fornicated for many years. But I'm sober now, by the grace of God and some damn hard work."

Tolliver nodded, to show we were registering her words.

"Both my girls are dead," Helen Hopkins continued. Her voice was absolutely steady and harsh, but the muscles in her jaw were taut with agony. "I ain't had a husband in years. No one here to help me but me, myself, and I. I want to know who brought you here, and what you are, and what you done out in the woods to find my girl. I didn't know anything about this till yesterday, when Hollis called me."

You couldn't get more straightforward than that. Tolliver and I looked at each other, asking a silent question. This woman was a lot like our mother—well, my mother, Tolliver's stepmother—except my mother had gone to law school, and she'd never gotten sober. Tolliver gave a shrug that couldn't have been seen by anyone but me, and I returned an infinitesimal nod.

"I find bodies, Mrs. Hopkins. I got hit by lightning when I was a girl, and that's what happened to me afterward. I found out I just knew when I came close to a dead person. And I knew what had killed that person—though not who, if the person was murdered." I wanted to be real clear about that. "What I know is how the person died."

"Sybil Teague hired you?"

"Yes."

"How'd she know about you?"

"I believe through Terry Vale."

"Are you always right?"

"Yes, ma'am."

"You think the Lord likes what you're doing?"

"I wonder about it all the time," I said.

"So, Sybil asked you to come here and find Monteen. She say why?"

"The sheriff told me that everyone was thinking her son had killed Teenie, and she wanted to find Teenie's body to disprove that."

"And you found Teenie."

"Yes, that's what Sheriff Branscom told me. I'm sorry for your loss."

"I knew she was dead," Helen said, eyes dry. "I been knowing since she vanished, that Teenie had passed over."

"How?" If she could be blunt, I could, too.

"She would've come home, otherwise."

According to Hollis, Teenie had been as out of control as her mother at one time. I doubted Helen Hopkins was speaking realistically. Her next words echoed my doubts so closely that I wondered if the woman was psychic.

"She'd been a wild girl," Helen Hopkins said slowly, "acting out because she could get away with it, because I was a drunk. But when I sobered up, she began to come around, too."

She gave me a wisp of a smile, and I tried to smile back. This dried-out husk of a woman had once had a jaunty charm not too many years ago. You could see the traces of it in her face and posture.

"I liked Dell Teague just fine," Helen said. Her voice was slow, as if she was thinking out what she was saying very carefully. "I didn't ever think that he'd killed my girl. I liked him, and I think Sybil's okay. But the kids wanted to get married, and I didn't want Teenie to marry early, the way Sally did. Not that Sally made a bad marriage. Hollis is a fine man, and I don't blame him for not caring for me none. He had enough reasons. But Teenie . . . she didn't need to be getting so tight with Dell Teague, so young. I just wanted Teenie to have some choices. It was good of Sybil to pay you to look for my girl, though. . . ."

"Hollis tell you we went out to the cemetery?" I was trying to make sense of this flow of thoughts.

"Yes. He come by yesterday, the first time I've talked to him in a long time. He told me that you said Sally had been killed, that it wasn't no accident." I saw Tolliver stiffen. He shot me a look. He didn't like me going off with someone, he didn't like me doing freebies, and he didn't like me not telling him everything.

"How do you do it?" she asked. "How can you tell? How can I trust you?"

These were all good questions, questions I'd been asked before.

"You don't have to believe a thing I say," I told Helen Hopkins. "I see what I see."

"You think God gave you this gift? Or the devil?"

I wasn't about to tell this woman what I really thought. "You believe what you want," I said.

"I believe that you saw both my daughters get murdered," Helen Hopkins said. Her huge brown eyes seemed to get even bigger and rounder. "I believe God sent you to find out who did this to them."

"No," I said immediately. "I am not a lie detector. I can find bodies. I can tell what killed 'em. But who, or why, that's beyond me."

"How did they die?"

"You don't want to hear this," Tolliver said.

"Shut up, mister. This is my right."

She was little, but persistent. *Like a mosquito,* I thought.

"Your daughter Sally was drowned in her bathtub. She

was grabbed by the ankles, so that her head went under the water. Your daughter Teenie was shot in the back."

All the strength seeped out of Helen Hopkins as we watched.

"My poor girls," she said. "My poor girls."

She looked over at us, without really seeing us. "I thank you for coming," she said stiffly. "I thank you. I'm in your debt. I'll tell the girls' fathers what you've said."

Tolliver and I got up. Helen didn't speak again.

"Now we leave," Tolliver said, when we were outside. And after we stopped by the bank to cash Sybil Teague's check, we got in our car and drove south out of Sarne.

We pulled into our motel in Ashdown a few silent hours later. Tolliver sat in the chair in my room after we'd eaten supper, and I perched on the foot of the bed.

"Tell me about going out with the trooper," he said. His voice was mild, but I knew that was deceptive. I'd been waiting for that shoe to drop all day.

"He came by while you were gone flirting with that waitress," I said. "He wanted me to take a ride with him." Tolliver snorted, but I decided to ignore that. "Anyway, he talked, and he talked, and we got a milk shake, and then I realized that he just wanted to take me out to the cemetery and get me to tell him what happened to his wife."

I could hardly bear to look at Tolliver's face, but I sneaked a peek. To my relief, he wasn't full of anger. He hated it when people took advantage of me, and he hated it more when the person was a man. But he didn't want me to feel bad, either.

"Don't you think he liked what he saw, and that's why he came by the motel?"

I ducked my head. Tolliver's hand smoothed my hair.

"No," I said. "I think all along he planned on getting me there to his wife's grave. I told him I had to be paid, Tolliver. So he took me by the bank and got the money." I didn't tell Tolliver it hadn't been the full amount. "But I left it in the truck, because I felt so bad about the whole thing." Bad and mad and guilty and hurt.

"You did the right thing," he said, at last. "Next time, don't go anywhere without telling me, okay?"

"You going to follow me?" I asked, feeling a little spark of anger. "What should I do when *you* go off without *me*? Make the woman promise to bring you back by ten? Take her picture so I can track her down when you're late?"

Tolliver counted to ten. I could tell by the tiny movements of his head. "No," he said. "But I worry about you. You're a strong woman, but a strong woman still isn't as strong as most men." This was one of those simple biological truths that made me wonder what God had been thinking. "If he hadn't taken you to the cemetery, he could have taken you anywhere else. I would have been looking for you, like we track other people."

"If anyone in this world is aware that she might be killed at any moment, Tolliver Lang, that person is me." I pointed at my own chest, my finger rigid. "Amazingly, every day millions of women go out with men who have no ulterior motive whatsoever. Amazingly, almost all of them come home perfectly all right!"

"I don't care about them. I care about you. How you could ever trust anyone when what we see, so many times a year, is murder. . . ."

"And yet, you have no problem inviting a woman you just met into your room!"

He threw up his hands. "Okay, forget it! Forget I said anything! All I want is to know where you are, and for you to be safe!" He stomped out of my room into his, which required going outside; no connecting doors in this cut-rate motel.

I heard the television come on in the next room. What had we been quarrelling about? Did Tolliver really want me to sit in my room while he had fun? Did he really want me to turn down every invitation that came my way, in the name of safety?

I was pretty sure the answer, if you asked him, would be yes.

During the night, the phone by Tolliver's bed rang. I could hear it through the thin walls. After a moment, it stopped. I tried to imagine who could know where we were and what we were doing, and in the middle of imagining, I fell back to sleep. I ran the next morning, and in the cold crisp air it felt great. The hot shower felt even better. While I was dressing, Tolliver knocked on my door. After I let him in, I finished buttoning my blouse. I was wearing better clothes since we would be meeting the Ashdown client for the first time. This would be a cemetery job, and I wouldn't have to change. A quick in-and-out.

"The call last night," he said.

"Yeah, who was that?" I'd almost forgotten.

"It was the police in Sarne."

"Who in the police?"

"Harvey Branscom, the sheriff."

I waited, hairbrush in hand.

"We have to go back."

"Not until we do this job. Why, what happened?"

"Last night, someone went into Helen Hopkins' house and beat her to death."

I stared at Tolliver for a minute. I was so used to death that it was hard to produce a normal reaction to news like this.

"Well," I said finally, "I hope it was quick."

"I told them we'd have to finish our business here first, then we'd drive back up there."

"I'm ready." I tucked my blouse in my gray slacks. I pulled on my matching blazer.

"Hey, the jacket matches your eyes," Tolliver said.

"That was my intent," I said dryly. Tolliver always seemed to think that if I looked good, it was a happy accident. The blouse I wore with the gray suit was light green, with a kind of bamboo pattern on it. I put on a gold chain that Tolliver had given me the previous Christmas, and slid into black pumps. I fluffed my hair, checked my makeup, and told Tolliver I was ready. He was wearing a long-sleeved cotton pullover sweater in a dark red. He looked very good in it. I'd given it to him.

We met the client and her lawyer at the designated cemetery, one of those modern ones with flat headstones. They're cheaper, and more convenient for the mower. Though not atmospheric, the "park" look does make for easier walking.

The lawyer, a woman in her sixties, made it clear she thought I was in the business of defrauding the desperate and grief stricken. I was getting a lot of red flags, not only from the lawyer's attitude, but from the twitchiness of the client. Following our standard procedure when I got vibes like those, I endorsed the check and handed it to Tolliver, indicating he should go to the bank while I did the "reading." The situation was showing all the indicators of a bad transaction.

The client, a heavy, peevish woman in her forties, wanted her husband to have died of something more dramatic than a radio falling into his bathtub. (Bathtubs had been big this month. Sometimes I got such a run of one cause of death that it made even me nervous. Last year, I had a streak of accidental drownings—five in a row. Made me scared to go swimming for a couple of months.) Geneva Roller, the client, had her own elaborate conspiracy theory about how the radio came to be in the bathtub. Her theory involved Mr. Roller's first wife and his best friend.

I love it when the location of the body is known. It was a little treat when the client led me directly to her husband's grave. Geneva Roller was a brisk walker, and I could feel the heels of my pumps sinking into the soft dirt. The lawyer was right behind me, as if I'd cut and run unless I was blocked in.

We stopped by a headstone reading *Farley Roller*. To give Geneva her emotional money's worth, I stepped onto the grave and crouched, my hand resting on the headstone. *Farley*, I thought, *what the hell happened to you?* And then I saw it, as I always did. To let Geneva know what was going on, I said, "He is in the tub. He has—um, he's uncircumcised." That was unusual.

This convinced my client I was the real deal. Geneva Roller gasped, her hand going up to her chest. Her bright red lips formed an O. The lawyer, Patsy Bolton, snorted. "Anyone could know that, Geneva," she said.

Right, that was the first thing I asked guys.

"He's whistling," I said. I couldn't hear what Farley Roller was whistling, unfortunately. I could see the counter in the bathroom. "There's a radio on the counter," I said. "I think he's whistling along with the music." This was one of the times when I saw more than the moment of death. This was not the norm.

"He did that when he bathed," Geneva breathed. "He did, Patsy!" The lawyer looked less skeptical and more spooked.

I said. "There's the cat. On the bathroom counter. A marmalade color cat."

"Patpaws," said Geneva, smiling. I was willing to bet the lawyer wasn't smiling.

"The cat's bracing to leap over the tub to the open window."

"The window *was* open," Geneva said. She wasn't smiling anymore.

"The cat knocked the radio into the water," I said.

Then the cat leaped out of the window and into the yard while Mr. Roller came to his end. The bathtub was an old one, an unusual shade of avocado green. "You have a green tub," I said, shaking my head in puzzlement. "Can that be right?"

Patsy the lawyer was gaping at me. "You're for real," she said. "I actually believe you. Their tub is avocado."

I got to my feet, dusting off my knees. I ignored Patsy Bolton. "I'm so sorry, Ms. Roller. Your cat killed your husband in a freak accident," I said. I assumed this would be good news.

"NO!" Geneva Roller yelled, and even the lawyer looked astonished.

"Geneva, this is a reasonable explanation," Patsy Bolton began, giving her client a formidable stare, but Geneva Roller had no emotional restraints.

"It was his first wife, that Angela. It was her, I know it! She went in the house while I was at the store, and she murdered him. Angela did it. Not my little Patpaws!"

I'd had disbelieving reactions before, of course, though most often these came when I'd discovered the death was a suicide. So it sure wasn't the first time I'd found that people invest a lot in their theories. In a Jack Nicholson moment, I very nearly told Geneva Roller that she couldn't handle the truth.

"I'll take my check back. I won't pay you a dime," she hissed. I was glad I'd sent Tolliver to the bank.

Looking over Geneva's shoulder, I could see our car turning into the cemetery. Relief gave me courage.

"Ms. Roller, your cat caused an accident, quite innocently. Your husband wasn't murdered. There's no one to blame," I said.

She launched herself at me, and the lawyer caught her by the shoulders. "Geneva, recall who you are," Patsy Bolton said. Her cheeks were red, and her brown-and-gray streaked hair had become a mess in the breeze that had sprung up. "Don't embarrass yourself like this."

With excellent timing, Tolliver pulled up beside me. Trying not to hurry, I climbed into the car while saying, "I'm so sorry for your loss, Ms. Roller." We sped out of the cemetery while Geneva Roller screamed at us.

"Got the money?" I asked.

"Yep. Good thing?"

"Yeah, she didn't want it to be an accident. I guess she

was hoping for an A and E documentary. 'Murder in Ash-down,' or something." I deepened my voice. "'The widow, however, suspected from the beginning that Farley Roller's death was a 'not what it appeared to be,' kind of thing. In-stead, all she has to blame is her stupid cat. Kind of a let-down, I guess.'"

"It's a lot more interesting to be the wife of a murder vic-tim than the owner of a killer cat," Tolliver said, but I had to wonder about that.

# Four

WE'D already checked out of the Ashdown motel, so we drove straight to Sarne. Tolliver went directly to the sheriff's office, and seconds after we sat down in the chairs in front of his desk, the sheriff came in, yanking his hat off and tossing it on a table behind him.

"I hear you went to visit with Helen Hopkins yesterday," Harvey Branscom said. He bent over and switched on the intercom. "Reba, send Hollis in," he said. A squawk came back, and in a minute Hollis Boxleitner came in, carrying a mug of steaming coffee. I could smell it from my chair, but I didn't ask for any, nor did I look him in the face. Beside me, Tolliver stiffened.

"Mr. Lang, I want you to go with Deputy Boxleitner here. I'd like to talk to Miss, Ms. Connelly."

I turned to look at Tolliver, trying not to let my anxiety show on my face. He knew I would hate for him to say anything out loud. I like to keep my fears to myself. He gave me a very steady look, and I relaxed just a little. Without a word, he stood and left the room with Hollis.

"How'd you make contact with Helen?" the sheriff asked me. His face was set in harsh lines. I could see the shadow of white whiskers on his face, as though his cheeks had been frostbitten. Lack of sleep made the lines across his forehead even deeper.

"She called us," I said, biting off any color commentary. Tolliver had always advised me not to answer any extra when I talked to the police.

"What did she want?" asked the sheriff, with an air of elaborate patience.

"Us to come visit her." I read the expression on Branscom's face correctly. "She wanted to know who'd hired me, and why."

"Sybil hadn't told her you all were coming?" Branscom himself seemed surprised, and he was Sybil Teague's brother.

"Evidently not."

"Was she angry about that?"

We looked at each other for a long second. "Not that she said," I answered.

"What else did you talk about?"

I spoke very carefully. "She told us she'd had a bad life for a while, but that she'd been sober for thirty-two months. She talked about her daughters. She was proud of both of them."

"Did she ask you about their deaths?"

"Sure. She wanted to know how I knew, if I were sure how they were killed. She said she would tell their fathers."

Harvey Branscom had been lifting his mug to his mouth as I spoke. Now the mug was lowered back to the desk. "Say what?" he asked.

"She said she would tell the girls' fathers what I'd said."

"The fathers of the girls. Both of them. *Plural*."

I nodded.

"She never would tell anyone who Teenie's dad was. I always thought she just didn't know. And Sally's dad Jay left years ago, after she put the restraining order on him. Did Helen mention any names?"

"No." I was in the clear on that one.

"What else did she talk about?" the sheriff asked. "Be sure you tell me everything."

"She wanted to know how I do what I do, if I thought my gift had come from God or the devil. She wanted to be convinced I knew what I was talking about."

"What did you tell her?" He seemed genuinely interested to know.

"I didn't tell her anything. She made up the answer she wanted to hear, all on her own." My voice might have been a little dry.

"What time did you leave her house?"

I'd thought about that, of course. "We left about nine thirty," I said. "We went by the bank on the way out of town. We got to Ashdown and checked into the motel about two, two thirty."

He wrote that down, and the name of the motel. I handed him the receipt that I'd tucked in my purse. He copied it and made some more entries in his notebook.

"What time did she die?" I asked.

He looked up at me. "Sometime before noon," he said.

"Hollis went over there on his lunch hour to talk to her about Teenie's funeral. He'd spoken to her for the first time in a year or two, when he went over to tell her what you'd told him about Sally. Which, by the way, I don't believe. I think you're just trying to mine for gold here, and I'm telling you, Hollis ain't a rich man."

I was puzzled. "He gave me money, but I left it in his truck. He didn't tell you that?" Maybe Hollis just hadn't wanted to tell his superior I'd asked for it in the first place—though why, I don't know. Sheriff Branscom didn't think much of me, and it wouldn't have surprised him at all that I'd wanted to be paid (for something I do for my living!). It would have confirmed his poor opinion. Yes, I expect even poor people who want my services to pay me. So does everyone else.

"No," the sheriff said, easing back into his creaking chair. He rubbed a hand over his stubbled jowls. "No, he didn't mention that. Maybe he was embarrassed at giving money to someone like you in the first place."

Sometimes you just can't win. Sheriff Branscom would never join my fan club. It's lucky I'm used to meeting people like that, or I might slip and get my feelings hurt.

"Where's Tolliver?" I asked, my tolerance all used up.

"He'll be in here directly," the sheriff said. "I guess Hollis ain't finished up his questions yet."

I fidgeted. "I really need to go to the motel and lie down," I said. "I really need Tolliver to take me there."

"You've got some car keys," the sheriff observed. "Hollis'll bring him over when they're done."

"No," I said. "I need my brother."

"Don't you raise your voice to me, young woman. He'll

be through in a minute." But there was the faintest look of alarm on the round soft face.

"Now," I said. "I need him *now.*" I let my eyes go wide so the white showed all around the irises. My hands wrung together, over and over.

"I'll check," said the sheriff, and he could hardly get up from behind his desk fast enough.

Most places, I would've gotten thrown in the cage or taken to the hospital, but I had gauged this man correctly. Within four minutes, Tolliver came in, moving quickly. Because Hollis was watching, he knelt at my feet and took both my hands. "I'm here, honey," he said. "Don't be scared."

I let tears flow down my cheeks. "I need to go, Tolliver," I said softly. "Please take me to the motel." I threw my arms around his neck. I loved hugging Tolliver, who was bony and hard and warm. I loved to listen to the air going in and out of his lungs, the swoosh of his heart.

He raised me up out of the chair and walked me to the front door, one arm wrapped around my shoulders. The few people in the outer office eyed us curiously as we made our way to the door.

When we were safely back in the car and on our way, Tolliver said, "Thanks."

"Was it going bad for you?" I asked, taking my hands from my face and straightening in my seat. "The sheriff thinks I made up everything I said, but the motel receipt was pretty conclusive."

"Hollis Boxleitner has a thing for you," Tolliver said. "He can't decide if he wants to go to bed with you or slap you around, and he's full of anger like a volcano's full of lava."

"Because of his wife getting killed."

"Yep. He believes in you, but that makes him mad, too."

"He's gonna burn himself up," I said.

"Yes," Tolliver agreed.

"Did he tell you anything about Helen Hopkins' murder?"

"He said he found her. He said she'd been hit on the head."

"With something there, something already in the house?"

"Candlestick."

I remembered the glass candlesticks flanking the Bible on the coffee table.

"Was she standing when she was hit?"

"No," he said, "I think she was sitting on the couch."

"So the killer was standing in front of her."

Tolliver thought about it. "That makes sense," he said. "But the deputy didn't say one way or another."

"Being suspected of a murder isn't going to help business," I said.

"No, we need to get out of here as soon as possible." He parked in front of the motel and went in to get our rooms.

I really did want to lie down by the time we were in our rooms, and I was glad when Tolliver came through the connecting door and turned on my television. I propped up on the pillows while he slouched in the chair, and we watched the Game Show Network. He beat me at *Jeopardy!* I beat him at *Wheel of Fortune*. Of course, I would rather have won at *Jeopardy!*, but Tolliver had always been better at remembering facts than I was.

Our parents were brilliant people, once upon a time; before they became alcoholic, drug-addicted disbarred attorneys. And before they'd decided their clients' criminal lifestyles were more appealing and adventuresome than their own. My mother and Tolliver's dad found each other on their way down the drain, having shed their original spouses. My sister Cameron and I had gone from living in a four-bedroom suburban home in east Memphis to a rental house with a hole in the bathroom floor in Texarkana, Arkansas. This hadn't happened all at once; we'd experienced many degrees of degradation. Tolliver had fallen from a lower height, but he and his brother had descended with his father, too. He'd been our companion in that hole in Texarkana. That's where we'd been when the lightning struck.

My mother and Tolliver's dad had had two more children together, Mariella and Gracie. Tolliver and I watched out for them as best we could. Mariella and Gracie had no memory of anything better than the life we were living.

What had happened to our other parents: my father and Tolliver's mother? Why didn't they save us from the terrifying turn our lives had taken? Well, by that time, my real dad had gone to jail for a long string of white-collar crimes, and Tolliver's mother had died of cancer—leaving our at-large parents to complete their own downward passage, dragging us and their own children behind them.

So here we were, Tolliver and I, in a run-down motel in a seedy Ozarks tourist town in the off-season, hoping to dodge being charged with murder.

But by golly, we were smart.

We were playing Scrabble when we heard a knock at the door.

It was my room, so I asked, "Who is it?"

"Hollis."

I opened the door. Hollis saw Tolliver behind me and said, "May I come in?"

I shrugged and moved back. Hollis stepped in far enough to allow me to shut the door behind him.

"You're here to apologize, I assume," I said in the coldest voice I could summon. It was pretty damn cold.

"Apologize! For what?" He sounded genuinely bewildered.

"For telling the sheriff I took your money. For implying I cheated you."

"You did take my money."

"I left it on the seat of the truck. I felt bad for you." I was so angry I was almost spitting; I'd gone from cold to hot in less than five seconds.

"It wasn't on the seat of the truck."

"Yes. It was."

He fished his keys out of his pocket. "Show me."

"No, you look yourself, so you can't accuse me of planting it."

Tolliver and I followed Hollis back outside. The sky was gray, and the trees around the motel were beginning to whip in the wind. I was cold without my coat, but I wasn't going back in to put it on. Tolliver put his arm around me. Hollis opened the passenger door of his truck, began thrusting his fingers in the crack at the back of the seat, and in about ten seconds he came up with the bank envelope, still fat with money.

He stared at it in his hand, flushed red, and then went white. After a moment or two, he met our eyes. "You told Harvey the truth," he said. "I'm sorry."

"There now," I said. "Are we all clear about this?"

He nodded.

"Okay, then," I said. I spun and walked into my room. Tolliver stayed outside for a bit. Then he came in, too.

We finished our game of Scrabble. I won.

We drove to a little town just five miles away to eat supper. Tolliver didn't seem keen on going back to the motel diner, and I didn't tease him about the waitress. We had country-fried steak, mashed potatoes, and lima beans at a near-duplicated Kountry Good Eats, and it was actually very tasty. The ambience was familiar: Formica-topped tables, cracked linoleum floor, two tired waitresses, and a man behind the counter, the manager. The iced tea was good, too.

"You know someone followed us here," Tolliver said, as the waitress took our plates and strode toward the kitchen. He fished out his wallet to pay our tab.

"A girl," I said. "In a Honda."

"Yeah. I guess she's a deputy, too? She looks awful young. Or maybe they just deputized her for this."

"She's probably cold sitting out there in that little Honda."

"Well, that's her job."

We paid, tipped, and left. The threatened rain was finally upon us, and Tolliver and I ran to the car. He'd clicked it unlocked as we left the restaurant, and I dove inside as fast as I could. I hate being wet. I hate storms. I won't talk on the phone when it's raining hard.

At least there was no thunder this time.

"I don't understand," Tolliver had said once, exasperated at not being able to call me when he was a few miles away. "Why? The worst has already happened. You've already been hit by lightning. What are the odds of that happening twice?"

"What were the odds of it happening once?" I countered, though my real reasons were probably not what he supposed.

We drove slowly, and the red Honda stuck with us. The roads around Sarne were narrow and flanked by some steep terrain, and there was the ever-present possibility a deer would dash across the road.

When we got to the motel, we had a debate about whether to stop and let the unknown girl see where we were staying (which she'd already know if she was a cop) or keep riding around until she tired of following us. Going to the police station, we agreed, felt silly. After all, she hadn't threatened us or done anything other than ride behind us.

It was my bladder that determined our course of action. We pulled in, I dashed into my room, and by the time I came out, Tolliver reported, "She's trying to make up her mind to come over and knock on the door." He was concealed behind the curtains, and he hadn't turned on a light in the room.

I joined him, and it was like watching a pantomime. The girl's car was clearly lit up by the lights in the parking lot, and she was recognizable; that is, I'd be able to pick her out in a police lineup now, though her features weren't crystal clear. She had short brown hair worn in a longer version of a standard boys' haircut, which looked cute on her, since she was a petite thing. She was maybe seventeen, maybe younger, and she had a pouting lower lip. She was wearing enough eye makeup for three ordinary women. Her small face had that look so common in teenage girls from homes where all is not well—part defiant, part vulnerable, all wary.

Cameron had worn that expression on her face all too often.

"How much are you willing to put down on this? I think she'll give up and drive away. We're too scary for her." Tolliver put his hand on my shoulder and squeezed it.

"Nah, she's coming in," I said with assurance. "I'd be taking your money too easily. See? She's daring herself."

Rain began to pelt down again as she made up her mind to brave us. She launched herself from the car and dashed for my door. She pounded on it twice.

Tolliver turned on the lamp beside the bed as I answered her summons.

She glared at me. "You the woman that finds bodies?"

"You know I am, or you wouldn't have been following us. I'm Harper Connelly. Come in." I stepped back, and, shooting me a suspicious look, she entered the room. She looked around carefully. Tolliver was sitting in the chair trying to look harmless. "This is my brother Tolliver Lang," I said. "He travels with me. You want a Diet Coke?"

"Sure," she said, as if turning down a soft drink was unthinkable. Tolliver got one out of the ice chest and handed it to her. She took it with her arm extended as far as she could reach, to keep her distance from him. I pushed the other chair out to indicate she should use it, and I perched on the side of the bed.

"Can I help you?" I asked.

"You can tell me what happened to my brother. I'm not saying I think what you're doing is okay, or even morally defensible." She glared at me. "But I want to know what you think."

I thought she had a good civics teacher.

"Okay," I said slowly. "Maybe first you could tell me who your brother is?"

She flushed red. She was accustomed to being a notable fish in a very small pond. "I'm Nell," she said, clipping off the words. "Mary Nell Teague. Dell was my brother."

"You can't be much younger than he was."

"We were ten months apart."

Tolliver and I looked at each other briefly. This girl was not only a minor, but the sister of a murder victim. And I was willing to bet she'd never been out of Sarne for more than a two-week vacation.

"Morally defensible," Tolliver repeated, as struck by the phrase as I'd been. He rolled the words over his tongue as if he was testing the taste of them.

"I mean, I think it's wrong, all right? Telling people what happened to their dead relatives. No offense, but you could be making all this up, right?"

No offense, my ass. I was sick of people telling me I was evil. "Listen, Nell," I said, trying my best to keep my voice under strict control. "I make my living the best way I know how. For you to assume I'm not honest *is* an offense to me. There's no way it couldn't be."

Maybe she wasn't used to her words being taken seriously. "Um, well, okay," she muttered, clearly taken aback. "But listen, can you tell me? What you told my mom?"

"You're a minor. I don't want to get into trouble," I said.

Tolliver looked as if he were mulling it over.

"Listen, I may be a kid, you know, but he was my brother! And I should know what happened to my brother!" There was a very real anguish behind her words.

We gave each other tiny nods.

"I don't believe he killed himself," I said.

"I knew it," she said. "I knew it."

For someone who'd been so sure I was a fraud, she was taking my word without a second thought.

"So if he didn't kill himself," she said, talking faster and faster, "then he didn't kill Teenie, and if he didn't kill Teenie, then he didn't . . ." She stopped with an almost comic expression of panic, her eyes popping wide and her mouth clamped together to block the crucial word in, whatever it might have been.

A pounding at the door startled Tolliver and me; we'd been staring at Nell Teague as if we could pry the end of the sentence out of her with our eyes.

"Wonderful," I said after I looked through the peephole. "It's Sybil Teague, Tolliver."

"Ohmigod," said our visitor, who suddenly looked even younger than her age.

I cursed very thoroughly but silently, wishing that Sybil had arrived five minutes earlier. I had a fleeting idea that we could sneak Nell out through Tolliver's room, but as sure as we tried that, we'd be caught. After all, we hadn't done anything wrong. I opened the door, and Sybil came in like a well-groomed goddess of wrath.

"Is my child here?" she demanded, though we were making no move to conceal Nell, who was sitting in plain view. It was like she'd preplanned the moment.

"Right here," Tolliver said gently, with an edge of sarcasm to his voice. Sybil flushed, her natural color warring with the carefully applied tints of rose and cream.

Sybil took in the sight of Nell sitting in the chair, unmolested and with a Diet Coke clutched in her hand, and she seemed to deflate. "Where have you been, young lady?" she asked, rallying almost instantly. "I expected you home two hours ago."

Fortunately for us, Nell decided to come clean. "I followed them. They went to Flo and Jo's for supper," the teenager told her mother. "They took their time. I followed them here, and then I asked them if I could come in."

"You drove back in the rain from that place, with the roads slick, in the dark?" Sybil Teague's face went even paler. "I'm glad I didn't know about it."

"Mom, I've driven in rain plenty of times."

"Oh, yes, in the two years you've been driving. You have nowhere near enough experience . . ." Sybil took a deep breath and made herself relax. "All right, Nell, I know you wanted to talk about what happened to your brother. God knows, I've wanted to find out, too. And I thought this woman would give me answers. I just have more questions than I started out with, now."

"This woman" felt like throwing up her hands in exasperation. "This woman" did not like being spoken of as though she weren't there.

Paul Edwards appeared in the doorway behind Sybil. His hair was dark with rain. He put his hand on Sybil's shoulder, I thought to move her farther into the room so he could get out of the weather. I also thought it would be nice if they shut the door, since the wind was gusting in. Sybil stepped forward reluctantly, but his hand stayed on her shoulder.

For the first time, it occurred to me that there might be more between the two than attorney-client privilege. I'm just not as sharp about the living as I am the dead.

Nell's face shut down completely when she saw Paul Edwards. All the youth slid out of her mouth and eyes, and she looked like a hooker with her heavy eye makeup and tight clothes, instead of a cute kid trying on her personality.

"Hello, Miss Connelly, Mr. Lang," Edwards said. He focused on Nell. "I'm glad we caught up with you, young lady."

I wondered if Edwards was related to Sybil Teague's deceased husband. His ears were the same shape as Nell's, though otherwise she looked more like her mother.

"Right," Nell said, in a voice as expressionless as they come. "Thanks for coming out to look for me, Mr. Edwards." You could have cut the sarcasm with a chain saw.

"Your mother doesn't need anything else to worry about, Nell," he said, with so much gentle reproof in his voice that I wanted to deck him. I had no doubt that Sybil Teague had suffered over the loss of her son, but I was pretty sure Dell's little sister had been missing him, too. If anything happened to Tolliver, I'd . . . I found I couldn't even imagine it.

I'd rather have been out doing "cause of death" for a whole cemetery than be standing in that room right then.

"Goodbye," I said, making a hostess gesture toward the door. I was sure no hostess actually indicated her guests should leave, but this was my room, and I could behave as I chose. Everyone looked astonished except Tolliver, who smiled, just a twitch of the lips. I smiled myself, and out of habit they all responded, though uncertainly.

"Yes, of course. I'm sure you're tired," Sybil said. Like a true lady, she was providing a reason for my discourtesy.

I opened my mouth to disagree, but Tolliver beat me to it. "We've had a long day," he said with a smile. Mary Nell

Teague suddenly looked at him with more interest. When Tolliver smiles, it's so unexpected it gives you a pleasant surprise.

Within a minute, the mother and daughter and lawyer were on the other side of the door, which was exactly where I wanted them.

"Harper," Tolliver said, in a reproving way.

"I know, I know," I acknowledged, without any regret. "What do you think she was really here for?"

"I'm trying to figure it out. Wait a minute, which 'she' do you mean?"

"I mean the mother."

"Good. Me, too. You think she was here to find out what Nell was saying to us? Or to keep us from telling Nell anything?"

"Maybe we should be wondering why Nell was so determined to talk to us. You think she might actually know something about her brother's death?"

"We're getting too wrapped up in this. We need to get out of Sarne."

"I agree. But I don't think the sheriff will let us leave." I drooped on the end of the bed, trying not to look at myself in the mirror opposite after one quick glance. I looked too pale and even a little haggard. I looked like a woman who needed a big mug of hot chocolate and about ten hours' sleep.

I could do something about that. I always carry powdered hot chocolate with me, and there was a little coffeepot in the room. After making sure Tolliver didn't want any, I had a steaming mug in hand. I scooted up against the headboard, pillows stuffed behind my back, and looked at Tolliver, who had slid down in the chair so that his long legs were fully extended. "What's our next appointment?" I asked.

"Memphis, in a week," he said. "Occult Studies at some university."

"A lecture?" I tried not to act as dismayed as I felt. I hated going back to Memphis, where I'd had the only easy part of life I could recall.

"Reading a small cemetery. I think they know the COD for most of the inhabitants." Cause of death. "It's a test. I could hear the professor gloating over exposing you, over the phone. Patronizing as hell. Is he going to be surprised or what?"

"Jerk," I said scornfully. "They paying us?"

"A nominal amount. But we should do it, because I figure the word-of-mouth on this one is gonna be great, and it's a private university, so some of the parents have money. Plus, we have an appointment in Millington the day after, which is real close."

Tolliver had arranged things very well. "Thanks, brother," I said, and I meant it with my heart.

He waved a hand to discount my gratitude. "Hey, what else would I be doing?" he asked. "Herding carts at Wal-Mart? Running a forklift in some warehouse?"

"Married with a couple of kids in a three-bedroom ranch, stable and happy," I almost said; but then I clenched my teeth over the words.

Some things I was scared to say out loud.

# Five

~

WE had no purpose the next day, which again dawned sunny and crisp. I went out for a run right after I got up, and I saw Tolliver trotting down the street in the opposite direction when I was almost back at the motel. After I'd showered, and he'd returned and cleaned up, we ate at a different diner.

About midmorning, I was so bored I got Tolliver to take me out to the older cemetery, the one I'd noticed the morning I'd found Teenie. I found it with my other sense, instead of asking for directions. This cemetery had graves over a hundred and fifty years old—well established, at least in American terms. The presence of so many old dead produced a constant, mellow reverberation, almost soothing, like giant ancient drums in the distance. Though the grounds were well tended, in the oldest section I spied a few overturned headstones with writing that time had obscured.

These stones would belong to families who had died out; there were no living descendants to tend the plots. I amused myself by going from grave to grave, reaching deep to pull from each collection of bones what information I could garner. The glimpses I caught of these faces were often blurred or obscured, as if the dead themselves had forgotten who they'd been. Every now and then I saw the features clearly, heard a name, caught a longer glimpse of death in the past.

"Childbirth," I called to Tolliver, who was sitting half-in half-out of the car while he worked a crossword puzzle.

"Another one," he said, hardly raising his eyes from the page. It was the third childbirth death I'd found.

"Kind of scary." I stepped to the next grave. Since this was simply to pass the time and keep in practice, I'd left my shoes on. It was a nippy day, and I didn't want to catch a cold, especially since I was just messing around. "You know, Tolliver, men didn't used to die of heart attacks."

"That so?"

"That's what I heard on the news the other day. Oh! This guy was crushed by a tree he was cutting down."

Tolliver didn't bother to look up. "Um," he said, so I gathered he wasn't listening. I moved to my right. "Asthma attack," I muttered. "Blood poisoning from a knife cut. Scarlet fever. Smallpox. Flu. Pneumonia." I shook my head. So many of these things could be cured, or at least eased, now. I couldn't fathom people who longed for the past. They weren't thinking about the absence of antibiotics, that was for sure.

The next grave was one of the oldest. The tombstone had broken in half, and someone had tried to set it back together. I couldn't read the name.

"Hey, gunshot wound," I called to Tolliver.

"That's Lieutenant Pleasant Early," Hollis Boxleitner said, from about a yard behind me. "He was shot during the Civil War."

If there'd been an open grave, I would've jumped into it. Tolliver looked up sharply and lay down the clipboard. "Where'd you come from?" he asked, in no very friendly tone.

"I was weeding my great-grandmother's grave over there." Hollis inclined his head toward the north side of the cemetery; sure enough, there was a bucket full of weeds and a trowel beside a grave with a leaning headstone.

"During a murder investigation, you have time to weed?" Tolliver's voice was sharper than necessary.

"It relaxes me." Hollis's broad face remained calm. "And the state guys are in town."

A gust of wind blew dry leaves across the graves. As they crossed the graveled drive that wended through the cemetery, they made a hissing sound. I liked it.

"So, is this kind of . . . recreation, for you?" Hollis asked, indicating the graves around us.

"Yes. Just kind of keeping my hand in." People always expect me to be embarrassed by what I do. Why?

"Have you ever been to a really old graveyard? Like in England?"

I ducked my head. "Not often. There are the Indian mounds, of course, and even more ancient people. Those are pretty interesting. And we went to a very early American one. In Massachusetts."

"Was it the same? Does the length of time they've been dead make a difference?"

I was pleased at the question. Not many people want to know too much about what I do. "Yes, it does," I said. "I get fainter pictures, less exact knowledge. Someday I want us to go to Westminster Abbey. And Stonehenge." Lots of ancient dead people there, for sure.

"You think you could get any more information by going back to Helen Hopkins' house?" The policeman had switched back to the here and now, putting an end to our conversation.

"No," I said. "I have to be with the body." I didn't want to go through that, not at all. It was very unpleasant, seeing the death of someone you'd known.

"The state police have taken over the investigation," Hollis said, after he'd retrieved his bucket of weeds. "I just answer the phones on my shift. There's a hot line number."

It took me a second to understand that he'd been banished from the investigation.

"That sucks," I offered. I've met enough cops to know that the best of them like to be in charge. The best ones have that confidence.

He shrugged. "In a way. I'm just a part-time cop, it's true."

"She was your mother-in-law."

"Yes," he said heavily. "They're waiting for you."

For a second, since I was standing on a grave, I was sure he meant all the dead people; and I already knew they were. Then I realized his meaning was much more mundane. The lawyer, Paul Edwards, and a uniformed man I'd never seen, were standing by the car talking to Tolliver. I was glad I'd left my shoes on. I took a breath and began walking toward the men.

"Good luck," said Hollis, and I nodded. I knew he was watching, and he would see.

WE had a dismal time at the police station. The state police thought I was a blood-sucking leech. I'd anticipated their attitude as we drove into town, but it wore me out anyway. The male faces followed each other in slow succession. Thin, heavy, white, black, intelligent, dense; they all shared an opinion of me they didn't take any pains to hide. I guess they thought Tolliver was the enabler of the blood-sucking leech.

I don't like being treated like a confidence trickster, and I'm sure Tolliver likes it even less. I retreat inside myself, and I don't let them touch my quick. Tolliver tries to do that, too, but he is less successful. He gets very upset when people impugn our honor.

"We looked into your file," said a thin man with a greyhound face and cold, narrow eyes. The interrogation room was small and beige. They'd taken Tolliver into the one next door.

I breathed in, breathed out, looked at the wall behind his ear.

"You and your 'brother' have been questioned lots of times," he said. His name tag read, *Green*. He waited to make sure I'd heard he'd put "brother" in quotes.

Since there was nothing to respond to, I did some of my own waiting.

"No one's ever put you behind bars," he said.

This was another indisputable fact, and I did some more waiting.

"Of course, they should've."

Opinion. Didn't call for a response. My parents hadn't been lawyers for nothing.

"You know what they say about people from this neck of the woods," Green said. "The kind of people who go to family reunions to get a date?"

Green was from somewhere else, I assumed. I slid lower in the plastic chair.

"I figure you and your brother are people like that," he said, with a most unpleasant smile.

Another opinion, and one he knew was based on incorrect information.

"He's not really your brother, is he?"

"Stepbrother," I said.

He was taken aback. "But you introduce him as your brother."

"Simplification," I said. I crossed my legs the other way, just to have a change. I was ready to eat lunch. Tolliver and I would go to a restaurant, or we'd get something at the grocery store to heat up in the little microwave we carried with us and plugged in at motel rooms. We'd talked about buying a little house outside of Dallas. We would have a bigger microwave there, or maybe I'd learn to cook. I liked to clean; that is, I didn't exactly love the process, but I did love the result. I might subscribe to a magazine, something it had never been practical for me to do. Maybe *National Geographic*. The December after we moved into the house, Tolliver and I would buy a Christmas tree. I hadn't had a Christmas tree in ten years.

". . . hearing a word I say?" Greyhound Green's face was drawn with anger.

"No, I haven't. I'm ready to go now. You know I didn't kill that poor woman. You know Tolliver didn't, either. There's not a reason in the world we'd want to do anything to her. You just don't like me. But you can't put me in jail because you don't like me."

"You prey on the grief of others."

"How?"

He glared at me. "They're grieving, wanting closure, and you and your brother turn up like crows to pick at the carcass."

"Not so," I said briskly. I was on sure ground, here. "I find the body. Then they have closure. They're happier." I got to my feet, feeling my legs prickle after sitting so long in the same chair. "We'll stay in town as long as you want. But we didn't hurt Helen Hopkins. You know it."

He stood, too, and tried to think of something to say that would stop me from leaving, convict me of some crime. But there was nothing, and he had to watch me leave. I knocked on the door of the next room. "Tolliver," I called. "Let's us go."

After a pause, Tolliver opened the door and stepped out. I looked up at him, and saw his eyes were filled with rage. I gently put my hand on his cheek, and when a moment had passed, he relaxed. Together, we walked out of the tiny Sarne police station and over to the car. The grass around the courthouse was starting to brown, and the big silver maple leaves cartwheeled across it exuberantly.

Following the path of one leaf, my eyes lit on Mary Nell Teague. She was waiting for us, her face eager. No, she was waiting for Tolliver. I was clearly a shadow walking beside him, in her eyes. She'd parked her little car right by ours, which must have been difficult. It was a Saturday, and the town was busy.

A group of teenage boys was clustered around the war memorial. They could have been teenagers from anywhere in the United States—jeans, T-shirts, sneakers. Maybe their haircuts weren't cutting edge, but that wouldn't bother anyone here. I wouldn't have had a second look at them if I hadn't realized they were watching us. They didn't look friendly. The tallest one was glaring from Nell to Tolliver.

"Hmm," I said, wanting to be sure Tolliver had noticed the boys.

"Psychics are all crap," the tallest boy said, loud enough for us to hear. Of course, that was his purpose. He was probably on the football team, probably class president. He was the alpha wolf. Handsome and brawny, he was wearing sneakers that had cost more than every stitch I was wearing added together. "The devil is in people who say they talk to the dead," he said even louder. Mary Nell was probably too far away to hear him, but she was glancing back and forth from the pack of boys to us, and she looked, in turn, indignant, horrified, and excited. I thought we had us a little love triangle going on here: Alpha Boy, Mary Nell, and Tolliver. Only, Tolliver didn't know about it.

I was becoming antsier by the second. The boys were moving to intercept us. Tolliver had gotten the keys out of his pocket and pressed the pad to unlock the doors.

Mary Nell, moving swiftly, intercepted us just before the boys did. "Hey, Tolliver!" she said brightly, taking his arm. "Oh . . . hi, Harper." I tried not to smile at my second-class status. It was easier not to smile when I saw there was no way to avoid some kind of confrontation with the boys. Alpha Boy laid his hand on Nell's shoulder, halting her progress, and therefore ours.

"You shouldn't be hanging around with these people," he said to Mary Nell. I could tell from his voice he had known Nell for a long time, and had a proprietary interest in her.

Alpha Boy might have known her for a long time, but he hadn't known her well. Her little face tightened with anger. He'd embarrassed her in front of her newest fixation, an exotic out-of-town older man. "Scotty, you don't have any say over me," she said. "Tolliver, let's us go to the Sonic and have a Coke."

Tolliver was caught between a rock and a hard place, and I waited to see what he'd do to get out of it. While he squirmed, I looked from young male face to young male face, trying to meet each set of eyes and smile, the squeaky non-sexual smile of a newscaster. Only two of them made the effort to nod to me; the others either evaded my gaze or scowled at me. This was not good.

"Mary Nell, I'd like to, but Harper and I have to go back to the motel and make some phone calls," Tolliver said. I could see him casting around for something to say that would simultaneously salvage her pride, get him off the hook, and mollify the angry columns of testosterone that were glowering at us. There was nothing that would serve all three functions.

"Maybe Mary Nell would like to have supper with us tonight," I said unwillingly. It was not so much that I was trying to show the girl some mercy; if she got angry with us, her anger would give the boys permission to attack.

I saw the conflict on Mary Nell's face pass in a flash; it was I who had asked, which negated the value of the invitation, but it did save her face, to some extent. "That would be wonderful," she said, giving me the barest glance. "I'll see you at six at the Ozark Valley Inn."

I had no idea where that was, but I said, "See you then," and Nell walked away to her car very quickly, her head held high. Just as quickly, Tolliver and I got in our car and drove away, stopping at the next light to buckle our seat belts.

Tolliver looked angry and embarrassed. "Too bad you don't want to be in a boy band," I said, after a minute of riding in silence. "You've obviously got the charisma."

"Oh, shut up!" he said. "How about you? You gonna be one of the Babes of Law Enforcement?"

"Well, at least Hollis is legal age. . . ." I began, but then I couldn't help smiling.

Tolliver managed a small upcurve of the lips. "Where the hell is the Ozark Valley Inn?" he said.

"I have no idea, but we better find it by six o'clock. Gosh, I have a headache. I sure hope it doesn't get so bad that I have to bow out of the dinner. . . ."

"You do and you die."

We picked up salads for lunch, and took them back to the motel. The phone rang just as we were settling down to read. We were in my room, so I answered.

"This is Hollis. Do you want to go to supper with me?"

*We could double-date with Mary Nell and Tolliver! Wouldn't that be fun?* I bit my lip to suppress the idea. "I'm busy for supper," I said hesitantly, knowing I should turn him down flat, but tempted nonetheless.

"A drink afterward?"

"Yes," I said cautiously, after I'd thought about it.

"I'll pick you up at the motel. Eight o'clock?"

"Okay, see you then."

"All right. Goodbye."

I said goodbye, too, and hung up. Tolliver was eyeing me sardonically. "Let me guess, Cop Boy?"

I nodded. "We're going to have a drink together tonight at eight, so we'll have to cut short our romantic rendezvous with Mary Nell. I'm sure you don't want to be unchaperoned."

"If there's anywhere here it would take two hours to eat, I'd be very astonished," Tolliver said, at his driest.

I agreed, and re-opened my book. But for a few minutes, I read the same page over and over.

When we stopped by the motel office to ask for directions to the Ozark Valley Inn, we noticed that the older man who ran the place was not too happy about helping us. We'd learned his name was Vernon, and he wore overalls and had the worn and wrinkled face of a basset. Vernon had been pleasant enough up to now, though we hadn't seen much of him. But tonight he was distant, his gaze disapproving. "You planning on moving your bags over there?" he asked, almost hopefully.

"No," I said, surprised. "We're just meeting someone for dinner in the restaurant at the inn."

"'Cause I been meaning to tell you, I'm going to need those rooms pretty soon. Hope you two wasn't planning on staying very long."

"I'm sure you have tons of business coming in," I agreed, maybe a little coldly. "And we won't stay a minute longer than we have to."

"Glad to hear it."

"I guess no one's going to ask us to judge the floats in the homecoming parade," I said to Tolliver when we were in the car.

He smiled, but it was a small smile. "The sooner we can get out of Sarne, the better," he said.

Mary Nell came in seven minutes after we were seated at a table in the inn, which was on the southern side of the town. Her face was flushed and her cell phone was in her hand. I was willing to bet she'd lied to her mother about where she was going and whom she was going to be with. I almost hated the girl at that moment, for the trouble she might get us into.

"Sorry I'm late," Mary Nell said, as she took a chair. "I had some things I had to do at home. My mom is so paranoid."

"She lost your brother," I said. "I'm sure that's made her more protective." I wouldn't have thought even a self-absorbed teenager could have missed that point.

The girl flushed deep red. "Of course," she said stiffly. "I just mean, she doesn't seem to know how old I am." She'd dressed with care, in new low riders with a tight green T-shirt. She wore a soft fuzzy cardigan sweater and boots.

"That's a common thing with mothers," I said. My own mother had forgotten how old I was, after she'd started chasing the drugs with alcohol. She'd decided I was much older and needed a boyfriend. She picked a doping buddy of hers who was willing to give her free samples for the privilege of being my first "date." Tolliver had gone off to college by then, and I'd had to spend a day locked in my room. I had known that eventually they'd go to sleep and I'd be able to get out of the house, but I was hungry and thirsty and had no access to a bathroom. After that, I kept bottled water and a box of crackers and an old cooking pot in my room.

"Have you lived in Sarne all your life?" Tolliver asked Mary Nell.

She flushed when he spoke directly to her. "Yes," she

said. "My dad's parents were born here, too. Dad died just before Dell." I was startled. When Edwards had told me Sybil was a recent widow, I hadn't realized how recent. "Dell, he really missed Dad. . . . He was closer to Dad than me." She sounded vaguely resentful.

"I want to ask you a question, Mary Nell," I said. "I don't want to upset you any more than I have to, but when you were talking to us the other night, you paused after you said one sentence. You said something like, 'I knew he wouldn't kill Teenie and . . . ' and then you stopped. What were you going to say?"

Mary Nell eyed me. You could tell her feelings were conflicted. "Please tell us, Nell," Tolliver said, and she crumbled when she looked into his dark brown eyes. He'd called her something special.

"Okay," she said, leaning across the table to share her big secret. "Dell told me, the week before he and Teenie . . . the week before they died, that Teenie was gonna have a baby." Her heavily made-up eyes were as big and round as a raccoon's. The girl was clearly shocked that her brother had been having sex with his girlfriend, and she just as clearly considered the pregnancy top-secret knowledge.

"No one knew?"

"He sure didn't tell my mom. She would've killed him." Then, as she realized what she'd said, Mary Nell turned red as a brick, and tears filled her eyes.

"That's okay," I said hastily, "we know your mom wouldn't really do that."

"Well, Mom never has liked Teenie's mom too much. I don't know why. Miss Helen used to work for us a few years ago, and I thought she was great. Always singing."

And I could tell that she suddenly remembered that Helen Hopkins had been murdered, too. There was a look on her face, a lost look, like she was drowning.

"If I'd killed everyone I didn't like, I'd be able to dress in their scalps," Tolliver said.

Mary Nell gave a startled giggle and covered her mouth with her small hand.

After all this time, could an autopsy establish Teenie's pregnancy?

"Dell didn't tell anyone but you?" I asked.

"No one knew but me," Mary Nell said proudly.

Mary Nell was sure her brother hadn't told anyone about the baby, but what about Teenie? Had she told someone? Her mother, maybe?

Her mother, who was . . . gee, let me think . . . dead.

# Six

AFTER Tolliver and I had exchanged glances, we steered off the subject quickly. Mary Nell's sad, tearful face had already attracted some attention from the sparse clientele. Her coloring cleared up and her demeanor brightened as she talked about happier topics, addressing her conversation almost exclusively to my brother. Tolliver found out that Nell planned to go to the University of Arkansas the next year, that she wanted to be a physical therapist so she could help people, that she was a cheerleader and didn't like algebra. Her cheerleading sponsor was totally cool.

I was free to think my own thoughts. Mary Nell didn't seem much different from any of the girls I'd known in high school, the girls with sober parents, the girls who had enough money to ward off worry and homelessness. She was bright but not brilliant, virginal but not saintly. The loss of her sibling had left her drifting, searching for a new identity when her old one had been shaken at its core. I could see the knowledge of her brother's secret life with Teenie had disturbed Mary Nell deeply, until that shock had been smothered by the greater trauma of Dell's death. Clearly, sharing her brother's secret had relieved the knot of tension deep inside Mary Nell Teague. It didn't seem to make a difference to Mary Nell that the people she'd shared it with were strangers.

The girl was fascinated with Tolliver. Since she was popular, pretty, and a teenager, Mary Nell was sure Tolliver would find her equally fascinating. I observed Mary Nell flounder through the conversation, trying to find the key to cajoling my brother into noticing she was a woman. Mary Nell would begin an anecdote about her homeroom teacher, realize that was a kid topic, and make a huge effort to switch to some conversational gambit she believed would appeal to an older man.

"Did you go to college?" she asked Tolliver.

"I went two years," he said. "Then I worked for a while. After that, Harper and I started our traveling."

"How come you don't get a regular job and stay somewhere?" Like real people do.

Tolliver looked at me. I looked back. "Good question," he said. I looked at him askance, determined not to answer. She hadn't asked *me*.

"Harper helps people," he said. "She's one of a kind."

"But she gets paid for it," Nell said, outraged.

"Sure," Tolliver said. "Why not? When you get to be a therapist, you'll get paid."

Mary Nell ignored this royally.

"And she can do that by herself. Does she have to have help?"

Hey, sitting right here! Listening! I spread my hands, palms up. Only Tolliver noticed the gesture.

"It's not that she has to have my help. It's that I want to give it to her," Tolliver said gently. I looked straight down at my plate. Mary Nell abruptly excused herself to go to the ladies' room. I had no intention of accompanying her—I would not be welcome—so Tolliver and I silently picked at the remnants of our food until she returned, her eyes red and her head held high.

"Thanks for dinner," she said stiffly. We'd insisted on treating her. "I enjoyed it." Then, holding her eyes wide and unblinking, she strode out of the dining room.

I watched her car pull out of the dark parking lot. I was a little surprised to find myself actually concerned about the girl. Her life was crashing in ruins around her, and that could make her careless. Too many things can happen to girls who don't watch where they're going. I find their corpses every year.

We got back to our motel in plenty of time for me to brush my hair and spray on a little perfume for my date. Tolliver watched without comment, his face harsh in the shadowy light of the room. "You got your cell phone?" he asked. "I'll leave mine on."

"Okay," I said. Tolliver went into his room, shutting the door behind him very gently.

Hollis knocked on my door right on time. When I opened it, he said, "You look pretty," sounding unflatteringly surprised. I was wearing jeans and a black blouse and some black heels. I wore a gold chain with a jade pendant, a gift from me to me after I'd gotten a bonus from a distraught husband who'd been looking for his wife's body for four years.

Hollis looked pretty good himself, solid and blond in a new pair of jeans and a gold-and-brown plaid shirt. He'd shaved, and he smelled of some cologne. He'd made an effort. Maybe this was a bit more of a date than I'd imagined.

We went to a small dive a little north of town. It was built of dark wood and had plastic banners on long ropes tied from the building to the trees and lamp poles around the graveled lot. If the brightly colored triangles had been fluttering in some breeze, possibly the effect would have been cheerful and festive. In the chilly, still night air, the banners were simply depressing, forlorn reminders of failed festivity.

The interior looked better than I'd imagined, given the exterior. The bar itself was polished wood and the floor had been redone recently in that fake oak flooring that actually looks pretty good. The tables and booths were clean. The décor was definitely Hunting Lodge, with deer heads and large fish mounted on the walls, interspersed with mirrors and old license plates. The jukebox was wailing country and western.

I was pleased with the place, and I smiled. Hollis asked if I wanted one of the small booths or a table, and I picked a booth. He asked me what I wanted to drink, and when I said a Coors would be fine, he went to the bar and returned with two longnecks. He also brought two napkins, one of which he solemnly placed on the heavily polyurethaned wood in front of me before he put my mug on it. I suppressed a smile.

So much for the preliminaries.

"What do you like to do?" he asked. "While you're traveling around the country?"

Not the opening I'd expected. "I like to read," I said. "Sometimes, we try to catch a movie. I run. I watch television. I like to watch the WNBA games, since I played a little basketball in high school. I plan my dream house."

"Tell me about your dream house," Hollis said, smiling.

"Okay," I said, slowly. This was something I didn't talk about too often. "It will have to be off the beaten road, of course. I want it to look like a log cabin, but without the inconveniences of a real log cabin. I found a plan on the Internet, and I bought it. But of course, I want to alter it a little."

"Of course," he said, taking a sip of beer.

"It would be two bedrooms and a study, with a family room. There'd be a kitchen here, with the washroom right off of it." I was looking down at the table, drawing with my finger. "Around back, there'd be a *porte cochere* for the cars, so you could carry groceries right into the kitchen without getting wet. There's a deck off the right side of the kitchen, see? Or maybe I'd put it off the family room. That's where the fireplace will be, and you could keep your firewood on the deck. And you could put your gas grill on the deck. For steaks."

"Who lives in that house with you?"

I looked up at him, startled. "Well, of course—" I began. Then I shut my mouth.

"Surely your brother will get married somewhere along the line?" Hollis asked gently, his eyes steady and his face calm. "You might want to marry, yourself. Cut down on your traveling, some."

"Yes, that might happen," I said after a moment. "What about you?"

"I'll stay here," he said, almost sadly. "Maybe I'll feel like trying something permanent again, who knows? I haven't been the man I was since Sally died. And before I met Sally, I was married for about ten minutes when I was just a kid. It might be hard to get some sweet thing to spend time with me."

"I don't think that'll be the issue," I said. Some women might be put off by Hollis, but it was hardly his fault that his second wife had been murdered. "Was being married . . . was it good? Living with someone full-time?"

He gave it some thought, staring down at his beer. Then he looked at me.

"The first time, it was heaven for two months. Then it was hell," he said, his mouth turning up wryly. "What a mistake that was. The only thing I can say, she was as eager to make that mistake as I was. We wanted each other so bad I couldn't sleep nights. At the time we married, we looked on it as a license to screw. And boy, did we. We didn't realize there'd be a lot more to it. We found out, right quick. When we split up, it would be a toss-up as to which of us was the more relieved."

After raising an inquiring eyebrow at me, he fetched us two more beers. "Sally, she was different," he said. "She was as sweet as her mom and her sister were wild. She wanted to get away from them, but she felt responsible for raising her sister, since her mom was such a lush. Then Helen kind of took a deep breath and got sober." He shook his head from side to side. "Now they're all gone, it don't make a difference, does it? Helen might as well have kept on drinking."

"Did the autopsy results come back on Teenie?" I asked.

His face became more guarded, cautious. "I can't talk to you about that." He looked at me for a long minute. "Why?"

It wasn't up to me to reveal the dead couple's secret. And I suddenly wondered why I even cared. I found bodies, and then I walked away. People died, died all the time, some in bed, some in the woods, some with a gun in their mouths. The end result was always the same. Why was this time different from any other?

"What is the worst case you've ever had?" Hollis asked me out of the blue.

I wondered if some expression crossing my face had triggered the question. "Oh, the tornado one," I said without even having to consider.

"Where was this tornado?"

"In Texas," I said. "Went right down the main street of this little town. I can't remember if the siren had gone off or not—or if it just came so suddenly there wasn't a chance to sound the siren. For whatever reason, this woman, her name was Molly Mathers, was running from her business to her car with her baby in one of those plastic carrying things with a handle. Little bitty baby."

"Storm took the baby?"

I nodded. "Snatched the carrier right out of Molly's hand."

We kept a moment of silence together.

"Everyone was sure the baby hadn't survived, of course, but the mom just couldn't let go of the idea that the baby was still in the carrier, maybe in some field, and was going hungry." I said this very evenly, because it was a hard thing to think of, a hard memory to carry around with me.

"You find the baby?"

I nodded, my lips pressed hard together.

"Deceased?"

"Sure. Up in a tree. She was still in the carrier."

"God."

I nodded again. Nothing you could say about that. "But mostly it's not so bad," I said, after a long moment of allowing the memory to dissipate. "Mostly it's girls who don't come home, or older people who wander away. Sometimes abducted kids—not too often, because if someone picked them up in a vehicle, of course there's no way to guess where the body would be."

"So you take cases where the body location is known?"

"Well, if it can be pinned down to a reasonable area. You couldn't say, 'Hey, he was hiking somewhere in the Mojave Desert,' and expect me to find anything. Unless you had unlimited money for the amount of time it'd take me."

"What's it like?"

"What?"

"The feeling, when a body's close."

"It's like a buzzing. A humming. In my bones, in my brain. It almost hurts. The closer I get, the more intense it gets. And when I'm close, when I'm in the body's presence, I see the death."

"How much of the death?"

"I see the few seconds before it. But the only person I see

is the one who died. Not any other people around. At the same time, I'm in that person, feeling it. So it can be pretty . . . unpleasant."

"That seems like an understatement." He took a long sip of his beer.

I nodded. "I wish I could see the face of the murderer, but I never do."

"Couldn't prosecute on your word alone, anyway."

"Yeah, I get that, but still." I shrugged. "I'd be more useful."

"You look on your job as useful?"

"Sure. Everyone needs closure, right? Uncertainty eats at you; well, I meant 'you' in the general sense, but didn't it make you feel better when you knew what had happened to your wife? Plus, if people believe me, I can save lots of money. Like, 'Don't dredge that pond or send in divers. No body there.' Or, 'You don't need to search through the land-fill.' Stuff like that."

"If people believe you."

"Yeah. Lots don't."

"How do you handle that?"

"I've learned to let it go and walk away."

"It must be tough."

"At first it was. Not now. What about your job?"

"Oh about what you'd expect. Drunk drivers, mostly. Neighbor disputes. Sometimes some shoplifting. Burglary. Not too much that's mysterious or even very serious. Every now and then a wife-beater, or someone with a gun on a Sat-urday night. I never get to see anyone at their best." He gave me a crooked half-smile.

I'd wondered what we could possibly find to talk about,

but the next couple of hours went easier than I'd anticipated. He talked about deer hunting, and told me about the
time he'd fallen out of his shooting stand and gotten nothing worse than a sprained ankle, the same year his friend
John Harley had fallen from a stand and broken his back. I
had once hurt my back playing basketball. He had played
basketball in high school. He'd had a great time in high
school, but never wanted to revisit those days. I didn't either. I had spent my high school years trying to keep my
head down and my mouth shut so no one would find out
how truly weird my life was. Because of my mother and my
stepfather, I didn't want to bring anyone home with me. I'd
managed pretty well until Cameron vanished. Her disappearance had been so spectacular, so media-saturated, that it
had drawn a lot of unwanted attention to me.

"Seems like I remember that," Hollis said thoughtfully.
He was on his third beer. I was still nursing my second.
"Wasn't she taken by a man in a blue pickup?"

I nodded. "Grabbed on her way home. She'd been deco-
rating the gym for some dance. I'd walked home earlier, so
she was alone. This guy took her right off the street. There
were witnesses. But no one ever found her."

"I'm sorry," he said.

I nodded in acknowledgment. "Someday I'll find her," I
said. "Someday it'll be her, when I feel that buzz. And we'll
know what happened to her."

"Are your parents still alive?"

"My father is, I think. My mother died last year." Her ad-
dictions had finally succeeded in eating up her body.

"What's your connection with Tolliver?"

"Tolliver's dad married my mother. We were brought up

as family, after that." If we'd been "brought up" at all, I added to myself. Mostly, we'd fended for ourselves. After a while, we'd become good at presenting a facade to the authorities who might separate us. Tolliver watched over Cameron and me, I watched over the two littler girls, Mariella and Gracie. Tolliver's older brother Mark stopped by on a regular basis to make sure we were eating. If we weren't, Mark would bring groceries. Tolliver got a job at a restaurant as soon as he was old enough, and he brought home all the food he could.

Sometimes our parents were both working, sometimes we got government assistance. But mostly the money went down their throats or into their veins.

We learned to survive on very little, and we learned how to pick clothes at the thrift store and at yard sales, clothes that wouldn't give away our situation. Mark would lecture us on how important it was to make good grades. "As long as you keep clean and neat, don't skip school, and make at least average grades, social services won't come by," he'd taught us, and he'd been right. Until Cameron vanished.

I tried explaining those years to Hollis.

"That sounds horrible," Hollis said. His face looked sad, sad for the girl I had been, God bless him. "Did they hit you?"

"No," I said. "Neglect was the key to their parenting system, even for Mariella and Gracie. My mom tried to take care of them when they were babies, but after that, it was kind of up to Cameron and me, mostly me. It was hard for us not to go down the same drain." I had clung to my memory of what life had been like before—before my mother had begun using drugs, before my father had gone to jail.

I'd promised myself I could have that life again. My two younger sisters hadn't had as hard a time; they had no memory of anything better.

The tension of maintaining the status quo had almost killed me. But we'd managed, until Cameron got snatched.

"What happened then?" Hollis asked.

I fidgeted, looked anywhere else. "Let's talk about something else," I said. "The summary is that I spent my senior year living with a foster family, and my little half-sisters stayed with my aunt and uncle."

"How was the foster family?"

"They were decent people," I said. "Not child molesters, not slavedrivers. As long as I did my assigned chores and finished my homework, I wasn't unhappy." It had been an acute pleasure to live in a household that valued order and cleanliness.

"Any trace of your sister ever found?"

"Her purse. Her backpack." I shifted my right leg, which tended to numb if I didn't move it around.

"Tough."

"Yeah, I'd say we've both had lives that had a few bumps."

Hollis nodded. "Here's to trying to live a better life," he said, and we bumped glasses.

We went to his small house later, gaining a little comfort and warmth from each other. But I wouldn't spend the night, though he wanted me to stay. About three in the morning, I kissed him goodbye at the door to my motel room, and we held each other for a long minute. I went inside by myself, cold to my bones.

# Seven

~~~

IT was a good morning for running: the third clear day in a row, chilly, with the promise of brilliance in the early sky. I ran a brush through my hair and put on my dogtag engraved with my name and Tolliver's cell phone number. I dressed in a sports bra and three-quarter length Lycra running pants. An old "Race for the Cure" T-shirt covered the little canister of pepper spray clipped to my pants. I'd found a plastic slotted cover with a hole punched in one end, and I slipped my room key in it and put it on the same chain with my dogtag.

After some warm-up stretches, I decided I'd run from the motel until I'd reached the Kroger that was at the other end of town. I didn't want to follow the main drag; even in Sarne, there'd be traffic, and I hated inhaling truck exhaust fumes. I had picked out a route that involved backstreets

lined with small businesses and homes. With an inner feeling of release, I began running.

When I was able to pick up my pace, it was possible to
think of something other than the act of running. A little to
my surprise, I felt better than I had expected: relaxed, not
guilty. Though I was fairly inexperienced, Hollis had
seemed a tender and considerate lover. He'd also seemed to
need the contact, the basic act of joining flesh, as much as I
had. *So*, I told myself, *that was actually an okay thing to do.*

Absorbed in my thoughts, I gradually realized a pickup
was moving just behind me. The growl of the motor had
been chewing at the edge of my awareness for a minute or
two. My heart began pounding with an unpleasant desperation when I realized the driver was definitely dogging me.
The dark shadow in the corner of my left eye turned into a
rumbling presence. Though I kept running at a steady pace,
all my attention was focused on the truck creeping along
like a lion through high grass, waiting for my inattention to
prove fatal. I flipped open the little holster and eased the
canister of pepper spray out of it. Was Arkansas one of the
states where the spray was legal? I couldn't remember, and
at the moment I decided that was the least of my worries. I
was at least half a mile from the motel, and there were few
cars stirring in the streets. I couldn't count on any help. The
little canister was almost completely concealed in my hand.

I was in front of a little strip of businesses that hadn't yet
opened; a laundry, a jewelry store, an insurance agency. No
cars, no passersby. The tension roiled under my skin as I
waited for whoever was in the pickup to act. If they would
just wait until we were closer to the main street, or if I could

angle through the downtown buildings to the police station . . . but then the suspense was over.

The pickup swerved to pull across the sidewalk, blocking my path, and three young men hopped out. Of course! Alpha male, the high school boy Mary Nell had called Scotty. He had his two buddies with him, naturally.

I stopped, and they ranged themselves in front of me, their faces ugly with tension. Incongruously, the three were wearing high school football jackets. Scotty was in the middle, and a smaller black-haired boy was on my right. There was a husky brown-haired boy, uniformly thick through the chest and middle, on my left. They didn't have weapons, at first glance. But they all had clenched fists.

"Hey bitch, we told you to leave town," Scotty said. His words' ugliness twisted his face. The three were suppressing so much excitement they were literally shifting from foot to foot, shoulders moving restlessly.

My eyes went from face to face as I wondered who would charge first. They were cocked and primed and ready to fire.

"You guys thinking of raping me?" I asked, wanting to have it clear in my mind.

They looked shocked. *Shocked.* The two followers looked at the alpha, so he could answer for them. Or maybe they needed to find out what they wanted to do.

"We don't want any part of you, you skanky ho," Scotty said, trying to sound scornful, to square his lack of rape aspiration with his need to assert his manhood. Of course, real men should be ready to have any sort of sex, any time. So if they didn't want to rape me, I must not be desirable.

"That's good," I said, and then I saw that the black-haired boy on my right had gotten too tense to hold back any longer. His arm had gone back to hit me. Stupid to telegraph like that. I sprayed him right in the face, and he turned red and began clawing at his eyes and shrieking.

"It's burning! I can't see!" he screamed. While his two buddies were staring at him with their mouths open, I sprayed them, too, though Scotty tried to dodge at the last minute, and I didn't get his eyes.

The blip of a police siren scared me out of what wits I had left. When I'd recovered from the shock, I was delighted to see the police car, and even more delighted to see that the driver was Sheriff Harvey Branscom.

He was not as glad to see me as I was to see him.

"What happened here?" he asked, surveying the young men with disgust. They were crying and moaning, and the black-haired boy was actually on the ground.

"They swerved in front of me and got out of the truck to threaten me," I said.

"No, Sheriff," wailed the black-haired boy who'd swung his fist first. "It was her! She—"

"She pulled your truck over to the sidewalk, dragged you out, and made you stand in a row in front of her so she could squirt you with pepper spray?" Harvey Branscom would have loved a credible reason to blame me, but he was honest enough not to manufacture one. "You three make me sick. Scot, if I see you even cast a glance at my niece after this little incident, I'll find a way to stick you in jail, and you won't like it one little bit."

I wasn't sure if Scot was absorbing any of Sheriff Branscom's threats, since he was doubled over rubbing at his burning face. That was exactly the wrong thing to do, according to the booklet that came with the pepper spray. Sheriff Branscom sighed heavily and pulled a six-pack of Ozark Mountain bottled water out of the police car. "Lucky I ride around with this," he muttered. He opened a bottle and made the boys stand still while he poured it over their faces.

"I hope you're all ashamed of yourselves. Not only were you on the edge of committing a felony, you were three big guys about to beat up a lone woman. Not only *that,* but you're tardy for school, and that means you're all going to be in detention this afternoon, which means you're going to miss football practice. I'm going to be interested to hear what the coach puts you through after I call him and explain the reason. And I will call him." Harvey raised his eyebrows at me. "That is, unless this lady wants to bring charges against you? If she does, you ain't going to get to school anytime today."

I knew a cue when I heard one. I hesitated. Then I nodded, and I saw the tension leave the sheriff's shoulders. "If you call their football coach, and you're sure he can give them a good punishment, I'll be satisfied with that. After all," I said pointedly, "if I bring charges against them, they'll be off the team, at least for a while."

Harvey looked relieved. "Yes, they would be off the team. And of course, their parents would know all about this little fiasco. I figure a felony arrest would sure screw up their college applications, huh? Your dad would love to hear your explanation for this, Scot, especially since he just had to pay for three new mailboxes on Bainbridge Road. Justin, I know your mama had a hard time buying that football jacket." Justin was weeping too hard to reply, but he did look a little more miserable. "Cody, what do you think your grandmother would have to say about you attacking a woman?"

"We just wanted her to leave town," Cody muttered. I must not have aimed well when I sprayed him.

My heart was still thumping like a rabbit's when it hears the dog in the bushes. It was an unpleasant and humiliating feeling, being this frightened. If I hadn't had my pepper spray, or if the sheriff hadn't intervened, by this time I'd have a broken jaw, or some fractured ribs. Three big boy/men, only a few years younger than I . . . they might have killed me by sheer stupid accident.

Harvey Branscom was as good as his word. He whipped out his cell phone and called the football coach at the high school, and without spelling out what the boys had almost done, he let the coach know they deserved the worst punishment the coach could hand out. I knew a football coach could hand out plenty, especially in season. I wasn't dissatisfied with the bargain I'd struck with the sheriff. I thought that in Sarne it was the best I would manage.

When he thought Scot could see well enough to drive his pickup, Branscom sent the boys on their way to school. After they'd driven out of sight, and my heart had calmed down to a normal rate, Sheriff Branscom said, "Miss Connelly, I guess you aren't popular here in Sarne." I sure wasn't popular with the elder law enforcement segment. His face was hard with repressed distaste. "I'm sorry that happened to you. Scot's had it bad for Mary Nell since they were in the first grade together."

I was still bouncing on the balls of my feet with adrenaline. "And he shows it by beating up another woman?"

"No, the idiot shows it by defending my niece against someone he imagines is going to hurt her," Branscom said heavily. He leaned against his car. At this moment, he looked far older than his years. "People around here just can't understand you or what you do, Ms. Connelly. It makes it worse that you're for real, I think. You did find Teenie, sure enough. But we're not closer to finding out who killed her, and there's still no way to prove Dale didn't. Somehow, finding Teenie has led to Helen getting killed, too. In fact, I guess we'll be burying Teenie and her mother at the same time, side by side, right in the plot with Sally. According to what you told Hollis, that's three murder victims in the same family. I wish that bolt of lightning had struck you a little harder. Maybe you would have seen enough to straighten out this mess."

Or maybe, his unspoken thought continued, I would have been killed and none of this would be a problem. I was swept with a wave of overwhelming disbelief. "You've had months and months to solve any mystery surrounding Dell's death and Teenie's disappearance," I said, almost whispering in an effort not to shout. "You have a police force and a police lab at your service in solving Helen's murder. I'm *one woman* who can find bodies, and I never claimed to be more. Don't you dare try to shift any of the blame for this whole mess to me."

Another police car pulled up behind the sheriff's. Hollis, creaking and heavily laden in his cop gear, was out of the car and beside us before I could make my mouth try to smile at him.

"Are you all right?" he asked, his hand cupping the curve of my shoulder. He leaned down to look in my face. What he saw there made him angry. "I stopped the Briscoe boy over by the high school for speeding, and he looked so bad I asked what happened to him. He told me everything, didn't understand why I didn't applaud."

I felt old. In the chilly breeze, my running clothes seemed inadequate, and the only warmth in the world was my skin under Hollis's hand. "I'm all right," I said steadily. "I think I'll finish my run and get back to the motel."

"Where's your brother? You want me to go get him and bring him here?"

Suddenly, my head felt as light as a balloon. I realized that the combination of intense fear followed by intense relief—and then equally intense anger—had just made me numb. And it was something, you know . . . hearing Hollis be intuitive enough to hit on the one thing I found I wanted above all else. But I wasn't going to ask him for it.

"I appreciate your concern," I said very softly. "But I'm just going to run, now."

I don't know if he understood or not; I hope he did grasp my sincerity. Since we were on the side of a public road, I didn't want to hug him. Even if we'd been in a more private situation, I'm not sure I'd have hugged him. But I tried to smile at him as I began to jog down the road. I moved very slowly, because my body chemistry was all screwed up; my muscles didn't know if they were cold from inactivity or warm from adrenaline, and my mind was scurrying around many different corners, but focused on one thing—finishing this run, out of pride.

I got back to the motel with no further incident. I had completed my self-assigned distance. I was walking around the parking lot outside my room, cooling down, trying hard to put the fear behind me. Stupid. I was stupid, stupid, stupid.

My brother came down the road, finishing up his own run. I hastily went to my own door and slid in the plastic card.

"No, you don't!" he called out. "You stay right there."

Shit. I kept my back to him.

He spun me around by one shoulder. He looked me up and down.

"Are you all right?" he asked.

He'd run into one of the lawmen.

"Yes," I said, trying not to sound sullen. "I'm fine. Who told you?"

"I saw Hollis Boxleitner," he said. "That where you were last night?"

I nodded, not meeting Tolliver's eyes.

"We have to get out of this place," he said. "We could go if they found out who did this."

"Maybe it would do some good if I could get to Helen's body," I said. "I might pick up something."

"Hollis said she got a phone call after we'd left her place that morning. The lawyer called her. Paul Edwards."

"What about?"

"Hollis didn't say. I don't guess he mentioned it last night?"

"No." I could feel my face heating up.

"But the sheriff still doesn't want us to go, because he still thinks we must know something."

"We could just leave anyway," I said. "There's no legal way he can keep us here, right?"

"I don't think so," Tolliver said. He'd been gripping my

arms, and when he let go, I got that tingly feeling as blood rushed back through the veins and arteries. "But you know one bad word from law enforcement will mean we'll lose a lot of jobs."

That was true enough. The last time a chief of police had been dissatisfied with me—he'd been convinced I had some prior knowledge of the body's location, that I was in direct communication with the killer and out to feather my own nest—I'd had almost no income for six months. It had been a hard time, and I'd had enough hard times. I didn't want any more, ever.

"Your boyfriend'll give us a good word," Tolliver said teasingly, trying to lift my spirits.

I didn't even protest over Tolliver's use of the term "boyfriend." I knew he didn't believe that Hollis was anything to me. As usual, he was both right and wrong.

# eight

GLEASON and Sons Mortuary was a place of heavy carpeting and dark corners. It was picturesquely located in an old Victorian-style home, and it was landscaped outside and painted a serene blue inside, with stained-glass windows that must have cost a small fortune. The restored Victorian held the two viewing rooms, an office where the families could select—and pay—for caskets and other services, and a kitchen to brew the constant stream of coffee consumed by mourners. A low, discreet modern addition in the rear held the grimmer rooms where the actual functions of the funeral home were conducted.

Elijah Gleason showed us the more public part before we went to the modern addition. He was proud of his accomplishments as the third Gleason in the funeral business in Sarne, and I had respect for following an honorable tradition. He was a short, stout man in his late thirties with slicked thick black hair and a wide, thin-lipped mouth.

"This is my wife Laura," he said as we passed an open door. The woman inside waved. She had very short brown hair and a rounded figure. "She does my books in the winter, and in the summer she's Aunt Hattie at Aunt Hattie's Ice Cream Parlor." The woman smiled and nodded in an abstract way and returned her attention to the computer screen before her. From the coatrack in the corner hung a soft, flowered bonnet and a matching long apron. I hoped Aunt Hattie's was air conditioned.

"I guess your business is pretty constant, rather than seasonal," I said, for lack of some better response.

Elijah Gleason said, "You'd be surprised. We get at least two deaths a summer from the tourists. Of course, those are usually just getting the remains ready to send to their home mortuary, but it all adds up."

I could think of nothing to say to that, so I just nodded. I reminded myself to stay away from Sarne in the summer. It was somehow embarrassing to think of these people dressing up to imitate a past that was hotter, smellier, more ignorant, and chock-full of deaths that nowadays could be easily prevented. Women in childbirth, kids with polio, babies with conflicting Rh factors, men whose fingers turned septic after little accidents with a saw . . . I'd seen all these during my little outing at the cemetery. Most people didn't think about this aspect of living in the past when they tried to imagine how it must have been. They saw the absence of what they perceived as modern ills: abortion, homosexuality, television, divorce. They saw the past in terms of Friday evening fiddling with the neighbors on the front porch, shoofly pie, gospel singing, long happy marriages.

I saw sudden, needless death.

Soon enough we were in the new part of the funeral home, and the director was showing us Helen. Hollis had asked him to do it, after assuring Gleason I wouldn't faint or throw up at the sight of the body. I like funeral homes. I like the attempt to make death presentable and palatable. It's a cushion to life. It's like the pretty padded lining to the coffin. The dead sure don't care, but makes the living feel better.

The buzzing in my head steadily increased as we grew closer to the room with the closed door. It reached a high drone when I stepped into the bright white sterility of the modern embalming room.

"I haven't started on her yet," Elijah Gleason said. "I just got her back from the state crime lab. It'll take them months to finish the toxicology, they told me, they're hundreds of cases behind."

"Would you stay outside?" Tolliver asked. "It's just that my sister has a pretty startling reaction sometimes, and it might alarm you."

"Sorry," Gleason said firmly. "Helen's body's under my care, and I'm staying with her."

Well, I hadn't expected much different. I nodded, all my attention focused on the form on the tilted table. I held up a hand to ask the two men not to speak.

I approached Helen. From her neck down, she was covered by a sheet. Her hair had been brushed. The hum of her presence filled my head. Her soul was still there. That was very unexpected. I jerked with surprise. For the soul to linger three days after death, especially when the body had been found, was almost unprecedented. I knew I would get more information since she was still intact. But I felt full of pity. My neck muscles began to jerk, almost imperceptibly, because I wasn't trying to search for her, she was right in front of me. And she was intact.

The funeral home director was eyeing me with ill-concealed disgust. "She's there," I said very softly, and I saw Gleason's face go slack with horror. I glanced at Tolliver, and he nodded, understanding. "I'm just going to touch her," I explained to Gleason. "With respect."

I stared down at Helen's battered face, my neck and facial muscles relaxing finally. All the bruising made her look as if someone had painted her in shades of dark. Under the edge of the sheet, my fingertips made contact with the skin of her shoulder.

From a distance, I could hear myself gasp—a deep, throaty, alarmed sound. I could see the arm upraised, the arm that held a candlestick. I was crouching down, trying to avoid the blow. The arm was a man's, in a long sleeve. An overwhelming sense of betrayal and shock. The glimpse of the descending arm. Pain and disillusionment, bitterness, the hope of resurrection, a terrifying blend of final emotions. And then nothing, nothing, nothing.

"I know," I whispered. "You can go, now."

And the soul of Helen Hopkins left her body.

This had only happened to me once before. I hadn't known what to do then, had only stumbled on the presence of the dead person by accident. This is what leads to the stories of haunting. The soul wants some acknowledgment of its struggle; the agony involved in the death of the body, and the emotional turmoil of being killed, somehow adhere the soul to the body. If not addressed before burial, this adhesion leads to hauntings.

I'd laid Helen Hopkins to rest before she was even buried. I had done something good.

But I'd endured her final moment with her, and the aftermath settled in. I was very shaky, and I felt Tolliver take my arm and lead me to a metal chair. What was in front of me finally registered in my brain, and I realized that Elijah Gleason was staring at me, mouth agape, eyes narrowed. I knew that look. It was a witch-burning look.

"Helen is at rest with our Lord," I said immediately, and I managed to smile. They like that.

Gleason looked a smidge less horrified. "You can tell?" he asked, at last.

"Yes," I said, my voice firm. "She is in heaven with all the saints, in eternal glory."

This toeing of the line always impressed them and got them off my back. It was a card I hated to play. I'm not saying I'm an unbeliever. Nor am I an agnostic. But I have to talk to other people about God in ways they'll understand, because my God doesn't seem to be anything like theirs. Even if they don't believe—really, truly—themselves, they're always reassured to hear the terms of fundamental Christianity. In fact, coming from me, it shakes their half-concealed disbelief.

And it keeps me safe. Tolliver, too.

Gleason flung the sheet over Helen's face, and I looked at the length of flesh draped in the bleached cotton. It was empty now, and it was just a collection of cells that would accelerate its dissolution now that it had served its purpose.

When we were back in the cool sunshine again, I asked Tolliver if we could track down a friend of Helen's. After a phone call to Hollis, who said Helen's best friend was Annie Gibson, we consulted a Sarne directory. Five minutes later we were sitting in a front room that was nearly a clone of Helen Hopkins'. The photographs of children as they aged, the big family Bible on the coffee table, the crowded clean furniture and the smell of cooking . . . it was all familiar. The only touch that differentiated the house was the set of newer pictures: Annie Gibson had grandchildren. There was a basket of toys in the corner, waiting for little hands to strew them around the small room.

Annie Gibson herself was nothing like Helen Hopkins, no matter if they shared the same concept of interior arrangement. Annie was fat, and her hair was short and curly. She wore glasses with blue plastic rims, and she breathed heavily. There was nothing stupid about Annie Gibson. She wouldn't let us sit down in her shabby house until we'd shown her our driver's licenses, and she offered us coffee in a way that let us know it was automatic courtesy and not heartfelt.

"Helen told me about your visit," Annie Gibson said. "I don't know if you're good people or not. But she spoke well of you, and that'll have to be good enough for me. I'm going to miss Helen. We had coffee together every other day, just about, and we went shopping in Little Rock together twice a year. We sent each other birthday cards." Tears began running down her plump cheeks, and Annie reached for the box of tissues on the table before her. She patted the tears and blew her nose, unself-consciously. "Our mamas were best friends, and they had us the same month."

I tried to imagine having the same person as a friend for so long. Annie Gibson was probably in her late thirties. I tried to imagine having grandchildren, but I couldn't even project how it would feel to have a child. Having a friend for as long as Annie had had Helen—that was something equally unimaginable.

*I would be lucky to live that long,* I thought. I watched the tail end of that thought trail out of sight and wondered where it had come from. At the moment, I had to pay attention to this woman across from me.

"I have to talk to you about something you may not like," I said. This was a direct woman, and I sensed it would be better to approach her head-on.

"You have to run it by me before I decide." Her face might be soft physically, but there was nothing soft about her will. "Some things ought to be secret."

"I agree," I said. I leaned forward, my elbows on my knees. "Ms. Gibson, Helen herself told us she had a bad time when she was drinking."

Annie Gibson nodded, her eyes not leaving my face. "That's so," she said.

"With Teenie being murdered, Helen was real upset when she asked us to come by to talk to her," I said, going so slowly, so carefully. "When I told her about Teenie and Sally, she said, 'I'll have to call their fathers.' What I want to know from you is, Who was Teenie's father?"

Annie Gibson shook her head. The brown curls moved with her, as if they'd been fixed in place with spray. Maybe they had. "I promised Helen I'd never tell," she said. "She told me not to tell even if Teenie came and asked me."

"And did she?" I asked. I blessed my brother for his silence.

"Yes," Annie said without hesitation. "Yes, she did. Right before she died."

"So, it seems like that was a pretty crucial secret," I said. "You see? She asked, and she died. Helen tells me she's going to call Teenie's father, and she dies."

Annie Gibson looked startled, as though she'd finally put two and two together. "But that can't be," she said. "He'd have no reason to."

"He must have," I said. I tried to keep my voice gentle and reasonable. "I told Helen that Hollis's wife Sally was murdered, too. All three members of that family are gone now. And they all knew who Teenie's father was."

"Not Teenie," Annie Gibson said. "Teenie never knew. I didn't tell her. I promised Helen I wouldn't. And I knew she'd asked Helen, many a time, after she began to suspect it wasn't Jay."

"Jay?" Tolliver asked.

"Helen's husband. Sally's father. He's coming back for the funeral. He may have been divorced from Helen, but I guess he inherits the house now. He called me this morning."

"Where is he staying?" I wondered if he would have a few words with us.

"He's at the motel where ya'll are at. But don't expect to get much sense out of him. Helen may have quit drinking, but Jay ain't. She had to take out a restraining order on him, I guess a year or two after Sally was born. Jay used to be a nice-looking man, and he had sweet folks, but he ain't worth a tinker's damn."

"We've had experience in dealing with drunks," I said.

"Oh, like that, huh?" She looked at me, with level eyes. "I thought I seen the mark on you."

"The mark?"

"Kids raised by drunks. They all got the same mark. I can see it. Not everyone can."

I was certainly not the only person walking this earth possessed of a weird little talent.

Tolliver and I rose to our feet, and Annie wiggled forward on her chair to rise with us. I looked around the small house, and I noticed she had good locks on the doors. And it was obvious a drove of friends and family came in and out all the time. The phone had rung twice while we were there, and she'd let her answering machine take the call. Annie seemed fairly well protected.

"If I were you," I said, very carefully, "I'd go to Little Rock for a couple of days to go shopping, or something like that."

"Are you threatening me?" she said right back at me.

"No ma'am, I am not. I liked Helen, the little I knew of her. And I saw her after she died. I don't want you to be as scared as she was."

"Sounds to me like you *are* threatening me," Annie Gibson said. Her jaw hardened, and she looked like a very determined pug.

"I swear I am not," I said, as earnestly as I could. "I'm just worried about you." She wasn't going to listen to a word I said, so I might as well save my breath. From now on, anything Tolliver and I told her would go straight to feed her conviction that we meant her ill.

"You all need to go to the gospel singing tonight, get some good thoughts in your head," she concluded, shutting the door behind us.

"I thought Helen was a tough nut to crack," I muttered. "I just hadn't met Annie Gibson."

We ate lunch at a McDonald's, which showed we were at the bottom of our spirits. Our parents had fed us from the fast-food place so often when we were little that we could hardly bear the smell of one now. When my mother had been married to my father, and we'd had the nice home in Memphis, we had a maid I'd been fond of. Her name was Marilyn Coachman. She was a stern black woman, you didn't back talk her, and when she told you to do something, you did it. The minute she'd realized my mother was using drugs, Marilyn quit. I wondered where Marilyn was now.

I looked down at the French fries in their grease-marked cardboard sleeve and shoved them away. She was a great cook.

"We need vegetables," I said.

Tolliver said, "Potatoes are a vegetable. And ketchup is made from tomatoes. I know technically they're a fruit, but I always think of them as vegetables."

"Very funny. I mean it. You know I have to avoid this shit. We need a place where we can live. I'll learn to cook."

"You mean it?"

"I do."

"You want to buy a house."

"We've talked about it before."

"But I didn't . . . You were serious, huh?"

"Yes." I was deeply hurt. "I guess you weren't."

He put down his Big Mac. He wiped his fingers on the paper napkin. A very young mother went by, carrying one child on her hip. The other hand held a tray full of food and drinks. A boy, maybe five, followed close on her heels. She put the tray down on a nearby table and began getting the children into their places and sorting out the food. She looked harried. Her bra strap kept falling down her arm; both her arms were bare. She was wearing a sleeveless tank top despite the chilly day.

Tolliver was giving me all his attention, now. "You're still thinking Dallas?"

"Or thereabouts. We could find a nice small house, maybe in Longview or even closer to Dallas, to the north. That'd be more central than the Atlanta area, which was the other place we'd discussed."

His dark eyes searched mine. "Dallas is close to Mariella and Grace."

"Maybe they won't always feel the same."

"Maybe they will. There's no point banging our heads against that wall."

"Someday they'll change."

"You think those people will let us see them?" Mariella and Grace now lived with my stepfather's sister and her husband. Tolliver's aunt Iona had never intervened to save me and Cameron, or her blood kin Tolliver and Mark. But when the end came, when Human Services discovered after Cameron's abduction how bad things were in our household and I'd been farmed out to a foster family and Tolliver had gone to his brother, Iona and Hank had swooped down to save poor precious Mariella and baby Grace, in a hail of publicity and denials of all knowledge of how low my mother had sunk.

After living with Iona and Hank two months, our little sisters had gone from regarding us as their saviors and defenders to reacting as if we had visible plague sores.

Out of many painful memories of that short era, the picture of Grace screaming, "I don't want to see you ever again!" when I'd gone to pick her up was the most shattering.

"It couldn't be them," I said for maybe the hundredth time to Tolliver, as we sat surrounded by the smell of cooking oil and lots of primary colors. "They loved us." He nodded, as he had every other time.

"Iona and Hank have convinced them we had something to do with how that household was run," he said.

"Or not run. How it was bungled," I said, out of the deep well of bitterness that separated me from other people.

"She's dead now," he said, very quietly. "He might as well be."

"I know, I know. I'm sorry." I waved a hand in front of my face, to dispel the recurrence of anger. "I just can't help but hope that someday the little girls will be grown up enough to understand."

"It won't ever be the same." Tolliver was my oracle, and he knew. He almost always said the things I was scared to even think. He was right.

"I guess not. But someday they'll need a sister and a brother, and they'll call us."

He bent back to his food. "Some days, I hope not," he said very quietly, and I couldn't think of anything to say.

I knew what he meant. We had no one to answer to. We had no one to take care of. We only had each other. After years of desperately plastering the cracks in our family so no one could see in, just watching out for each other in the here and now seemed relatively simple and even soothing.

Hollis sat down at our table, his meal in a bag in his hand. "I hope I'm not interrupting anything," he said. "I was going through the drive-through and I saw you two in here. You looked mighty serious."

Tolliver gave the policeman a sharp glance. Hollis was in

uniform. He looked good in it. I smiled down at what was left of my lunch.

"We're ready to leave this town," Tolliver said. "But we can't go until the sheriff gives us the nod."

"What happened at the funeral home?" Hollis wisely ignored Tolliver.

I told him that Helen had been killed by someone she knew and trusted, which was no revelation. Her little house had been as neat as a house can be that's the site of a violent murder. No one had broken into it. No one had rifled it.

"Someone wearing long sleeves, not a uniform." I knew that.

"That's all you got?"

"*No, I released Helen's soul to heaven,*" I wanted to say. But there are a lot of things that are better left unsaid, and this was definitely one of them. "Tell me, Hollis . . . someone told me that Helen had taken out a restraining order on her first husband, Jay. Is that so?"

"Yeah, Jay was a drunk like Helen was, at least at the time. He was drunk at Sally's and my wedding, for sure. My uncle had to take him out of the church because he was getting loud. It embarrassed Sally real bad." Hollis shook his head at the recollection. "He's back in town, I hear. Evidently, Helen had made a will. Jay inherits the house and what little Helen had in the bank."

"Why would Helen leave what she had to a man who abused her so badly?" That hadn't fit the Helen Hopkins I'd met, however briefly.

Hollis cleared his throat. "Ah, well, she might have been grateful that he was willing to acknowledge Teenie as his."

"No one knows for sure who Teenie's dad was?"

"No, but there must have been at least a chance that Jay was. They never had a DNA test, though. Jay acted like she was his, and Helen put his name on forms, so—"

"Why would he agree to that?" Tolliver asked, his eyes still focused on the food wrappers. He was crushing them into balls and putting each ball on our tray.

"If he said she wasn't, he'd have been admitting his wife wasn't satisfied with him," Hollis explained, as if the answer were self-evident.

"He'd rather acknowledge a bastard than admit his wife had slept with someone else?" Tolliver was openly skeptical.

"And it was the gentlemanly thing to do." Hollis did some staring in another direction himself this time. He was looking at me, and I could feel the heat rising in my face. "Sometimes men do the right thing," Hollis said, very seriously.

"But if Teenie wasn't his, he was denying another man the chance to do the right thing," I said.

"Weren't a lot of men clamoring for the honor of claiming the baby," Hollis said.

I remembered high school all too clearly. There was something that had baffled me from the start, and now seemed as good a time as any to ask Hollis about it. "There's something I don't understand. Dell Teague didn't mind dating a girl with such a bad reputation? He's from the best family in town, right? Or at least the one with the most money. And yet . . . he's dating a girl who has an alcoholic mother and an absent father, a poor girl, a wild girl." I waited, with my eyebrow cocked, for Hollis to comment.

Hollis ruminated for a minute or two. "They didn't run with the same crowd, until Helen started working for Sybil.

She'd have Teenie come over there, after school, and do her homework. They were drawn to each other from that time, is all I know to tell you. When Teenie got into trouble after that, it was when Dell's parents decided to interfere between them, or when Helen was on a tear. If Teenie couldn't go out with Dell, she'd raise hell."

That was interesting. It didn't lead anywhere, but it was interesting.

I folded my own wrappers neatly and put them on the same tray with Tolliver's.

"Before Helen had to get a restraining order against Jay, was their relationship violent? Did the cops have to go there every weekend? Or did something specific spark that episode?"

Hollis looked thoughtful. "If it came to that, it was before my time on the force. You'd have to ask one of the older guys about that. One of 'em runs the hotel where you're staying at, Vernon McCluskey? He'd know about that."

We weren't exactly popular with Vernon McCluskey, if he was the skinny older guy in overalls that was usually behind the motel counter, the one who'd hinted broadly that we weren't welcome anymore.

Tolliver got up to dump the trash from the tray into the garbage bin. One of the uniformed workers, a woman about twenty-five, watched him from her spot at one of the cash registers, an avid look in her eyes. She was short and dumpy and the McDonald's uniform didn't suit her. I'll give her this, she had outstandingly beautiful skin, something Tolliver's a real sucker for, maybe because of his own scarred face. I don't think it would occur to Tolliver to list "good skin" if someone asked him to make a list of things he found attractive, but I'd noticed that everyone he hit on had a clear complexion.

Today, this woman longed in vain, because Tolliver never once glanced her way. He went to the men's room, and while he was gone, Hollis asked me if I would see him again that night. "We can go to the gospel singing on the lawn at the courthouse. It's the last of the season. There won't be many tourists there, and you might enjoy it."

"I might, huh?" I thought about Annie Gibson's recommendation, and his big hand covered mine.

"Please," he said. "I want to see you again."

There were a lot of things I almost told him, but I didn't say them.

"All right," I finally said. "What time?"

"I'll take you out to eat first, okay? See you at the motel at six thirty," he said. His radio squawked, and he rose hastily, telling me goodbye at the same time he was taking his own tray to the stand by the door. As he pushed open the glass door, he was talking into his shoulder set.

Tolliver came back, swinging his hands in an exaggerated arc. "I hate those damn hot-air dryers," he said. "I like paper towels." I'd heard him complain about hot-air dryers maybe three hundred times, and I gave him an exasperated look.

"Rub your hands on your jeans," I said.

"Well, you got another date with lover-boy?"

"Oh, shut up," I said, mildly irritated. "Yes, as a matter of fact, I do."

"Maybe he's talking his boss into keeping us here so he can have another date with you."

Tolliver sounded so serious that I actually considered the

idea for a minute, before I caught my brother's smirk. I smacked him lightly and got up, hanging my purse on my shoulder. "Jerk," I said, smiling.

"You two gonna go watch the sidewalks roll up?"

"No, we're going to a gospel singing on the courthouse lawn, evidently." When Tolliver raised his eyebrows, I said seriously, "It's the last one of the season." He laughed out loud.

I felt a little ashamed of myself, though, and when we were going back to the motel I said, "He's a nice guy, Tolliver. I like him."

"I know," he said. "I know you do."

# nine

WE talked about approaching Vernon McCluskey when we were back at the motel. I was redoing my fingernails in a deep brown, and Tolliver was working a puzzle in a *New York Times* Sunday crossword collection. I knew what I was getting Tolliver for Christmas: some book containing the Hebrew alphabet. The Hebrew alphabet was a major feature of crossword puzzles, at least according to Tolliver, and he was totally ignorant about it. I might get him a world atlas, too. That way, if the question was "river in Siberia" he could damn well look it up, instead of asking me.

"Why are we talking to this asshole?" Tolliver asked. "He's made it clear he wants us out of here. Do we really need to find out about Helen Hopkins' relationship to her ex-husband? Why don't we just lie low until the sheriff lets us go? How long can he actually keep us here? Not long. One phone call to a lawyer, and we're out of here."

I looked at Tolliver, the polish brush suspended over my little fingernail. "We don't want to be remembered here as people who were released because they couldn't find anything to pin on us, do we? You know how we operate. People will be calling Branscom to find out what kind of job we did. They'll ask him how cooperative we were. We need to look as though we're taking him seriously, that we're trying to get to the bottom of these deaths, too. That we care."

"Do we care?" He tossed his pencil on top of the crossword puzzle book. "I think you do."

I hesitated, taken aback by what sounded very much like an accusation. "It bothers you?"

"That depends on what you care about."

"I kind of liked Helen Hopkins," I said at last, very carefully. "So, yeah, I'm upset that someone cracked her skull. I care that two young people were shot, that they died out in the woods, that people think the boy killed her and then himself. That's not what happened."

"Do you feel like they're asking you to investigate?"

"They?"

"The dead people."

I felt a big light bursting behind my eyeballs. "No," I said. "Not at all. Nobody knows better than I do that dead is dead. They're not wanting anything. Well, maybe Helen Hopkins was, but now she's released."

"You don't feel an obligation?"

I polished my little fingernail. "Nope. We did what we were paid for. I don't like thinking about someone getting away with murder, but I'm not a cop, either." I wished immediately that I hadn't added the last phrase.

Tolliver got to his feet, suddenly in a hurry. "I'm going

to go wash the car. I'm pretty sure there's an Easy Klean right off Main Street. But I'll stop by the office to ask the McCluskey guy for the location. It'll give me an excuse to talk to him. I'll be gone about an hour, more or less."

"Sure, that sounds good. You don't want me to talk to McCluskey?"

"No. He thinks you're the great Satan, remember? I'm just Satan's assistant."

I smiled at him. "Okay, thanks. You want me to tell Hollis you're coming with us, tonight?"

"No, Harper. You go enjoy being a girl for a while."

He didn't sound like he meant it. "What's that supposed to mean?"

"Did you ever stop to think we could settle down in a town like this? We could quit what we're doing? We could get regular jobs?"

Of course I'd thought of it. "No," I said. "It's never crossed my mind."

"Liar. You could date some guy like Hollis for real. You could work in a department store, or in an office. Somewhere with live people."

I looked away from his face. "You could date a hundred Janines, or even wait for Mary Nell Teague to grow up," I countered. "You could get a job at a Home Depot. You'd be manager in no time."

"Could we do that?" he asked. He didn't mean, could we do it if we had the option; we had the option, all right. He meant, was it possible for us to settle down to being regular citizens.

"It would be pretty hard," I said, after a pause, in a noncommittal voice.

"Getting a house might be the first step," he said.

I shrugged. "Could be."

He shut the door behind him very quietly.

We didn't talk much about the future.

Of course, I'd had plenty of opportunities to think about it. We spent a lot of time driving. Though we listened to audiobooks and the radio, inevitably there were long periods of silence.

Though I didn't want to tell Tolliver this, I thought way too much about our past. I tried not to dwell on the squalor of daily life in that house in Texarkana. Maybe if I hadn't been raised so gently to start with, it wouldn't have bothered me quite so much. But the descent from pampered princess to virgin pussy peddled for drug money had been too shocking, too abrupt. I hadn't seasoned slowly enough. I'd acquired a hard brittle shell instead of toughening all the way through.

"Bullshit," I said out loud. "To hell with this." I pushed introspection right out of my brain and turned on the television. My nails were beautiful by the time I finished with them.

Tolliver returned about four o'clock, a lot later than I'd expected. When he came in, I smelled a whiff of beer and sex. Okay, I told myself. Steady. Tolliver almost never drank much, and he wasn't drunk now. But the fact that he'd had a beer during the day, and the fact that he'd stayed away to have sex when he knew I'd be anxious—those were significant facts.

"Well, the car is clean," he said, "and I talked to former police officer McCluskey, who is without a doubt one of the most repellent people I've ever had a conversation with."

"That's good, about the car," I said. I was pleased with how level my voice was. "What did McCluskey have to say? Anything interesting?"

"It took me forever to get him soothed down and to the point," Tolliver said.

"This is part of your build-up, to let me know what a tedious job I gave you?"

"Damn straight. I worked for this information."

"Um-hmmm."

"And I expect you to appreciate that."

"Oh, believe me, I do."

"Do I hear some sarcasm in your voice?"

"God forbid."

"Then I'll finish what I was saying."

"Please do."

Tolliver sprawled on my bed, lying on his back with his arms flung out on either side.

"McCluskey—did I mention how nasty the man is? McCluskey's decided I'm your bodyguard, and he wanted to know how I managed to stay around you, since surely you were marked by the devil."

"Oh, yeah? And I thought I'd showered real well."

"You probably missed some Satan behind the ears."

"Sorry about that."

"Well, he thinks anything to do with contacting the dead, or seeing the dead, is a big church no-no, and anyone who claims to be able to do that is—"

"Let me guess—Evil?"

"How'd you know? Amazing! You're right!"

"Just lucky."

"Anyway." Tolliver yawned. "He heard about the boys

this morning, and though he thought young men shouldn't hurt women, he also thought putting a scare in you was a good thing."

"Oh, gee, thanks."

"I told him it wasn't." Tolliver sounded suddenly sincere. "I told him if anything happened like that again, I'd be forced to display some of my amazing bodyguard skills, learned at the Special Forces camp."

"What Special Forces camp?"

"Obviously, the one that exists to train specially vicious and lethal bodyguards."

"Oh, that one."

"Right. Anyway, he swallowed some of that story, and he said that he was sure nothing else like that would happen to you here in Sarne, since Sheriff Branscom was so put out about your being threatened."

"Well, actually, that's nice to know."

"That's what I thought. Do you think it's safe for you to go out tonight?"

I stopped looking at my fingernails and started looking at Tolliver.

"I'm not trying to stop you," he said hastily. "You go on with Officer Friendly, if you want to. I'm just reminding you, this is a fundamentalist community and they don't admire your ability."

I held my tongue for a long minute, trying to think through Tolliver's advice. But I heard myself saying, "It's okay for you to go out and get laid while you're getting the car washed, and it's not okay for me to go to a gospel singing?"

Tolliver's skin reddened. "I just don't want anything to

happen to you," he said steadily. "You remember what happened in West Virginia."

In West Virginia, the entire populace of a tiny hamlet had thrown rocks at our car.

"I remember," I said. "But it was a smaller place, and it had a strong leader who hated the whole idea of me."

"You're saying there's no united front here in Sarne?"

I nodded.

"You may be right," he said, after a long moment. "But I just hate that anything . . ." his voice trailed off.

"I don't want to be the target of any kind of attack," I said, after a pause. "I do *not*. But I also don't want to cower in this hotel room."

"And you want to see Hollis again."

"Yes."

He looked away for a second. "Okay." He made himself nod. "It'll be good to go to something different. Have a good time."

I definitely didn't want to stand out, but I also thought it might be disrespectful to under-dress. I had a hard time imagining what you'd wear to an al fresco gospel concert. I picked what I thought of as neutral clothes: good slacks, a sweater set, loafers. I snatched up a heavier jacket when Hollis picked me up. He was wearing new jeans and a corduroy shirt—the softest narrow-wale corduroy I'd ever seen. He had a jacket, too. And he was wearing cowboy boots, which surprised me.

"Nice footwear," I said.

He looked down, as if he'd never seen his boots before. "I used to do a little riding," he said. "I got to like 'em."

He asked me how I was feeling after the incident of the

morning, and I told him I was fine. That wasn't entirely accurate, but close enough. I didn't want to think about it
anymore, and *that* was the truth.

There were cars parked all around the square, and the
pretty streetlights that had been put up for the tourists lent
the area an air of prosperity and quaintness. The broad
courthouse lawn was strewn with folding chairs of all kinds.
Little children were dashing through the gathering crowd,
shrieking and excited in the chill evening air. Since I was an
outsider, I couldn't tell the leafers from the locals, but Hollis told me the ratio was about forty to sixty.

The stage that had been thrown up at the base of the old
courthouse was not very high, and it was crowded with the
equipment of the first group to perform. A woman in a long
full skirt and a wide turquoise belt was tuning a guitar. Her
gray hair fell to her waist, and her face was deeply lined, intent and calm. The men behind her were in their forties and
fifties, and they all shared her air of professionalism.

"This here's Roberta Moore and her Sons of Grace," Hollis said. "They're from over to Mountain Home."

"How many groups will play?"

"We just see who shows up," he said. "Sometimes six or
seven, but tonight I only see three others. Bobby Tatum, he
sings by himself." Bobby Tatum was a very young man in a
cowboy hat and a very elaborate cowboy shirt and boots. His
jacket was Western-tailored, of course, and his clean-shaven
face gleamed with eagerness. He was chatting with a cluster
of girls who looked about Mary Nell's age, and they were
giggling at everything he said.

The other entertainers seemed to be groups like Roberta
Moore's. I eyed the amount of expensive equipment piled up

behind the stage and was taken aback. This wasn't slapdash and amateurish. These people knew their stuff.

As the darkness gathered closer, Hollis got a blanket from the truck and moved his chair right by mine so we could share its warmth. Terry Vale, the mayor, made some public service announcements. He was far from the anxious man I'd met at the sheriff's office. He was happy, relaxed. "The tan Chevy Venture blocking the driveway to Martin's Pharmacy, be advised you've blocked Jeb Martin in, and he sure wants to go home. Unless you want him to call the tow truck, you better get over there with an apology on your lips," Terry Vale said, and the crowd laughed. A very young man with a sparse mustache got up, abashed, and headed for the pharmacy. After a couple more public service announcements, including a reminder to pick up trash when the concert was over, Terry Vale introduced Roberta Moore and the Sons of Grace to a big round of applause. The gray-haired woman nodded absently at the crowd and continued tuning her guitar. When she felt she was ready, Roberta Moore gave her band a signal, and she began to sing.

It was just great. I was sure these people were pharmacists and pest control sprayers and farmers by day, but by night they were talented musicians, and I was enthralled. I didn't know any of the songs, though I had a vague feeling that when I was very young I'd heard one or two of the spirituals. The voices, twangy and plangent, rose through the clear night air. From time to time, one of the singers would say, "Now we're gonna do an old favorite, and if you know it, you sing along." But it was not an old favorite of mine or my parents, or even my grandparents, as far as I knew, and I realized how ignorant I was. It wasn't the first time I'd reflected on that, and it wouldn't be the last.

Hollis sang along with "The Old Rugged Cross." To my surprise he had a nice baritone.

Just when I was thinking I was getting too cold to enjoy any more singing, Hollis produced a thermos of hot chocolate, and I was glad to drink some. I felt so relaxed. No one was paying me any attention, and that was just fine. Hollis's hand was warm and dry when he held mine, and the hot chocolate was good.

The singing drew to an end after a couple of hours, and people began to pack up their blankets and chairs. Children were carried to cars, their sleeping heads resting on parental shoulders. I gathered up the blanket and the thermos while Hollis toted the chairs. I was surprised to cross the path of Sybil Teague. She was doing exactly the same thing; the man in charge of her chairs was Paul Edwards.

It was a draw as to which one of us was the more astonished. "I didn't know you were in town," Sybil said. She looked a bit more expensive than anyone else in the crowd. So did Paul, for that matter.

"The sheriff doesn't want us to go just yet," I said. I thought Sybil had certainly known we were in town. I thought Sybil had to have heard about the incident this morning, especially since the boy who was the ringleader was such a follower of Mary Nell's. I thought Sybil was just surprised to see me here on the courthouse lawn. Paul Edwards didn't make any effort to charm or greet me, he just stood behind Sybil with their two chairs slung across his back.

"I don't understand why," Sybil said. "I'm sorry you're being, ah, inconvenienced this way." She looked at me as if she had no idea how to end the encounter, and I was petty enough to leave her in the lurch. "Why don't you come to lunch with me tomorrow?" she suggested, I guess since she couldn't think of anything else to say. "You and your brother. Noon okay? Do you know how to get to my house?"

"Thanks. I expect we can find it." I gave her a very small smile and nod, and then Hollis and I moved on to his pickup.

Hollis made a choked noise, and I realized he was trying not to laugh out loud. "What's up with you?" I asked, smiling a little myself.

"She couldn't get out of that one," he said.

"Nope. She feels obliged to the hired help."

"You could have helped her out some," he said, but not as if he were too worried about Sybil's social dilemma.

"Nah. I figured she'd come up with an idea. And she did."

We deposited our burdens in the bed of the pickup and climbed into the cab. Hollis put his hands on my waist and gave me an unnecessary but pleasant boost.

When we got to the motel, I asked him in.

He said, "I always did want to make love to someone in a motel."

"That's my goal . . . expanding your horizons."

The motel bed was much nicer with someone else in it.

# Ten

HOLLIS slipped out at five o'clock. He whispered that he had to go home, shower, and get to work. He kissed me, and I hugged him close for a long moment, wishing he didn't have to go. Though finesse would never be Hollis's trademark, either in making love or conversation, that wasn't a bad thing. He was warm and big, and he had a delicate snore that made me feel all cozy. It was like being in bed with a giant, enthusiastic teddy bear.

I would not mind being with him for lots of nights.

That thought woke me up completely.

I almost never had sex. One reason I picked a sex partner so rarely was the sure brevity of the connection. One-night stands were about scratching an itch, and I'd rather do that by myself than enlist a human dildo. Oh yeah, I knew consenting adults could give and take a little of themselves in one night. I knew it didn't have to be tawdry and cheap. But most often it was; and it left me feeling a little nauseous and dissatisfied with myself, no matter how satisfying the physical act had been.

This was the other downside. Now, I'd been with Hollis two nights, and already I found myself wanting extended time with him. But I knew damn good and well that the nature of my life precluded more.

It seemed so much easier for Tolliver. He made eye contact with a woman, she agreed to have sex, they did it, and she left. She knew he was leaving town, of course, as suddenly as he'd blown into it. Or did some of these women think, "It'll be so good, he'll like me so much, he'll send his sister away by herself and he'll stay with me for a while." Since I didn't have any women friends, hadn't had for years, I couldn't say what other women thought. But maybe, some day, that would happen.

Despite that niggling worry, I dozed back to sleep, but by seven I was in the shower. I was dressed when Tolliver knocked carefully on the outer door to my room.

He looked around quickly when I let him in and relaxed when he saw we were alone. "How was the gospel singing?" he asked.

"Really good. You would have enjoyed it." I didn't ask him what he'd done instead. "You ready for breakfast?"

"Yeah. Let's go to the Denny's."

Maybe Denny's fruit plate would be better. Like many lightning-strike survivors, I have trouble with terrible headaches, and my right leg is much weaker than my left. I can lessen those symptoms by avoiding fried food and starches. Our lunch at McDonald's the day before had been a serious fall from grace, and my leg had twitched all night.

Luckily, Hollis hadn't noticed. But I'd been too uncertain on my feet to run this morning.

"Oh, we've been invited to lunch," I told Tolliver as we buckled our seat belts. The day was cloudy and chilly. Soon there'd be a rainstorm with high winds, and it would whip all the beautiful leaves off the trees—oak and maple and gum. Sarne would roll up the few sidewalks it had left out for the leafers. Its people would put away their hillbilly costumes and close their fruit and crystal stands, and Sarne would be alone for the winter.

"Where?" Tolliver asked, drawing me back into the present.

"At Sybil Teague's." I told him about running into Sybil and Paul the night before.

"That's interesting," he said. "Before we go in the restaurant, let me tell you what I learned from Janine last night. Paul Edwards was the lawyer Helen hired to get her restraining order and then her divorce from Jay Hopkins. And he'd represented Jay and Helen before, in a lawsuit they brought against Terry Vale."

"What'd they sue the mayor for?"

"Maybe he wasn't the mayor then. He owns the local furniture and carpet sales company. Jay Hopkins said the carpet Terry sold them wasn't stain resistant, and Terry wouldn't make good on the warranty."

"Hmm," I said. "I'm not sure what that all means." And I needed a cup of coffee before I even began to figure it out.

"It means," Tolliver said, "that Paul Edwards is in a position to know all the secrets of both families."

"Like?"

"Who Teenie's father really was, for one."

"Oh."

"And maybe he knows why Teenie and Dell were out in the woods that day. What could have made them go out to that place, on land that neither family owned, to be killed?"

"Who does own that land?"

"I guess we don't know."

"Could we find that out this morning?"

"Sure. We can go to the county clerk's office. But why should we go to the effort?"

"I'd rather have something to do than go back to the motel room and work crossword puzzles."

"Yeah, me, too." We worked out a plan for the day.

First thing after breakfast, we did our laundry in the Sudsy Kleen Laundromat, owned by (not to our surprise) Terry Vale. His representative at the Laundromat was a seamed old woman with a walker who dispensed correct change for the washers and dryers. She also sold little boxes of detergent and dryer sheets from behind a dilapidated desk. We learned by observation that the old woman also washed and folded laundry upon request. Sudsy Kleen did a great drop-off business.

This stout old woman performed a great service and did a good job, we decided, but she was determined to be as unpleasant as possible while she did it.

Initially, the fluffy white hair and the crocheted white sweater suckered me into believing I should be gently polite with this old bat. But when I asked for change for a dollar bill so I could feed the dryer, she drew in her breath as if I'd made a nasty suggestion. I stood transfixed, trying to figure out what I'd done. Dumbly, I held out the money. Granny Grump fumblingly took the dollar from my hand and examined it, since I was obviously a counterfeiter, I guess. Then she very slowly counted out the correct change, casting quick glances at me all the while as if she suspected I was going to snatch the money box and run. Her glasses glinted with every glance, just a quick flash in the overhead lights, as if she had bionic eyes. When I took the coins to my brother, I was half amused and half angry.

"She's charming, you need to go meet her," I said, in a conversational tone, dumping the quarters into the slots on the machine.

Tolliver glanced her way, started to say something, tried not to smile.

"I mean, it's just adorable when she glowers," I told him. "What a character! You just can't find old ladies like that anymore!"

"Shh," he said, but not as if he meant it.

I wasn't sure if she'd heard me or not—her expression of extreme disgust never changed. Was there something personal about us that she loathed? Or did she distrust us simply because we weren't from Sarne? Hard to tell. I wasn't sure I cared.

We finished washing and folding our clothes pretty quickly, since the Laundromat had few customers early in the morning. Maybe the dragon had driven all the self-serve customers away.

Our next stop was closer to the center of town. The county clerk's office was in the old courthouse in the square. It was the first time we'd actually entered the building. The ceilings were just as high as I'd imagined, and the windows just as huge; obviously this building predated the wide-spread use of air-conditioning. The room we entered was so disproportional, the distance from floor to ceiling to much more than from wall to wall, that I felt a little uneasy. I couldn't imagine working in such a room.

The two women who did work there were definitely surprised to see strangers come in, but the older of the two, a very round woman with dyed brown hair, immediately rose from her desk and came to the counter. When we asked to see a map of the county, she pointed silently to the wall behind us.

"Snake," I muttered to Tolliver after we turned around. There was a huge map of Colleton County right there. He nodded, understanding that I'd meant, "If it had been a snake, it would have bit us." I tried to orient myself by following the two main roads that formed a waggly X through Sarne, but I was still working it out when Tolliver pinpointed the area where we'd gotten out of our car when we'd been searching for Teenie's body.

After some cross-referencing, we decided which parcel of land that was, and the clerk handed us the appropriate ledger. According to the ledger, Colleton County Land Development was the owner of the property, and of several other parcels on both sides of that road. I couldn't see that we were any further along than we had been. Tolliver asked the county clerk if she knew who was actually behind Colleton County Land Development.

"Oh," she said, smiling. "That's Paul Edwards, Terence Vale, and Dick Teague. They bought up quite a bit of property over the years, thinking that someday we'd become another Branson. I don't think that's ever going to happen."

"The same names keep showing up over and over," I said when we were alone in the car.

"That's going to happen in a small town with a long history," Tolliver said, logically enough. "I'm not sure it means anything. Where next?"

We got to the newspaper office about nine forty-five, where we discovered that all the past issues of the *Colleton Mountain Gazette* (at least for the past ten years) were on computer. We were free to look through the computer archives, all we wanted, right there at the newspaper. This unexpectedly enthusiastic reception was due to a woman about my age, a brand-new reporter, who hoped we might be good for some kind of story. She was plump and dark-haired and wearing a color I'd call mustard. I am no clotheshorse, and fashion trends aren't of much interest to me, but even I could tell it was maybe the worst color she could have picked. But she was a person who liked bright things, as attested by her gold chain and gold bracelet and shiny bronze lipstick, so maybe the mustard was part of the same syndrome. Her name was Dinah Trout, according to the plate on her desk. She offered us coffee, she strode past us about eleven more times than was necessary, and she eavesdropped on every word we said to each other. Today was our day for meeting challenging women.

In self-defense, Tolliver and I took turns sitting at the computer. The one who was not reading had the job of deflecting the extremely curious Ms. Trout. If some of the people of Sarne knew about my unusual career, they apparently hadn't shared it with Ms. Trout, and I was really grateful.

In about an hour, I was sure we'd read every article that dealt with the death of Dell Teague, the disappearance of Teenie Hopkins, and the "tragic accident" of Sally Hopkins Boxleitner. I was fascinated by pictures of the Hopkins sisters. It was a shock to see them living.

I'd been so overwhelmed by the multiplicity of pictures in Helen's living room that I hadn't taken any time to examine the subjects.

The sisters didn't look alike. Sally, Hollis's wife, had been light in coloring, with reddish-blonde hair and freckles. She had a broad face and broad shoulders and a pleasant look about her. I couldn't see anything lurking in her eyes—no hidden misery in her stance, nothing that hinted she knew she was going to die. I tracked down her wedding picture (it was eerie to see a much younger Hollis feeding her wedding cake) and an employee photograph taken at Wal-Mart, where she'd been the manager of the baby department.

Her younger sister Teenie was shown in her school picture, the saddest accompaniment to an obituary. She'd been a little over made-up for the occasion, and her hair was dramatically combed in two solid falls of darkness on either side of her face. She had her mother's narrow features and small build, and she had a sharp nose, perfectly straight. It was hard to extrapolate anything about her character from a class picture. She was smiling, of course, but it was just an arrangement of her lips. There wasn't anything genuinely happy about it. She was a deep well, and I wasn't surprised Dell Teague had been intrigued.

Dell Teague was blond like his mother. I found a shot of Dell on an old sports page, where he was shown dressed in his football uniform. It was enough to break your heart—even my heart—seeing the young man standing there smiling at the camera, full of youth and pride and strength. I wondered if he'd known what was happening to him, or if the shot had been a complete surprise—if he'd had a chance to worry about his girlfriend's fate. The feeling I'd gotten, while I stood on his grave, was that he had known what was happening. I felt sorry for that.

I looked at Dell's picture, then back at Teenie's. Then again. They shared something, these two. I checked the years the pictures had been taken. Teenie's had been taken earlier in the fall, so had Dell's. Too early for Teenie to think she might be pregnant. What secret was it they shared? I wanted to print out the articles and take them with me. Then I realized I was getting too caught up in the lives of these two teenagers who were dead and buried.

While I was getting so much good stuff, I searched the computer for any stories or pictures including Mary Nell Teague. Mary Nell was in lots of pictures; she was a cheerleader (no surprise there), she was her class president, she'd been on the homecoming court. I even took a second to look at a picture of Dick Teague, the deceased husband of Sybil. He was a medium man; medium stature, medium brown hair, light complexion, narrow shoulders, and a tentative smile, at least in the newspaper pictures. He had a definite overbite, a generous nose, and he'd died of a sudden heart attack in his home.

Nonetheless, it was sad to hear that such an abrupt end had come to a man who'd done a lot for the community, at least according to his obituary. Dick Teague had been a county judge. He'd been in the Lion's Club and the Rotary. He'd been a member of the Chamber of Commerce, and he'd been on the Board of the Boys and Girls Club. He'd even been a local leader for Habitat for Humanity. I wondered if Sybil was upholding his banner in the civic department. Somehow I doubted it.

Speaking of Sybil . . . I glanced at my watch.

"We need to go," I murmured to Tolliver, who was smiling at Dinah, maybe dazzled by the gleam off her many polished surfaces. "Could we print out these articles?" I asked, trying to be charming.

"Sure, for twenty-five cents a page," she said. Guess I wasn't charming enough. "We don't mind doing it, but we have to pay for the ink cartridges, of course." I could understand that, and I tried to maintain a pleasant expression as the printer slowly spit out the pages I'd designated.

Dinah Trout urged us to come back any time, which I didn't think was likely. She was wearing a wedding ring, so I knew Tolliver wouldn't ask her out, even if she sent a clear signal she would be willing.

Seeing we were slipping from her grasp, Dinah thought of a few more questions to ask us, and we dodged them more or less politely. "The Ozarks breed women of strong character," I told Tolliver. He nodded a little grimly.

The most unremarkable woman I'd talked to all day was Sybil Teague, and she was no slouch in the grooming and looks department. She was wearing a skirt and sweater set in red and white, and she looked really good. I wondered if she was the kind of mother who scoured her deceased child's room, or if she was the kind of mother who kept that room intact as a shrine. I would have put money on her being a scourer, but I was wrong. When I slipped into Dell's room after lunch, excusing myself to use the bathroom, I found it was probably neater and cleaner than a teenage boy would leave it. But the dead boy's clothes were hanging in the closet, and though he didn't have a bulletin board of pathetic souvenirs as Teenie had, a framed picture of the girl sat on his computer desk. I thought the better of Sybil that she had left it there.

It had taken some maneuvering to get a look at the house, but fortunately Sybil was egotistical enough to take my gap-mouthed admiration at face value. Tolliver and I got a tour the minute I showed interest; no "it's not in its best shape" protestations from Sybil, no "please excuse the mess." The house was in perfect order, and probably always was. Even Mary Nell's room was spick and span—no clothes tossed on the floor, no unmade bed. The bathroom was scrubbed and there were clean towels out. If Mary Nell married a local boy, he'd have a hard act to follow.

There was a maid, of course, whom I had to credit with all this cleanliness and order. She was a gaunt older woman in a snagged knit shirt and baggy stretch pants. Sybil didn't introduce her, but the woman gave us an openly curious look as we strolled through the kitchen. Through glimpses of the backyard I caught at various windows, I spotted a man raking and burning the fallen leaves. I couldn't discern his features—that was how far it was to the back fence. This was a mansion, or as close to a mansion as Sarne could offer.

I wondered again how Sybil must have felt when Dell had picked a girl from the bottom stratum of local society. Having seen her house, I knew her talk of having accepted Teenie as a potential daughter-in-law was pure bullshit. I wondered how far she would go to prevent Dell from being trapped in that relationship by fathering a child on the girl; because I was pretty sure that was how Sybil would see it. Whatever part she'd played in the death of Teenie Hopkins, Sybil had surely loved her son Dell.

Mary Nell came home while we were sitting at the dining table. She dashed in, calling, "Mom? Mom? Look at my skirt!" Mary Nell turned red when she saw us in her home. I didn't know if that was because she was upset at seeing Tolliver, or because she was appalled at facing me after what her admirer had done to get me to leave town. Maybe both.

"Mary Nell, what are you doing home?" Sybil asked, obviously surprised.

"Stupid Heather spilled her stupid drink on my skirt," Mary Nell said, after a second's pause. She held her leg out to show the splotch on her denim skirt. "I asked Mrs. Markham if I could sign out for thirty minutes and run home to change."

"Mrs. Markham is the cheerleader sponsor," Sybil explained to us, as though we cared. "Well, go change, honey," she said to Nell. She might as well have said "Shoo!" and flapped her hands. Nell darted away, her cheeks flushed. In five minutes she was back, dressed in a dark blue long-sleeved T-shirt and a khaki skirt. I was willing to bet her previous outfit was on the floor of her room. "I'm gone, Mom!" she called as she went down the hall to the kitchen. The kitchen had a door leading into the garage, and I was sure that Nell had her own car. Sure enough, within a minute I saw a Dodge Dart zipping down the graveled driveway.

"She's so active in her school," Sybil said.

"And what year is she?" I asked politely.

"Oh, I'll have her for one more year," Sybil said. "Then it'll just be me rattling around in this big empty house."

"You might remarry," I said, in a completely neutral voice.

Sybil looked startled, maybe at my offering a suggestion

about a subject that was clearly none of my business. "Well, I suppose that's possible," she said stiffly. "I hadn't thought about it."

I didn't believe that for a minute. From the way the maid cut her eyes toward Sybil (she was carrying out the used plates), she didn't, either. We'd had iced tea with our salad and our chicken divan served over rice, but I'd only had one refill. I wanted to get into Nell's room, but I could hardly say I had to use the bathroom again. That would just be too suspicious. There was no way I could tell Tolliver what I needed, and he was not very good at sneaking, anyway.

A picture presided over the dining room, and I assumed the portrait was of Sybil's dead husband. I was seated opposite it, so I had forty-five minutes to stare at the painted features and look for their traces in the pictures of Dell and Mary Nell that were hanging on either side.

"Your husband?" I offered, nodding toward the picture. I thought it had been painted from a snapshot, but it was interesting. The eyes looked alive, and the tension of the seated body suggested that Teague was going to leap up at any moment.

She turned her head to look at the picture, as if she'd forgotten it was there. "He was a good man," she said softly. "He was just nuts about the kids, of course. He'd had pneumonia, one of those strains that's resistant to antibiotics, so he'd been in the hospital in Little Rock. He'd had a little heart trouble, but the doctors kept telling us it wasn't much, not to worry. They were going to do more about it when he got over the pneumonia, you see. But one afternoon, while he was recuperating, he was in his study with all the medical records from the past year. He wasn't satisfied with our insurance, or he thought that they should have paid more on his doctor bill, or something. I don't even remember now. But it had been a big year medically, you have those sometimes, I guess. Mary Nell had had a tonsillectomy, and Dell was the passenger in a car that had a little accident. The driver had a broken leg, and Dell had a little knock on the head and some stitches. Bloody, but really after it was cleaned up, he wasn't hurt too badly. And I'd had high cholesterol. So Dick had this pile of papers he was going through, and sometime in the afternoon he just . . . passed. When I went in to get him for supper, he had his head on the desk."

"I'm so sorry," I said. Sybil had had a lot to bear in her life, and I had to respect that, no matter how cold I found her.

"I'm curious, Sybil," my brother said, sounding as if going from one subject to another was simply logical. Sybil blinked and refocused on Tolliver. "Why didn't you ask Harper to come to Sarne earlier?"

"I'm sorry?" Sybil's attractive face was blank.

"Why didn't you ask Harper right after Teenie went missing?"

"I . . . well, I . . . of course, at first I was shocked by my son's death, and I just couldn't think about Teenie. Frankly, I just . . . didn't care, in the face of my own loss." Sybil gave us a noble face, telling us she was ashamed of that, but so what?

"Of course," I said. "Of course." This was just noise, to get her to continue.

"But when I heard all the rumors that were going around town, about how there was only justice for the rich, and why wasn't anyone looking for Teenie, and people seemed so sure that Dell had done something terrible to her . . . I was talking to Terry at Sunday lunch at the country club, and he told me what he'd heard about you. Paul was dead set against it, but I just couldn't leave a stone unturned. There had to be something I could do besides get out there and search the woods myself. You know, they should have brought in tracking dogs right away. But no one knew Teenie was out there with Dell. When he got found, it was assumed he was a suicide. By the time Helen realized Teenie was missing, too, it was late at night. It rained real heavy. When they resumed the search the next day, the scent was gone, I guess. I don't remember any of that, at all. I was far from worrying about Teenie."

"No cadaver dogs?" I asked.

"They're different from trackers, right? No, I guess not. After Helen thought about it, she said she was sure Teenie would turn up somewhere alive, and bringing in the cadaver dogs would be like saying she was dead. I thought for sure she'd back down on that one, but she said everyone was telling her it was not the right thing to do." Sybil shook her head. "Terry thought it would give the town a bad name, too, but the hell with that. If a young one's missing, you got to look for 'em. Maybe if Jay had been around . . . Oh, he wants you to come by the house, by the way. He called here this morning to find out more about you. Anyway, Jay and Helen's relationship wasn't all bad. Helen was more of a woman after she lay off the alcohol, you understand, but she had more backbone altogether when she was with Jay. She'd just listen to this one and that one and end up all confused after she separated from Jay."

That was totally not the impression I'd gotten of Helen

Hopkins. It sounded as though Sybil and Helen hadn't communicated face to face at all.

As if she'd heard my inner comment, Sybil said, "She never wanted to sit down and talk to me, so we could work out what to do. I'd call and get someone else. I'd send a message, and she wouldn't respond." Sybil shook her head. "And now it's too late," she said dramatically, able to be insincere now that she was no longer talking about the tragedy of her son. "Poor Helen. But at least she was spared the burial of her daughter. Harvey will catch the one who did it. The son of a bitch'll try to sell something he stole from Helen, or he'll get drunk in a bar and tell some buddy of his. Harvey says that's the way it works."

Sybil Teague herself would never know how things worked, I thought. In some way I had yet to define, she was so far from the truth she wouldn't know it if it bit her in the ass.

# eleven

"WHY aren't you one of those computer hackers?" I asked Tolliver. "Then I could tell you all this, and you'd have some brilliant idea, and you'd hack into the law enforcement system, or the Teagues' home computer, and find out some critical information, and I'd put it to brilliant use."

"You need to stop reading mysteries for a while," Tolliver said, braking gently for one of the town's numerous four-way stops. "Or get a new sidekick."

"Sidekick?"

"Yeah, if you're the brilliant sleuth, I must be the slightly denser but brilliant-in-my-own-useful-way sidekick, right?"

"Yes, Watson."

"More like Sharona," he muttered.

"That'd make me Monk?"

"If the shoe fits."

Actually, that hurt a little bit, the way a joke does when it's just a tad too close to the truth.

"Of course, you're a lot cuter," he said in a judicious voice, and I felt better. A little.

"Listen, did that sound like Helen Hopkins to you, all those things Sybil said?"

"No," he said promptly. "By the way, where are we going?"

"To Helen Hopkins' house. Jay Hopkins wants to meet with us."

"Why?"

"I have no idea."

"Well, it sounded like neither of them really wanted to make the effort to talk to each other, despite the fact that one was the mother of a dead teenager, and the other was the mom of a missing teenager. And those two kids loved each other. But it must have drenched them with a bucket of ice water, finding out Teenie was pregnant."

"Yeah. And evidently, she hadn't told her mom. And Dell hadn't told Sybil, that's for sure. But he had told his little sister. Don't you think that's strange?"

"No. I'd tell you anything before I'd tell my dad or your mother."

I felt warmer immediately. "But those were our circumstances. These two were brought up normal."

"Normal? Helen was an alcoholic, and she divorced her husband because he drank and beat her. Sybil Teague is one of the coldest women I ever met, and if she didn't marry that poor guy to get his money . . . well, it seems to me that what she loves is one, her son Dell, two, herself, and running a long third, Mary Nell."

"Okay," I said. "Okay." Sometimes Tolliver astonished me, and this was one of those times.

We drove around town, taking in the limited sights and sounds of Sarne. With the weekend over, the town had returned to its own preoccupation with battening down for the winter. The banners were being taken down from the ornamental streetlights. No one was wearing a cute costume. Aunt Sally's had a "Closed for the Winter" sign in the window. The horses and carriages were gone from the square.

Our cell phone rang as we made our way once again to the little house on Freedom Street. I answered it since Tolliver was driving.

"Hello," I said, and a remote voice asked, "Harper?"

"Yes?"

"It's Iona. Tolliver's aunt."

"Iona," I whispered to Tolliver. I put my mouth back to the receiver. "Yes, what do you want?"

"Your sister's run off."

"Which one?"

"Mariella."

Mariella had just turned eleven. Tolliver and I had sent a card, enclosing money. Of course, we hadn't gotten a thank-you of any kind, and when we'd called—okay, I'd called—on the actual day, Iona had told me Mariella was out. I'd been sure I heard her in the background, though.

This seemed horribly like Cameron's history. I made myself say, "Did she run off with someone, or did she just disappear?"

"She ran off with a little boy who's thirteen. Some delinquent named Craig."

"And?"

"We want you to come back and look for her."

I held the phone away to give it the look of incredulous amazement her statement deserved.

"You told her for years how awful Tolliver and I were," I said to my aunt Iona. "She wouldn't come back with me if I found her. She'd run the other way. Besides, I only find dead people. You look for her. Call the police, of course. I bet you haven't." I pressed the button to end the conversation, if you could call it that.

"What?" Tolliver asked. I recounted Iona's words.

"Don't you think you were a little hasty?" His words were mild, but they stung me.

"We're due in Memphis and Millington, and we've been delayed here already. There's no telling where Mariella is, or this Craig either. How far could they be? They can't drive. They're right down the road from Iona, I bet. She hasn't gone to the police because she's too proud to let them know Mariella's run away."

"You remember what Cameron was like at eleven?" Tolliver asked. "I didn't know her then. But I bet she ran off, too, huh?"

"No," I said. "We were still safe when Cameron was eleven." Though probably the signs of our parents' dissolution had been there by then, we'd just been too young to interpret them. We'd still been cocooned in upper middle class assurances. "Maybe Mariella and her friend went to join the circus," I suggested. "Or travel with a rock band."

"I think you're being old-fashioned," Tolliver said. "Girls now want to be fashion designers or supermodels."

"Well, Mariella will never make it," I said. The last time

we'd seen our sister Mariella, she'd been on the short and plump side, and models notoriously aren't. It was a little early for her to have gotten her growth spurt.

"They'll call Mark next," Tolliver said. His older brother lived not too far from Will and Iona.

"Poor Mark," I said. He always helped other people, and he needed a break himself. His first marriage had failed spectacularly and quickly, and he'd been dating a string of losers ever since. Mark was a nice guy, and he deserved better, but he always sought worse. "We should call him tonight."

"Good idea. Well, here we are again."

The little house seemed drenched in gloom today. Jay Hopkins might have a hard time selling the place, though the paint was fresh and the yard in good condition.

Jay Hopkins was as thin as his ex-wife had been. I had a fleeting image of their skeletons clacking together during sex, an image I was quick to banish from my mind. He was sitting on the front steps, so I was able to get a good look as we crossed the yard. Helen's ex had the malnourished face of a longtime drinker, and he could have passed for anywhere between his probable age—which would be in his early forties—and sixty. His hair was sparse and silver-blond, and he smoked with quick jerks of his hand.

"Thank you all for coming by," he said. "You must be the psychic lady."

"I'm not psychic," I explained, for maybe the thousandth time. I started to add I wasn't a lady, either, but that would become evident, and the topic bored me. "I just find bodies."

"I'm Tolliver Lang, Harper's brother." Tolliver extended his hand. "I'm sorry for your loss."

"My whole family is dead now," Jay Hopkins said, matter-of-factly. "Both my daughters, and my wife. You couldn't get a much bigger loss than that."

I groped around mentally for something to say, but came up speechless. Maybe there just wasn't anything.

"Have a seat," Jay said, when the pause became painful.

"Before I do," I said abruptly, "I have a question for you. Did your wife leave Teenie's room just like it was?"

"Yes, because she always expected her to come back," he said unsteadily. "Sally and Teenie shared that room until Sally married Hollis, and then Teenie had it all to herself. What are you wanting to know?"

"May I see it?"

"You said you weren't psychic. What are you hoping to find out?" Jay Hopkins was sharper than I'd given him credit for. Maybe he hadn't started drinking for the day.

I hesitated. "I want to see if some of her hair is left in her hairbrush," I said finally.

"For what reason?" He lit another cigarette. It was his house, I reminded myself.

"I want to have it tested," I said.

"To find out what?"

Now he'd asked one question too many.

"I think you know," Tolliver said unexpectedly. "I think you wonder, too."

Jay stubbed out the cigarette with vicious jabs. "What're you talking about, mister?"

"You wonder who her father was."

Jay froze in position, I guess amazed that someone had actually been rude enough to say it out loud. "She was my daughter," he said finally, in a final voice.

"Yes, in every way that mattered. But we need to know whose daughter she was in the biological way," Tolliver said.

"Why? I'm burying that child. You can't take that away from me." This was the voice of a man who had lost many things, though I was sure he'd tossed some of it away himself.

"If her father hasn't made a sound toward claiming her yet, he's not going to now," I said reasonably.

"There's every chance I could be Teenie's father. I don't want anyone thinking bad of Helen."

Too late for that. "I think everyone knows Helen was human," I said gently. "I think the shame would be on the father, for not owning up to his responsibility." I was thinking, Tolliver can hold him down and I'll run back to the room . . .

"All right, then," Jay Hopkins said. He sounded defeated, beaten down, and I knew caving in to my request was one more item in a line of items that marked his unmanning. But at the moment, his sense of self was not too high on my list of things to preserve. I doubted he had much self left, anyway.

"What'll you do with her hair?" he asked.

"Send it to a lab, have it tested for her DNA."

"How?"

I shrugged. "Via UPS, I guess."

"Her room's on the left." His elbows were propped on his bony knees, and he bent his head over his clasped hands. There was something smug about him, now. I should have been warned.

The house was so small there was little question of which room he meant. It still held twin beds, with a nightstand

jammed between them. The walls were covered with posters
and memorabilia. There were dried corsages and party invi-
tations, notes from friends and buttons with cute sayings, a
big straw hat and a napkin from Dairy Queen. Little things
like that would only evoke a memory for the one who saved
them; and now those memories did not exist anymore. I was
willing to bet that all Sally's memorabilia had come down
when she married. All these items were Teenie's. There
wasn't any hair in the brush on the shelf under the small
mirror. I wondered if the police had taken it when she'd
vanished, to get a DNA sample. I spied a purse was on top
of the battered chest of drawers. I dumped it out on the
nearest bed and was rewarded with a smaller hairbrush
choked with Teenie's dark hair. I put the brush into a brown
envelope I'd brought with me and glanced around the
crowded space. I was sure various people had already
searched this room thoroughly—the police and Helen, of
course. I would search my daughter's room if she went missing. I would tear up the floorboards. There didn't seem to be
any point in me combing it for clues.

I got a hair sample from Jay Hopkins, who made a wry
joke about how little of it he had to spare. Now I had hair
samples from both Teenie and Jay, and a fat lot of good it
would do me. But I would send them in, nonetheless.

Tolliver had a friend in a big private lab in Dallas. He
could get things done that I couldn't. His friend was a
woman, and he had to give her a certain amount of sweet
talk, but that never killed anyone. Well, it made my stomach clench, but I wouldn't die of it.

I was anxious to leave, but Jay wanted to know about our
last talk with Helen, and I felt obliged to recount it just as I

had to the police. He gave me permission to get hair from Helen's brush, too, and he suddenly seemed more interested than upset by the idea that now he could find out if he was Teenie's biological father.

"And you're paying for this?" Tolliver asked as we drove away. We went to the UPS pickup spot, which was in an auto parts store many blocks from the square. Small businesses in Sarne—in the south in general—had to diversify, but I was used to that and kind of enjoyed it. I got some mailers and followed the advice of Tolliver's friend at the lab in packing the samples I had.

"Yes, I am," I said. "I'm paying for this."

"Why, in God's name, are you doing this?"

"I don't really know. I want to leave. I want justice done. I feel terrible that Helen lost both her daughters to a murderer."

"Or is this all about Hollis?" Tolliver asked, his voice sharp. "Is this about you wanting to impress a law man?"

I felt like slapping Tolliver, or screaming. But I stared up at him and did neither of those things. After a long moment, he said, "Okay, I'm sorry."

"She said it would take three days to get a preliminary answer?" I responded.

"Yes. Longer for a definitive answer, but three days for a quick yes or no. Since it's from hair follicles, and not blood samples."

We were leaving the store when a patrol car pulled up beside ours. A deputy got out, a man I hadn't seen before. He was tall, thin, and middle-aged, his colorless hair shaved close to his head. He wore ugly glasses and he was tense as a coiled snake. He stalked to the rear of the car and looked at our Texas license plate like it was in German.

"I run your license plate," he said. "You got a warrant out for your arrest in Montana."

"No we don't," I said, but Tolliver gripped my arm.

"And you got a busted out taillight back here." He pointed, but I wasn't fool enough to get close to him to look. He waited for a reaction from us, seemed a little disappointed when he didn't get one. "You, sir, you're the legal owner of this car?"

"Yes," Tolliver said carefully.

"Lean up against your car with your hands on the hood. I'm going to have to take you in."

I felt a humming start up in my head, just a distant little humming. I stood frozen while my brother silently, almost casually, complied. Tolliver had seen the tension in the deputy's body, too.

"What . . ." I had to clear my throat. "What are you doing?"

"Outstanding warrants, he's got to go to jail while I clear this up."

"What?" I couldn't understand him because the humming felt louder.

"Judge'll come to town soon. If there's any mistake, he'll be out quick as a New York minute."

"What?"

"Ain't you understanding me?" the tall man said. "Can't you speak English, woman?"

"You're arresting my brother," I said.

"You got it."

"Because you say there's a Montana warrant out for him."

"Yes'm."

"But that's not true. The charges were dismissed."

"That's not what the computer says. And, ma'am, aside from that, there's the matter of the taillight." And he pointed. While Tolliver stayed where he was, I edged carefully around the car, keeping a safe distance from the deputy. The taillight was smashed.

"It was okay when we went in the store," I said.

"You'll excuse us if we can't take your word for it," the deputy said, smirking. He walked around the end of the car, taking care to stay as far from me as I wanted to be from him, and he patted Tolliver down. I could see shiny pieces of the broken light scattered on the street.

"When can I get him out?" I asked, pretending with all my might that the deputy didn't exist. This was sheer bullshit, but there was nothing I could do about it.

"After the judge sets the fine for the taillight, and we get this warrant thing settled," the deputy said. "We don't have a sitting judge here; have to wait for the judge to come around."

I gasped. I couldn't help it. Every fearful reaction I gave fed the deputy's sense of power and gloating, but there was nothing I could do about it. I was on the teetering edge of panic, and I was scrabbling around in my head for some way to put this right, *right now.*

"What's your name?" I asked.

"Bledsoe," he answered, not too happily.

"Harper," my brother said. He was handcuffed now, and the humming level rose higher and higher as I looked at the metal around his wrists. The deputy was looking at me uneasily. He'd quit grinning. "Just call Art. He'll recommend someone." Art Barfield was our lawyer. His office was in Atlanta, which was where we'd been the first time we needed an attorney.

The deputy looked even more jittery as he absorbed the implication that we had a high-powered lawyer at our backs (which wasn't exactly true), and he began to say something. Suddenly he thought the better of it and stopped, a word half out of his mouth. Then he made up his mind again. "Don't go crazy about this, young lady. Nothing's going to happen to your brother in our jail."

I hadn't even thought about that. My focus had been on my own selfish need for Tolliver, my panic for fear of how I'd manage without him. I had been frightened of the wrong thing, I saw immediately. I realized Tolliver would be in the hands of this deputy, who was a fool with power.

Tolliver began trying to make his way around the car to me, and the deputy yanked him back by his cuffed wrists.

I had to pull myself together. I concentrated, completely, on pushing the terrified child inside me back into her hole. I breathed slowly, deeply. I had to focus on Tolliver now, not myself and my trembling hands. My brain began to function again; maybe not well, but it began to produce thoughts.

I looked directly into Bledsoe's eyes. "If anything happens to Tolliver in your jail, it would be very, very unfortunate." That wasn't a threat, was it? I didn't want to give him any excuse to lock me up, too.

"I'm going to get our cell phone from my brother, now. It's in his pocket," I said, in a voice barely above a whisper. I put my purse on the hood of the car so that I was obviously unarmed and unencumbered. No one moved as I held up my hands and walked very slowly over to Tolliver. I wanted the deputy to die. I wanted to stand on his grave. I never lowered my stare from his eyes, which were narrow and watery blue. His lids fluttered, and he looked away at his patrol car, pretending to be fascinated by the querulous voice coming over the radio.

I slid my hand in Tolliver's pocket, pulled out the phone.

"Proud of you," he murmured, and I smiled up at him, as much of a smile as I could manage. I lay my head against his shoulder for a second, and then I straightened, widening the smile as much as I could, while the deputy shoved Tolliver into the back of the patrol car. The policeman climbed in, and while I watched him, he backed out and drove Tolliver away.

I stood there until the man inside the auto parts store came out to ask me if I was all right.

# Twelve

~~~

I drove back to the motel very slowly and carefully. I felt like my right hand had been amputated, or one of my feet. I felt exposed and as vulnerable as if a target were attached to my back, as conspicuous as a giraffe would be if it wandered down the streets of Sarne.

When I was back in my room, with the door locked, I felt how close I was to the edge. My right leg, damaged by the lightning all those years ago, was trembling and would barely take my weight. But I got a grip, if only by my fingernails. I stared into the mirror over the sink. "I'm going to hold on," I told myself out loud. "I'm going to hold on, because I'm the only one Tolliver has to get him out of this." I felt better after I'd stared at myself for a minute and seen my own resolve. I looked like a person who could cope.

I called Art Barfield. Art was not a nationally famous lawyer, nor was he a member of a huge firm. He was well respected in the south for his old and wealthy family, and well known in Atlanta for his eccentricity. He was in a partnership with two other lawyers, lawyers only a bit more traditional than Art.

His secretary was a straight arrow, and she was not amused to hear me demand to be put straight through to Art. But after she checked with her boss, I heard his booming southern voice, and the dreadful tension that had gripped me eased off a fraction.

"Where are you, honeychild?" Art asked.

"Sarne, Arkansas."

"My God almighty, what the hell are you doing there?"

I almost smiled. "We had a case here. But there were complications. When we came out of the auto parts store, there was this asshole deputy waiting to arrest Tolliver." I explained about the open warrants and the broken taillight.

"Hmmm. So, Tolliver is in jail?"

"Yes." That was way too close to a whine. I gripped the cell phone so tightly my fingers were white.

"You're there all by yourself, darlin'?"

"Yes."

"That's not good. Of course Tolliver's not wanted in Montana. We got that all cleared up. He couldn't be arrested for a broken taillight, so the cop trumped up something else for some reason."

That really wasn't the point I'd make if I were defending Tolliver, but I was glad to talk to someone who took Tolliver's innocence for granted.

"Are you going to be able to handle this, sweet thing?" Art's voice was very gentle, but also brisk, as if he expected a quick answer.

"Yes, I'll be fine," I said, pretty sure I was lying.

"That means you're going to try real hard," Art translated.

"Yep."

"Good for you, darlin'. Tell you what, I know a lawyer in Little Rock who can drive up there and steer you through this. Her name is Phyllis Folliette. Write that down, now."

There was nothing wrong with my memory, but I did write it down, along with the lawyer's phone number.

"I'm calling her as soon as I hang up the phone with you, and she'll be in touch with you right away, or at least very soon."

"That's good," I said. "That's real good. Listen, Art? They can't open packages we were sending via UPS, can they?"

"No," he said. "I guess they'd have to have a warrant to do that." Then he told me to call him if I needed anything more and hung up.

I was hoping that Bledsoe didn't know what we were doing at the auto parts store; he hadn't gone inside to enquire while I was standing there, and he hadn't asked me. So maybe sending off the hair samples hadn't been the trigger for Tolliver's arrest. Maybe there had been something else.

Harvey Branscom, while not my favorite guy, had seemed like a pretty independent fellow to me, and one who knew his business. Why would he consent to be part of the charade outside the auto parts store? Who could influence him so heavily? He had to know what his deputy was doing.

What was gained by having Tolliver in jail? That was the crucial question. What was the result of his incarceration?

Well, the first thing to pop up in my mind was that we'd have to stay in Sarne longer now. But I couldn't understand why that would be to anyone's advantage. A wild thought crossed my mind, and I made myself consider it. Could Hollis have become so nuts about me in such a short time that he was willing to frame Tolliver to keep me here? I just couldn't swallow that. Actually, it was somewhat easier to believe a scenario in which Mary Nell sprung the same trap on Tolliver, because the phony warrant and the broken tail-light seemed like such desperate and amateurish steps. But it seemed very unlikely that Mary Nell would even know we'd been in trouble in Montana once upon a time, and even if she'd learned about the episode somehow, she wouldn't be able to go on the police computer network and somehow enter a false incident.

I tried to imagine a credible progression of cause and effect, opportunity and motive, sitting in my lonely hotel room. When my mind remained persistently blank, I opened the door to Tolliver's room and went and sat there. The maid had done the beds and put fresh towels out, so there wasn't even a trace of Tolliver in his room, at least to my eyes. For a little while, though, being there made me feel a tad better; but after a bit, I felt foolish, and then I felt like an intruder, so I went back.

There was a knock at the door, and I nearly jumped out of my skin. I glanced down at my watch. I'd been sitting there, with my thoughts scurrying around like hamsters in an exercise wheel, for over an hour.

At the door, Hollis said, "I'm sorry."

"Did you . . . you didn't have anything to do with this, right?"

"No," he said, not sounding offended. He sounded almost too gentle, the way you sound when you're afraid a dog might turn on you. "Marv Bledsoe and Jay Hopkins, they used to drink together."

I remembered the smug look on Jay Hopkins' face, and I felt sure he'd called Marv and told him where to catch hold of us. No wonder he hadn't minded us getting the hair samples. He hadn't believed we'd have time to get them in the mail.

"I've never trusted Jay, or Marv for that matter. Unfortunately, Harvey does, or at least he acts like he does. And the state guys are gone. They went off to check out another teen date murder they think might be related to Teenie's and Dell's. So there's no brakes on Marv, like there ought to be."

"So, have you seen this warrant?"

"No, not me. I gather there was some problem in Montana while you worked up there, last year?"

"Yeah, but it was all resolved. There's no warrant for Tolliver's arrest. I'd know for sure. And we didn't have a busted light this morning when we got up."

"Did you see him do it?"

"No, we didn't."

"If Marv made all this up, he would have some way to stop you," Hollis said, sitting down heavily on the foot of my bed. He caught my eyes, and said hesitantly, "I thought I better stop by to see how you were doing. I got the impression you depend a lot on your brother."

"I do," I said simply. "But I'm going to be okay. I've already called a lawyer in Little Rock. She's going to call me back."

"That's good," Hollis said heartily. "You're doing real good." Again, the encouragement was too overdone.

I was well aware that I wasn't, you know, Miss Stability.

But there's a difference between knowing you have a flaw and seeing other people reacting to it. "You can't hide how weird you are," was the unspoken message. "You require special handling and careful treatment." I began to tense up all over again.

"Hollis," I said, hearing my voice come out as a growl. "You make sure nothing happens to Tolliver in that jail. You hear me?"

I could see his resentment at the implication, but at the moment, that wasn't important to me. What mattered to me was that I see in his face the assurance that nothing could happen to my brother in that jail, that he would be treated fairly and guarded well.

I could not find that in Hollis's expression.

"Hollis, you listen to me," I said, in the quietest voice I could manage. "I know you love this town and you love the life you have here. But something's going on in Sarne, there's a rotten apple somewhere spoiling things. There's a lot we don't know about these deaths. Someone you know murdered Dell Teague and Teenie Hopkins. Someone you know killed your wife Sally and beat Helen Hopkins to death. And someone you know doesn't want my brother and me to leave, for some reason. Now, we have to find out who that someone is. I came here, and I did my job, and I did it quick and I did it right. Now, Tolliver and I should be able to leave you all to solve your own damn problems."

"You were beginning to care about me until this happened," Hollis said, completely to my surprise. It seemed more like the kind of thing men expect women to say; if life were like a sitcom, that would have been my line.

"Yes," I said. "I was."

"I know someone is responsible for all the deaths," he said. "I know that. And I realize it's someone I know. But I can't imagine why. Sally was a good woman, a nice woman, and I loved her." Hollis was apparently having as hard a time keeping his thoughts on track as I was.

"She knew something," I said intently. "She knew a secret, a big secret. She died first."

We thought about that for a second.

"Can you remember anything about her, in the days before she died? Was she excited, upset, worried?"

Hollis looked profoundly depressed. I wanted to touch his hair, stroke it, but I kept my hands locked together in my lap. "She seemed like someone who had a secret," he said heavily. "She would talk to me about almost anything, but some things about her family and the mess her mother had gotten into—I guess it's not too surprising that she didn't want to talk about their drinking and fighting and their divorce, or her mom's and dad's . . . well . . . infidelities."

I worked my way through that sentence. "So, she'd be open and honest with you about almost anything except her family," I said.

He hesitated. "Yes," he said finally, firmly. "Anything but her family."

"Do you think she had a secret because she had just figured something out—like, 'Oho! Eureka!'—or because her mom or Teenie had confided in her?"

Hollis tried hard to remember, while I tried hard not to be impatient. I was sorry he had to go through even more pain, but I thought it was necessary. Actually, part of me was asking, "Why didn't he do all this before?" Of course, he'd thought his wife had died accidentally. Now that he knew she'd been murdered, though, surely he'd been turning that time over in his head?

"I think she'd figured out something," he said. "It's almost impossible to say what was going through someone's mind, you know? And I've been thinking maybe I didn't know Sally as well as I thought I did. If we'd been married longer, trusted each other more, she would have told me what she was worried about, thinking of. We could have worked on it together. We just hadn't been married that long. We hadn't been tested."

This wasn't getting us anywhere. "Did anything happen right before she died?" I asked, realizing I might sound callous. "Anything that might have triggered her death?"

"Only Dick Teague dying," Hollis said.

"When did he die?" I asked. I'd seen the newspaper stories, but I hadn't noted the date.

"I think in February. That sounds right," Hollis said, after a moment's thought. "When Sybil found him, she couldn't cope with cleaning up everything for the funeral, so she hired Helen and Sally to clean the house. Did you know Sybil used to have Helen clean her house, before Helen began drinking so bad and all? Sybil hired Barb Happ after that. I didn't much want Sally cleaning for anyone, but Sally really enjoyed cleaning and she said she might as well do it on her day off from Wal-Mart, not only because she felt sorry for Sybil, but because she wanted some extra money for Christmas. Sally came home that day feeling real concerned about something."

"But she didn't give you any hints?" I'd been assuming that Sally had discovered her sister's pregnancy, but Sally had died months before the event.

"Of course, I asked her how the job went. She said she cleaned the downstairs while her mom took the upstairs, and that's about all she said. The study was just like it had been when Dick fell over dead, and that made her feel a little funny, she said. But that night, she searched out one of her high school textbooks. The school system discontinued this book, so the students could keep it if they wanted to, and she did. Sally was interested in some things that surprised me."

"What book was it?"

"She had several. I can't even remember now. I only recall it because she seemed so . . . like she was thinking real hard about something else, and then when Sally found the book, she studied over it for the longest time. That was unusual."

"So, do you think you could remember?"

"Maybe. I'll look this evening, see if I can find it. Seems like I remember it had a red back cover . . ." Hollis looked distant, as if his eyes were seeing a distant scene, and I guess they were.

The phone rang. I jumped about a foot. "Hello?" I said.

"Ms. Connelly?" It was a woman's voice, heavily southern and somehow really smart.

"Yes."

"This is Phyllis Folliette? With Huff, Moon, and Greene?"

"Right. Oh, good." Hollis was pointing at the door, indicating he needed to leave, and I nodded and waved before returning my attention to the lawyer.

"Okay," she said, and her voice became carefully soothing. "I hear you're in kind of a jam, over in Sarne."

"Yes."

"I just wanted to tell you, I called the sheriff's office and they said your brother wouldn't be arraigned for two more days. I can't bail him out until the judge sets the bail, you understand?"

"Yes, I understand."

"And the judge won't be there until the day after tomorrow."

Okay, I wasn't dumb. "I understand that two days means the day after tomorrow," I said clearly.

"Um. I get that . . . Sorry if I was talking down," the lawyer apologized. "Occupational hazard."

"Umm."

"So, I'll be there in Sarne, day after tomorrow, to get your brother out of jail," she said. "These charges sound like a bunch of crap, but I'm calling Montana first thing in the morning to get this straightened out. In the meantime, don't do anything rash, and don't worry. Art especially charged me to tell you that. Okay?"

"Yes."

"Okay. Now I'm going to switch you over to our financial office, so you can take care of that part of it."

Everyone wants to be paid, even me—especially me, since I figure at any moment my gift could be taken from me. I want to use it while I have it, and it's really my only marketable skill. It should support me, I figure. It robbed me of a normal life.

After I fixed things with the financial office, I hung up and tried to figure out what I should do next. I packed up Tolliver's stuff and stowed it in my room, then I walked up to the motel office and told horrible old Vernon McCluskey that we wouldn't be using the second room for now. He said he was about ready for me to check out, and I said I had to stay in

Sarne a few more days. He couldn't throw me out, not legally—though today I'd had a big hint that the legal system in Sarne wasn't exactly on the up and up. If he did somehow make me leave, I'd just go to the next town, which was in a different county.

While I ran through all these contingencies, I returned to the room. I found myself shaking my hands vigorously in the air like in a children's exercise, to refocus my mind. It was time to eat, and I opened a granola bar. I needed more than that, better food, but I didn't want to go out by myself. It was one thing when I knew Tolliver was waiting for me back at the motel, or that he was somewhere in the same town: it was entirely another thing when Tolliver was locked away in a jail. I wondered what they'd fed him for supper, and when I could see him. I wondered if he had a cellmate. I wondered how ruthless his cellmate was.

The most important person I knew in Sarne, aside from the sheriff, was Sybil Teague. I didn't know if she'd even care, and I doubted she'd help, but I called her anyway.

"My brother's in jail on a trumped-up charge, Sybil," I said, after she'd told me she was glad to hear from me.

"Paul Edwards mentioned that to me this afternoon," Sybil said, in her cool rich-woman's voice. "I'm so sorry for your trouble."

This didn't sound promising. "Tolliver isn't wanted by police anywhere," I said, as calmly as I could.

"I know my brother's the sheriff, but you must realize that I can't interfere with legal matters," Sybil said, and her voice was frosty rather than cool.

"Tolliver is my brother, and your brother's deputy set him up, for reasons best known to himself."

"Which deputy?" Sybil said, and that did surprise me.

"The one named Bledsoe. Some coincidence, right?" I wanted Sybil to confess that she'd sicced the deputy on to me, so I'd know who my enemy was.

"That would be Marv," she said slowly, and now she sounded distinctly unhappy, whether because I'd tried to involve her or for some other reason. "Paul's second cousin. But that doesn't mean anything."

Was everyone involved in this case related?

Sybil wasn't willing to do a thing to help me, and I wasn't even sure I could think of anything concrete for her to do. She wasn't happy, and I definitely got the feeling she didn't think Tolliver was guilty of anything. But she also couldn't or wouldn't intercede with the sheriff. We hung up, equally unhappy with each other.

I thought long and hard. Then I called Mary Nell Teague on her cell phone. She'd given the number to Tolliver, and I'd fished it out of his jacket pocket when I packed up his stuff. She'd drawn a little curlicue under "Nell."

Mary Nell wasn't happy at hearing my voice on the other end of the line.

"Tolliver himself can't call you," I said, "since your uncle Harvey put him in jail." This was not entirely accurate, but I wasn't interested in being fair.

She shrieked and carried on for a full minute while I waited patiently on the other end of the line.

"Of course, he isn't wanted by the police in Montana," she said. "That's just crazy."

Though Mary Nell was just basing her opinion on her sexual attraction to Tolliver rather than any factual basis, it was nice to hear someone so positively on his side. To set the outspoken teenager on the right track, I told her that her mother had refused to help. I didn't put it as bluntly as that, but I made sure the picture got transferred. This would ensure that Sybil's life would be irritating and unpleasant for at least twenty-four hours, which was no more than she deserved. I'm not above being petty.

I called Hollis next, and got no answer. Considering his earlier exit, as if he urgently needed to be somewhere else, I wondered if he'd had to return to patrol. Or maybe he was just being a cowardly rat bastard? Possibly the sheriff had told him to stay away from me if he wanted to keep his job? Hollis probably did want to keep his job badly enough for that. I tried not to blame him, but I was miserable enough to think that it made him a rat bastard, anyway.

I considered my next course of action. The likelihood that I'd break down crying lurked just over the horizon, trembling and shivering. But that would be counterproductive, and there must be something I could do besides sit in the damn hotel room. I could go beat up Bledsoe; and at the moment I felt like I could dig out his liver with my fingernails. But surely there was something more constructive . . . I considered everything I knew, and then I had it. I called Hollis again and left a message on his machine.

"If you aren't picking up because you don't want to talk to me, that's okay, but know this: I'm going to your house right now, and I'm going to want to search your bookshelves." I was sorry I'd been honorable enough to return his money, since I could have used that as an extra incentive if I'd kept hold of it.

I ran to Hollis's house, since I needed the exercise. It might help keep me calm for a while longer. The leg faltered a couple of times, but didn't give out utterly. There was no truck parked under the carport. I had planned on getting in whether Hollis was home or not, so I didn't care. But I didn't want to be arrested while doing it. Fortunately, the back door was fairly well screened from the neighboring small houses by thick bushes. Since it was a working day, quite possibly the neighbors were gone.

For a policeman, he sure had lousy security. I found his spare key in the third place I looked—hanging from a little nail in the roof over the porch. It was in a dark corner, and partially hidden from view, but my fingers patted around until they felt the nail, and in a second the key was in my hand. I was glad to find it; it would spare me from breaking one of the panes of glass in the back door—also a security risk, as any cop should know.

Since the day was once again gloomy and overcast, I switched on a lamp in the living room. I'd only passed through on my way to the bedroom the last time I'd been here, so I wasn't familiar with the layout. The little room was comfortable and . . . cozy, with an overstuffed love seat and matching recliner. There was the usual coffee table in front of the love seat, and an occasional table cluttered with a lamp, some magazines, and a book, plus various remotes by the recliner. Within arm's reach was a particle-board bookcase crammed with books, mostly romantic suspense-type paperbacks by Jayne Anne Krentz, Sandra Brown, Nora Roberts, and the like. There were a few adventure/mystery paperbacks—Lee Child and Thomas Cook—which more likely belonged to Hollis.

I did a quick tour of the house to make sure I was looking in the right place. The bedroom didn't have any bookshelves, and the second bedroom (used as a computer room/storeroom now) held only computer manuals and video game guides. The kitchen had a couple of cookbooks, and the bathroom a wicker basket of magazines. Back in the living room, I squatted by the jammed shelves.

Hollis had told me his wife had gotten out one of her old school textbooks. I was willing to bet he hadn't packed them away yet, and I was right. Sally Hopkins Boxleitner had kept a book of British poetry, a copy each of *Julius Caesar* and *The Merchant of Venice,* and an American history textbook. There was a basic biology textbook, too, much battered and torn.

According to Hollis, the book had had a red cover. Both the history text and the biology text were predominately red, at least on their spines.

"What the hell are you doing in here?" I guess part of me had absorbed the small sounds of Hollis arriving home, because I didn't jump. He sounded pretty mad.

"I'm looking for whatever Sally was thinking about that night," I said. "I found your spare key in less than two minutes. Here. Here's the history book. Is this the one she had?"

"Why didn't you just wait for me to get home?" Maybe he sounded a tad bit less angry.

"I thought you were avoiding me, and I figured you wouldn't let me in."

"So you decided right away to just break in my house? You know that's illegal?"

"So's putting a man in jail on trumped-up evidence. Is this the book she had?"

"It might be," he said, distracted. "Is there another red one?"

"Yes, the biology book, here."

"That might be it, too."

"Okay. You look at the history, I'll look at the biology."

I turned the book upside down and shook it, and a piece of paper fell out. I figured I'd discovered an old grocery list or a note she'd written the boy who sat beside her in fourth period in high school. I found it was something much less straightforward.

It was half a sheet of blank paper, and on it was written, "SO, MO, DA, NO."

"If you'd left it in there, we'd know which section it fell from," Hollis pointed out.

"You're absolutely right," I said absently. "I messed up. Does this mean anything to you?"

"No, not at first glance. But that's her handwriting . . . Sally's."

There was a new note in his voice that penetrated even my overloaded emotional system.

"I'm sorry," I said, making a great effort. "I know this is dredging up stuff for you that you're trying to put behind you."

"No, I'm not trying to put Sally behind me," he said. "But I am trying to think about the rest of my life. And the ideas of the last few days, the idea that Sally was murdered, that the son of bitch who did it has been walking around this town, talking to me, free, has been curdling my gut. And the fact that every time I see you, I want to screw you so bad it hurts. You practically break in my house, my damn house, and I want to fuck you right here on the floor."

"Yeah?"

"Yeah."

It was like he'd flipped a switch. Suddenly, I was thinking about it, too, thinking that it would feel good to forget about my problems for a few minutes, and I rolled over on my back and pulled my shirt over my head.

It was short and violent and the most exciting encounter I'd ever experienced. Nails and teeth, slick skin against slick skin, the thud of body against body. Afterward, he lay beside me on the floor in the small space we'd had available and said, "I need to vacuum." He was panting heavily, and the words came out slowly.

"A few dust bunnies," I agreed. "But they were good company."

He wheezed as he laughed, and I pulled my bra back up because there was a draft along the floor. I rolled to my side and propped up on one elbow.

"I made your back bleed," I said, looking from the scratches to my fingernails. "I'm sorry."

"It felt good when it happened," he said, and he was beginning to drift off to sleep. "I don't mind."

While he dozed, I rolled onto my stomach and flipped through the biology book. It was a very basic text, with chapters on plant cells and reproduction, the human nervous system, how eyes work, and . . .

I glanced at the scratches on Hollis's shoulder and shook my head. I looked back down at the graph on the page.

I pulled my jeans back on.

"Hollis," I said, very quietly.

"Mmph?" he said, opening his eyes.

"I have to go."

"What? Wait a minute. Where's you car?"

"I ran from the motel to your house. I'll walk back."

"No, just wait a minute, I'll run you to the motel. Or you can stay here. I know you don't like to be alone."

It wasn't being alone that made me so antsy. It was being without my brother. But I didn't want to explain that. "I need to go back to the motel," I said, as regretfully as I could manage. "I think the lawyer may call me." Okay, that was a lie, but I was trying to spare his feelings. I had a few things I needed to do, and I'd have free reign to do them when I wasn't around Hollis, the lawman. He pulled on his uniform swiftly.

"Have you eaten?" Hollis asked practically, as we drove down Main.

"Ah . . . no, I guess not." I hadn't even finished the granola bar.

"Then at least let me take you to Subway to get something."

"That would be good," I agreed, suddenly aware that I was hungry.

The truck filled with the good smell of the hot chicken sub; my mouth was watering.

When Hollis pulled into the slot in front of my room I hopped out of the truck with the bag containing my sandwich; I wanted to use the glare of his headlights to help me fit the key in the lock. The motel was anything but well-lit. Hollis began backing up as I pushed the door open. I turned to wave at him with one hand while the other hand clutched my bag of food. I could vaguely see Hollis's arm move as he switched gears to pull out of the lot.

Suddenly, from inside the room there was a grip on my upper arm that spun me around, then I was stumbling into the room and meeting the rug with a speed that was terrifying.

I rolled to my feet and launched myself at my attacker, pushing him right back out the open door. Never let yourself get cornered. You have to fight instantly, I'd found as a teenager, or your opponent has the upper hand; your injuries hurt too much, or you get scared. And you have to go with it with every fiber of your being. Pull, bite, strike, scratch, squeeze; let go completely. If you're dedicated to hurting someone else, it doesn't register so much when they hurt you. I hardly felt the two pounding blows the man got in on my ribs before I grabbed his testicles and clamped down, and then I bit him on the neck as hard as I could. He was shrieking and trying to pry me off when Hollis separated us.

I sat back against the wall of the motel, sobbing and shaking with the aftermath of unleashing all that, and stared at my assailant, whom Hollis handcuffed with a few economical motions. It was Scot, of course, the teenage admirer of Mary Nell; Scot, who'd tried to attack me before. He was whimpering now, little snot-nose bastard.

"Are you crazy?" Hollis yelled at him. "Are you nuts? What are you doing, attacking a woman like that?"

"She's the one who's crazy," Scot said. He spit out a little blood. "Did you see her?"

"Scot, what the hell made you decide to do this?" I could see that Hollis was absolutely stunned. "Who let you in her room?" He shook the boy.

The teenager stayed silent, glaring up at Hollis.

Vernon McCluskey hobbled out of the office and down the sidewalk to where we were poised in our strange tableau.

"Vernon, did you let this boy into Harper's room?" Hollis bellowed.

"Naw," Vernon said. He looked down at the boy contemptuously. I knew it wasn't because the boy had been poised to attack a smaller woman, but because the boy had failed to attack hard enough, and at the wrong time. "I rented him a room, the room this lady's brother was in earlier. If she happened to leave the adjoining door unlocked, ain't my fault. I had no idea Scot would do anything like this." Vernon shook his head with insincere regret.

Son of a bitch.

If I was feeling paranoid, it was with some justification.

"Get up, Scot," Hollis said. "You're going to jail. Harper, you're going to press charges?"

"Oh, you bet." I needed a hand up, but Hollis was escorting Scot to his truck, and I wouldn't have asked Vernon for a place to spit on the sidewalk. Shakily, I worked my way to my feet. My thigh muscles were trembling, and I felt weak and sick. I hated pretty nearly everyone. "I may have to wait until tomorrow, but I'm definitely going to press charges. I was willing to forgive the first time, when he looked to be a teenager driven nuts by jealousy, but this is above and beyond."

What on earth could have induced this boy, who'd been so scared of his parents and his coach, to attempt something like this? What had he been ordered to do? Kill me, or beat me up?

"Paid," I said. Hollis stopped, halfway through pushing the handcuffed boy up into his truck. "I'll bet someone paid him to do this."

And I saw by Scot's face that I'd struck oil. "Were you

supposed to break some bones?" I asked him, conversationally. "Or kill me?"

"Shut up," he said, turning his face away from me. "Just don't talk to me anymore."

"Coward," I said, and I remembered that Harvey Branscom had called him the same thing the morning before. Harvey had been right.

"Burn in hell," Scot said, and then Hollis slammed the door on him.

Vernon was still standing there when they pulled away.

"You do anything but take my key when I leave, I'll slap you with a lawsuit that will bankrupt this motel," I said. I knew damn good and well I'd locked the interconnecting door. "If any harm comes to me, my brother will see to it. Any harm comes to him, our lawyer will do it."

He didn't say anything, but he watched me with old, hostile eyes while I shut and locked my door. I picked up the bag of food from Subway. Luckily, I hadn't gotten a drink, since I had bottled drinks in the ice chest in my room. Vernon probably would have had me arrested for defacing his property if I'd spilled a Coke on his green carpet.

I shoved a chair under the doorknob and moved the ice chest against the connecting door. It wouldn't hold the door, but it would slow down an entrance and provide noise. I used my cell phone to call Art in Atlanta, and I left a detailed account of what had just happened on his answering machine. Just for the record.

I was so lonely I cried.

Then I ate the food in the bag, not because I wanted it (it was nasty and cold by that time), but because I had to have fuel. I peeled off my clothes with shaking fingers. I was a mess; I'd had sex and a fight in the same evening, and I needed a shower. I looked at myself in the mirror over the sink. My ribs were already turning blue on my left side where Scot had gotten in the two good punches. I breathed deeply, trying to decide if I had any broken ribs. I didn't think I did, after a few experimental movements.

It gave me some satisfaction to think that if it had been a bad day for me, it had been a worse day for Scot. He'd turned from being football team quarterback and suitor for Mary Nell Teague into a soon-to-be felon. Hurt pride had done it; that, and a bribe, I figured. I could conjecture he'd felt embarrassed after the morning incident. The coach had probably made him feel like a fool, after the sheriff had called him a coward. Instead of taking their words to heart, he'd gotten angry, and when he'd been offered money, he'd jumped at the chance to recoup his self-esteem. It was one of those situations where you learn what you're made of. Unfortunately for Scot, it turned out he was made of lesser things.

Hollis called after he'd booked Scot into the jail. He wanted to find out how I was and to reassure me that nothing would disturb my night. "We'll figure out what the initials mean," he said. "I knew my wife, and I'll understand it sooner or later."

I didn't think we had "later," and I didn't know if understanding Sally would help or not. She'd known exactly what she meant, and she'd been referring to something simple and obvious. With all due respect to Sally, if a girl who'd graduated from Sarne High could make some significant discovery after a glance at her biology textbook, then I should be able to figure it out. So should any number of people, and that was what had me worried. "SO MO DA NO" I wrote on the little pad of paper kept by the phone. I wrote it as one word. I wrote it backwards. I tried to make a word out of the letters. I fell asleep with the pencil clutched in my hand.

# Thirteen

A pounding on the door woke me up. I rolled an eye toward the clock on the bedside table. It was seven in the morning.

"Who is it?" I asked cautiously, when I'd stumbled over to the door.

"Mary Nell."

Oh, wonderful. I moved the chair to open the door, and she strode in. "We've got to get him out," she said dramatically, and I felt like smacking her.

"Yes," I said. "I want him out, too." If there was a little sarcasm in my voice, it was lost on Nell Teague.

"What have you done about it?"

I blinked, sat on the side of the bed. "I've hired a lawyer, who'll be here tomorrow," I said.

"Oh," she said, somewhat deflated. "Well, I called Toby Buckell, but he just laughed at me. Said he wouldn't take a case unless a grown-up called him."

I could just imagine. "I'm sorry he treated you with dis-
respect," I said, trying hard to sound like I meant it. "I appreciate your effort. But Tolliver is my brother, and I have to
be the one who works on this." I wanted to be nice to this
girl, whose only fault was that she was sixteen, but she was
wearing me out. Talk about drama. Then I reminded myself
she'd lost her brother and her father in a very short period,
and I forced myself into a more hospitable mode.

"Would you like some coffee, or a soda?" I asked.

"Sure," she said, going over to the ice chest and pulling
out a Coke. I brewed a little pot of coffee from the motel
coffeemaker, and poor coffee it was, but it was hot and con-
tained caffeine. I looked at my visitor. Mary Nell's face was
bare of makeup, and her hair was pulled back into a very
short ponytail. She looked her age, no more. She should be
at home working on her English composition paper, or on
the phone with one of her friends about last night's date,
rather than in a motel room with a woman like me.

"You said you called another lawyer," I said. "Why not
Paul Edwards?"

She said suddenly, "I think my mom might marry Mr.
Edwards."

"You don't like him?" I was groping around for what to say.

"We get along okay," Mary Nell said. "He's always been
around. He and my dad were friends, and my mom always
got his opinion on everything. Dell never liked Mr. Edwards much, and they had a big argument before Dell
died."

"What was that about?" I asked, trying to sound casual.

"I don't know. Dell wouldn't tell me. He'd found out

something, and he went to Mr. Edwards to talk about it, but Dell didn't like whatever Mr. Edwards said."

"Something he'd found out about Paul?"

"I don't know if it was about Mr. Edwards, or someone else. Dell just thought Mr. Edwards would be able to help him out with it, give him an answer."

"Oh." None of the letters had been a P or an E, assuming the letters Sally had written referred to a person. Damn, why didn't people just write what they meant? To hell with shorthand.

"I thought you and Dell were so close," I said, which was tactless and stupid. "I'm surprised he didn't tell you what he was mad about."

She gave me an outraged stare. "Well, for brother and sister we were close."

"What does that mean?"

"There's stuff brothers and sisters don't talk about," she said, as if she'd been requested to explain snow to an Eskimo. "I mean, there's stuff you and Tolliver don't talk about, right? Oh, I forgot. You're not *really* his sister. So you wouldn't know."

Touché.

"Brothers and sisters don't talk about sex, I bet not even when they're grown up," she instructed me. I remembered how shocked she'd been when she'd told me her brother had said Teenie was pregnant. "Brothers and sisters don't talk about which of their friends are doing it, either. But other stuff, that's what they talk about."

"Did you and Scot talk about him coming here to beat me up?" I asked.

She flinched. "What are you talking about?"

So the Sarne grapevine hadn't gotten in gear yet, and she didn't know. "Someone paid Scot to come here and hide in my room last night. He was supposed to beat me up. It was just like the other morning, except this time he was by himself. If Hollis Boxleitner hadn't been with me, I could be in the hospital by now."

"I didn't know," she said, and again I felt guilty. But there's no gentle way to tell someone a tale like that. And I couldn't minimize it any more than I had. "What's happening to our town? We were okay until you came!"

That was a fine turnaround. "Your mother invited me," I reminded her. "All I did was find Teenie's body, like I was supposed to."

"It would have been better if you'd never found her," Nell said childishly, as if I could have predicted this outcome.

"That was my job. She shouldn't have been lying out there in the woods, waiting to be found. I did my job, and it was the right thing to do." I said this as calmly as I could.

"Then why is all this happening?" she asked, like I was supposed to supply her with an answer. "What's going on?"

I shook my head. I had no idea. When I got one, one that would release my brother, I was never going to put foot in Sarne again.

Nell left to go to school, looking stunned and very young.

I stopped in the police station to give a statement about the incident of the night before and ask when I could see Tolliver. I was almost scared to ask the desk clerk, the round woman who'd been there the first time I'd come in the week before. I was scared that once they found out I wanted to see him, they'd find some way to keep me from it. And I didn't even know who "they" were.

"Visiting hours are from two to three on Tuesday and Friday," she said, looking away from me as if I were too loathsome for her eyes to behold.

Since it was Tuesday, I could see him that afternoon. The relief was enormous. But until two o'clock, I didn't have anything to do. I was sick to death of that motel room.

I went out to the cemetery, the newer one. I wanted to have another visit with the rest of the Teagues, the deceased side of the family. This time I was able to park very close to the Teague plot, and I was bundled up pretty heavily, because the temperature was dropping. This was Arkansas in early November, so snow wasn't too likely; but in the Ozarks, it also wasn't out of the question. I had a red scarf wrapped around my neck and wore my red gloves. I was wearing a puffy bright blue jacket. I like to be visible, especially in Arkansas in hunting season. It was the first time I'd wrapped up quite so much this fall, and I felt as padded as a child being sent out to play in the snow for the first time.

I looked around me at the people-empty landscape. Across the county road, to the west, was a stand of forest. There was a small group of houses, perhaps twenty, to the north; they had half-acre lawns and sundecks and gas grills outside their sliding glass doors. No visible cars; everyone worked to maintain that slice of suburbia. The cemetery stretched south over the swell of a steep hill, part of a line that also blocked the view to the east. This was a peaceful place.

It was easy to locate the Teague plot. There was a large monument on a plinth in the center, with TEAGUE carved on it twice, once to the north and once to the south.

I moved through the Teagues, slowly working my way from grave to grave. They were not a family that had long lives, as a whole. Dell's grandfather had lived only until he was fifty-two, when he'd had a massive heart attack. Two of Grandfather's sibs were there, dead in infancy. Dell's grandmother had come from hardier stock. She'd been seventy-two, and she'd died just two years ago—of pneumonia, basically. I gave Dell a hello; his gunshot death brought the average down sharply, of course. I did the subtraction on his father's tombstone and found that Dell's dad had only been forty-seven when Sybil found him facedown on his desk.

Of course, Dick Teague had been my goal all along. When I stepped onto his final resting place, I felt an edge of anticipation, like you feel before you bite into a gourmet dessert. Down through the rocky soil my special sense went, making contact with the body below me. I examined Dick Teague with the careful attention he deserved. But I found the barrier of shoes and dirt and coffin were muffling my response. I needed more contact. I sank down in front of the headstone to lay my hands on the earth. Just as I did so, there was a cracking noise from the woods to the west of the cemetery, and something stung my face sharply enough to make me cry out.

I put my gloved hand to my cheek, and it came away with blood on it. My blood was a different red than the cheerful scarlet of the glove, and I looked at it with some bewilderment. I heard the same crack again, and suddenly I realized that someone was shooting at me.

I launched myself from squatting to prone in one galvanic motion. Thank God I wasn't in the Delta, where the land was so flat I wouldn't have been able to conceal myself from a fly. I crawled to take cover on the east side of the big monument in the middle of the plot. It wasn't as wide as me, but it was the best I could do.

For a miracle, I'd put my phone in my pocket, and I stripped off one glove and called 911. I could tell the person who answered was the woman I'd just talked to at the desk at the police station. "I'm at the cemetery off 314, and someone's firing at me from the woods," I said. "Two shots."

"Have you been hit?"

"Just by a piece of granite. But I'm scared to move." I'd started crying from sheer terror, and it was an effort to keep my voice level.

"Okay, I'll have someone out there right away," she said. "Do you want to stay on the phone?" She turned away for a minute, and I heard her ordering a patrol car to my location. "Probably just a hunter making a mistake," she offered.

"Only if deer here are bright blue."

"Have you heard any more shots?"

"No," I said. "But I'm behind the Teague monument."

"Do you hear the car coming yet?"

"Yes, I hear the siren." It wasn't the first time I'd been glad to hear a police siren in Sarne. I wiped my face with the clean glove. A police car pulled to a screeching halt behind my car, and Bledsoe, the deputy who'd arrested Tolliver, stepped out of it. He sauntered over to the spot where I crouched.

"You say someone's firing at you?" he asked. I could tell that for two cents he'd whip out his own gun and take a shot.

I got up slowly, fighting a tendency on the part of my

legs to stay collapsed. I leaned against the granite monument, thinking a few deep breaths would have me back up to walking speed.

He looked at my face. His demeanor became a lot more businesslike. "Where'd you say these shots came from?"

I pointed to the woods across the road to the west, the closest cover to the cemetery. "See, look at Dick Teague's tombstone," I said, pointing to the jagged little white scar where a chunk had been blown off the edge.

Suddenly, Bledsoe was scanning the woods with narrow eyes. His hand went to his holster.

"What's the blood from?" he asked. "Were you hit?"

"It was the chip from the stone," I said, and I wasn't happy with how uneven my voice was. "The bullet was that close. The chip hit me in the cheek."

I spotted it on the ground, picked it up and handed it to him.

"Course, you coulda done it yourself," he said, with no conviction.

"I don't care what you think," I told him. "I don't care what report you write up. As long as you showed up and stopped him shooting at me, I don't care."

"You say 'him' for a reason?" he asked.

"No reason at all." My breathing was about normal by now. As I adjusted to the fact that no one was going to try to kill me in the next second or so, I reverted to my former opinion of the deputy.

"What were you doing out here, anyway?" He, too, was reverting to hostility.

"Just visiting."

He looked disgusted. "You're some piece of work, you know that?"

"I could say the same. Listen, I'm leaving while you're standing here, because I don't want to die in this town. Thanks for coming. At least . . ." I stopped before I finished with, "At least the police here aren't totally corrupt." I figured that would be less than tactful, especially since the deputy wasn't standing there pointing at me and yelling, "You can go on and shoot her!"

He gave me a curt nod. As I was shutting my door, he said, "You were standing on Dick Teague's grave?"

I nodded.

"You wanted to know what killed him?"

I nodded again.

"Well, what was it? According to you?"

"Heart attack, just like his dad." I looked at the deputy, making sure my face was smooth and sincere.

"So, the doctor was right?"

"Yes."

He nodded, rather smugly. I started my engine and turned the heater up. When I stopped at the turnoff from the cemetery onto the county road, I glanced in the rearview mirror. Deputy Bledsoe was right behind me. I realized at the same time that I needed to stop by the motel before I went to see Tolliver, unless I wanted to give him his own heart attack. My cheek was spotted with drying blood, and some had spattered on my coat, too.

I hated the motel by this time, but (since no attacker leaped out at me when I unlocked the door) I had to admit it felt safer than the streets. Sarne was beginning to represent one big danger zone to me. With the dead bolt and the chain employed on the door, I washed my face and put on some makeup, including bright lipstick. I didn't want to look like a ghost when I went to visit Tolliver. Possibly the little butterfly strips I put across the cut on my cheekbone detracted from the effect, but I had to use them. I put the blood-spotted jacket and glove in the bathtub to soak in cold water and I got out a black leather jacket.

On the drive to the jail, I caught myself checking my surroundings every few seconds. I tried not to feel ridiculous. No one was going to try to kill me in broad daylight in a busy town, I told myself. But then, I'd thought I'd seen the last of Scot, too; that he was a basically harmless teenage lunk whose punishment I could safely leave to his football coach. Ha.

I'd visited jails before. Being searched and having to let the jailer keep my purse was nothing new or extraordinary. It was far from pleasant, though. The sudden movements I'd made at the cemetery had reawakened the painful bruises from the night before. I was just a mass of misery, and I hated being so needy.

Seeing Tolliver enter the room in an orange jail jumpsuit made my brain flicker. When a jailer ushered him in, I had to cover my mouth with my hand. Two other prisoners entered the room with him (neither of them Scot), and they went to their visitors at their little separate tables. The rules at the Sarne jail were: Keep your hands on the table so they're visible at all times. Do not pass anything to the inmates unless you'd had it cleared with the jailers first. Do not speak loudly or rise suddenly from your chair until the prisoners have left the room.

Tolliver took my hands. We looked at each other. Finally, he said, "You've been hurt."

"Yes," I said.

His face was rigid. "Your face. Did one of them hit you?"

"No, no." I hadn't prepared a story for him. It would be stupid to try to conceal what had happened to me since he'd been in jail. I couldn't think of a lie that would cover everything, not even for Tolliver's peace of mind. "Someone shot at me from the woods," I said flatly. "I wasn't hurt, except for this scratch. I won't go back to the cemetery."

"What's going on in this town?" Tolliver was having a hard time controlling his voice. "What's wrong with these people?"

"Have you seen Scot?" I asked, trying to put a little perkiness in my voice.

"Scot the kid?"

"Yeah."

"They brought someone in last night, someone I haven't seen yet. What's he in for?"

"He was in my motel room when Hollis brought me back last night, and he . . ."

The expression on Tolliver's face stopped me.

"You have to calm down," I said, very quietly and intently, holding on to his hands as if they were lifelines and I was drowning. Or he was. "You have to. You just have to. You can't get into trouble in here, or they'll keep you. Now you listen, I'm going to be okay. I've called the lawyers, and a lady, Phyllis Folliette, from Little Rock, is coming tomorrow for your arraignment. She's a friend of Art's, so she's good. You'll get out, and we'll be okay." I adjusted my position in the hard chair, suppressing a wince.

"That Scot's a rat bastard," Tolliver said. His voice was misleadingly calm.

"Yeah," I said, and gave a little snort of laughter. "Yeah, that's what he is, all right. But I think someone paid him to be more of a rat bastard than he actually is."

I told Tolliver about the death of Dick Teague, the fact that Sally had been hired to clean the study, the fact that she'd seen something on Dick Teague's desk that had aroused her curiosity or her interest, so much so that she'd come home and consulted her textbook about what she'd noticed. "SO MO DA NO" didn't mean anything to Tolliver, either.

"Maybe an anagram?" he asked.

"I haven't been able to make a word of it, if so," I said. "And those aren't anyone's initials. I tried writing it backwards. I tried assigning numbers. I tried moving the letters one forward in the alphabet, and one backward. I don't think Sally Boxleitner was up to a more complex code than that."

Tolliver thought for a minute. Under my fingers, I felt his pulse, steady and vital.

"And what was on his desk?" Tolliver asked.

"Insurance forms."

"Whose?"

"According to Sybil, he was reviewing the family's medical bills for the year."

"And he really had a heart attack?"

"Yeah, that was what I was checking at the cemetery. He really did. It runs in his family; at least, Dick's father died the same way, real early—though not as early as Dick."

"I can sure give it a lot of thought, since I don't have anything else to do," Tolliver said, trying hard not to sound bitter.

I cleared my throat. "I brought one of your books. They're searching it for hidden messages, I guess, and they'll pass it on to you when you go back to your cell."

"Oh, thanks." There was a pause while he struggled not to say anything, but he lost. "You know, I ended up in here so I can't stop someone when they try to hurt you."

"I know."

"I feel as angry as I've ever felt in my life."

"I got that."

"But we have to know who wanted me in here so bad."

"Surely . . . surely it must be Jay Hopkins?"

"What's your figuring on that?"

"Marv Bledsoe is a good buddy of Jay Hopkins. And Marv's a cousin of Paul Edwards. Or else it was Harvey the sheriff, himself, who told Marv to arrest you."

"Of the three, I'd rather this be Jay's doing."

I nodded. Jay was the weakest of the three.

"Time's up," the jailer said, and the other two visitors stood. Tolliver and I looked at each other. I was making a huge effort not to look as anxious as I felt. I suspected Tolliver was doing the same.

"I'll see you tomorrow in the courtroom," he said, when the jailer showed signs of impatience. I let go of his hands and pushed back the chair.

Five minutes later, I was standing out in the cold, bright day, wondering what I should do next. I couldn't stop myself from wondering if anyone was looking at me, and if that anyone had a rifle in his hands. I wondered if I would live long enough to get Tolliver out of jail. I despised myself for my fear, because at least I was free; my brother was not. He was probably not any safer in jail than I was walking around, especially if our enemy turned out to be the sheriff.

I could see from the traffic that school had let out for the day. So I wasn't surprised when my new best friend, Mary Nell Teague, pulled up in her little car. "Come for a ride," she called, and I climbed in the front seat. I was surprised she was by herself, and I was also surprised that she would want to approach me so publicly.

"Have you seen him?" she asked, backing out and driving away at what I could only think was a reckless speed.

"Yes."

"They wouldn't let me, since I'm not family or a spouse." She said this with sullen amazement, as if it was extraordinarily bull-headed of the jailers not to let a lovesick teenage girl visit a prisoner. I was getting so tired of this girl, with her burdensome crush and her sense of privilege. But I also felt a certain amount of pity for her, and I hoped she could still be useful in helping us figure out what was really happening in Sarne.

And she needed to start doing that now. "Mary Nell, what do you know about Jay Hopkins?"

"He used to be Miss Helen's husband," she said, "you know that."

"Did he have any contact with Dell?"

"What difference does that make? I don't think about trashy people like him."

"This isn't going to be easy, but it's time for you to grow up a little."

"Like I haven't, this past year?"

"You've had some tragedy this year, but as far as I can tell, it hasn't matured you any."

She pulled to the side of the road, tears in her eyes. "I can't believe you," she said chokingly. "You're so mean! Tolliver deserves a better sister than you."

"I agree. But I'm what he's got, and I have to do everything I can for him. He's all I've got, too." I noticed she still hadn't answered my question. But I figured that was a kind of answer in itself.

She wiped her face with a tissue and blew her nose. "So why do you keep asking me about people?"

"Someone took a shot at me today. Someone paid your teenage admirer to beat me up, and someone let him into my room. I don't think he thought of that on his own, do you?"

She shook her head. "When I talked to Scot yesterday, he was mad at me, and mad at you, but he was going to stay away from you. Mr. Random, the football coach, he got onto Scot in front of the entire team and gave him twenty bleachers, and then Scot's dad grounded him from television or the telephone for a month."

"So what could have happened in the meantime, to make him hide in my room like he did?" Running up the bleachers and back twenty times, and no TV or telephone. Glad to know terrorizing me came with a stiff penalty.

"Did you ever think it might have been your *lover-boy*, Hollis, who asked him?" Mary Nell had decided to counterattack.

"No, I never did. Why do you suggest that?" Mary Nell was trying to make me angry, and she was pretty close to succeeding, but I made myself hold on to my temper with a ferocious effort.

"Well, just maybe Hollis wanted the chance to save you from something bad, so he could look like a big hero? And maybe he shot at you, too, which I have only your word for—that it ever happened, I mean."

"Why would he shoot at me?"

"To make you need him," she said. "To make you hold on to him. Now that your brother's out of the way, you need an ally, right? So maybe Hollis even got Tolliver arrested."

I was impressed with Mary Nell. This was deep and indirect thinking from a seventeen-year-old. What she said made sense, sort of. I didn't want to believe her theory about Hollis, and I don't think I really did believe it, but I had to consider her idea for a second or two. It made as much sense as any of my theories, and maybe more than some of them. I remembered having sex with Hollis the night before, and I had a bleak, black moment of wondering if he might have betrayed me from the start. Then I realized, more rationally, that Mary Nell was striking back at me for many reasons, most of all for having a closer relationship with my brother than she would ever have.

Silly girl. But looking at her, as she mopped at her face and then brushed her hair, I realized that she was only seven years younger than I. Mary Nell's life had been no picnic, of course, but probably it had been better than mine. By the time I was Mary Nell's age, even aside from the lightning strike, my life had changed forever. I had watched adults I knew and loved, as they threw their futures away. Then I had lost my sister Cameron; literally, lost her.

"Don't look at me like that," Mary Nell said, her voice quavering. "Do you even know where you are? God, stop it!"

I blinked. I hadn't realized I'd been staring.

"Sorry," I said automatically. "Your mother says you had a tonsillectomy this past year?"

"You are so weird. So fucking weird," she said, daring to say the bad word in front of me, daring me to admonish her.

I didn't give her any reaction. "Answer me," I said, after a pause.

"Yes, I did," she said, sullenly.

"You were in the hospital here?"

"In the next town, Mount Parnassus. Our little hospital closed two years ago."

"Dell was in the same hospital when he had to have stitches?" I was dredging up Sybil's conversation from when we'd seen her house. It was hard going. I wasn't sure what I was probing for; maybe I'd know it when I heard it. "He had a broken leg, or was that someone else?"

"That was the boy who was driving the car. Dell had stitches in his head. At first the emergency doctor thought he might have other problems, and he was unconscious for a little while, but they just kept him overnight."

"And your dad was in the hospital, too." I was trying to make something out of nothing.

"Yes, he had pneumonia." Mary Nell's face grew sad. "He had a bad heart, and the pneumonia just weakened him. I told him he'd get better, but the day before he died, he said, "Nelly, I'm just not the man I was before I caught that bug.""

"He called you Nelly?"

"Yeah, or Nell. He liked me and my brother being Nell and Dell." The teenager's little face collapsed as I watched her. "I don't have a brother or a father. Probably nobody'll call me that again in my whole life."

"Sure someone will," I said, trying to figure out what had

rung a bell in my head. "You're a pretty girl, Mary Nell, and you have a lot of spirit. Someone will come along who'll call you anything you want him to."

She brightened, happy to hear this even from someone she thought she despised. What she actually felt toward me was probably something closer to envy.

"You think so?"

"Yes, I think so."

"Harper," she said, and I realized she'd never spoken my name before, "what's going to happen to Tolliver?"

"Like I said, I called our lawyer. He gave me the name of an Arkansas attorney. She'll be here tomorrow. She's coming from Little Rock. She's going to appear at Tolliver's arraignment. I know she'll get him out."

"You fixed that up yourself?"

I nodded. "Sure."

"I couldn't do that," she said, subdued. "I wouldn't know how to begin."

I didn't want to sound like Ozark Granny Wisewoman, but I said, "You'll know when you need to."

"I liked Miss Helen," Mary Nell said, surprising me yet again.

"You told me that before," I said mildly. "I did, too. How well did you know her?"

"Well, she worked for us for a while. That's how Dell got to know Teenie. I mean, he knew who she was from school, because we all know each other, right? But he probably never would have spent time with her if Miss Helen hadn't worked at our house. That's how he got to know what she was really like. Then Miss Helen got to drinking so much she didn't get to work on time, and Mom had to let her go, and hired Mrs. Happ to help. But Dell and Teenie were sneaking off to see each other by then."

I'd heard pretty much the same thing from Hollis.

"Then Mr. Jay, Jay Hopkins, he beat Miss Helen up, and I heard my mom and Uncle Paul arguing about whether we should get Miss Helen back to work in the house. Uncle Paul said Miss Helen was sober and deserved a second chance, and Mom said after what she knew now, she wouldn't have Helen back in the house for love nor money. Especially love, she said."

"What do you think she meant by that?" I asked. With Mary Nell around, you wouldn't need a tape recorder.

"I have no idea," the girl answered. "I never did understand. I think my mom thought Miss Helen took something from her. But they wouldn't tell me." Familiar bitterness tinged her voice: the teenager vs. the adult world.

"Mary Nell, could you drop me back by my car?"

She sounded a little hurt when she told me she could.

I'd been too abrupt; but I had to think, and I knew Mary Nell would keep on talking as long as I was available to be her audience.

Once I was by myself, I felt both visible and vulnerable. I drove to my motel by the most direct route and shut myself in the damn room with the damn green bedspread. I had no messages. I couldn't decide if that was a good thing or a bad thing. My leg was tingling, as it sometimes did, and I peeled off my jeans and rubbed the skin, with its fine tracery of purple spiderwebs. Cameron had called me Spiderwoman for a while, before we'd figured out that the branching lines weren't going away. My stepfather had been fond of ordering me to show the leg to his friends.

Hollis never mentioned it. Maybe he didn't understand it was lightning-related. Maybe he thought it was a birthmark of some kind and didn't want to hurt my feelings.

I lay down on the bed. SO MO DA NO, I thought. It might almost be the chorus to a Caribbean song. Okay. Reverse it. ON AD OM OS. NO DA MO SO. Dams, moon, soon, mad, mono, moans, nomad. Damon, doom, moods. Amos. Samoa? Nope, only one A. Why one A? Every other phrase ended with O.

Okay, what if the second letter was some . . . condition? What if the first letters stood for names? S could be for Sybil, D for Dell, N for . . . oh, Mary Nell had said her dad had called her Nelly. That could be N. But then, who was M? No one's name started with M, that I could recall. D could be for Dick Teague, if not Dell.

For the first time, I wished that I could ask questions of the dead. I could only take what they gave me. They gave me a picture of their deaths. They gave me what they'd been feeling at the moment. But they never told me why, or who, just how.

*A bullet in my back . . . an infection in my lungs . . . my heart stuttered and quit pumping . . . I was just too old and worn out . . . the car hit so hard . . . the fall was from too high . . . I picked up the razor blade . . . I couldn't breathe, couldn't breathe, my inhaler was too far away . . . the meat lodged in my throat . . . the virus traveled through me and laid waste to my body . . . the knife traveled through my liver, then my stomach, then . . .*

The dead all had stories, but they never explained or condemned. I'd heard, on odd little message boards that I visited, that some others like me—people who'd been French-kissed by electricity—could see the dead, could even communicate with them. No one else had confessed to having my truncated sort of relationship with those in their graves. There were lightning-struck people who could see the future, who now walked with a limp, who were blind in one eye. One woman had said no one in her family would help her right after she'd been hit because they were convinced she was charged with electricity. On a more private board, a board with far fewer members, a man in Colorado Springs posted that he was accompanied everywhere he went by his dead brother, who'd been killed by the same lightning bolt. No one else could see the brother, of course; his family had even had him committed for a time.

I stayed in my room all night. I ordered a delivery pizza. Hollis called to tell me he was working that night, all night, and to remind me to call him if I needed anything. I got one heavy-breathing anonymous call, a call I figured came from one of the teenage boys who'd confronted me. Paul Edwards called to tell me he was sorry about my brother's "situation," and he offered to help me in any way he could.

Since it was his cousin who had arrested my brother, I was pretty sure there would be a conflict of interest there, but I thanked him politely. He hinted that he wanted to come over and hang around with me. I turned him down, much less tactfully.

He was handsome, and he was a lawyer, and I could probably use a handsome lawyer friend, but Paul Edwards didn't offer to come hang around with a woman for no reason at all. He wanted something, and maybe it wasn't sex. He didn't seem to be a constant lover. The relationship between the lawyer and Sybil Teague wasn't clandestine, yet here he was with his ulterior motives.

I got a few hours' sleep that night, which was more than I expected. I drank coffee in the room. It wasn't good, but I didn't have to face anyone to drink it. I couldn't have eaten anything, so a restaurant was a waste of time.

I'd arranged to meet Phyllis Folliette at the courthouse. I didn't know what the lawyer would look like, but she proved to be very easy to pick out. The second I saw her I knew she wasn't from Sarne. Phyllis Folliette was a tall woman in a dark green suit and bronze silk blouse, with beautiful cordovan leather pumps that matched her bag and her briefcase . . . even her hair. Somewhere in her forties, Folliette exuded confidence and intelligence. That was what we needed.

I felt almost embarrassed to approach someone who was so obviously a star. I think few women would feel very well groomed or attractive when they looked at this woman, and I was no exception. I was all too aware of my messy hair and my wrinkled pantsuit. I'd made the effort to pull "meet the client" clothes out of my suitcase, but I'd lacked the energy to iron them. With Phyllis Folliette so ably making a great impression, I regretted not having stuck with jeans.

"I'm glad to meet you," she said. "You've impressed Art Barfield, and that's saying something." She shook my hand and began to tell me what she'd learned in talking to the law enforcement people in Sarne. "I've been over to the jail," she said. "Something is up. For one thing, if they were taking the story about Montana warrants seriously, Mr. Lang would be appearing before a different court. I don't know how much you know about the legal system in Arkansas." She raised her eyebrows.

"Assume I'm ignorant," I said, which was pretty much the truth.

"They would never have arrested him for a broken tail-light unless he did something else, like shove a cop or try to evade arrest, something like that. What gave the patrolman the juice to arrest Tolliver was the allegation that he had open warrants in Montana." That's what Art had said, too. "Now, if they were sticking by that story, your brother would be appearing in circuit court. But he's not. He's going to appear in the Sarne District Court, which only handles misdemeanors. You'll see when we get in there. We'll have to wait our turn, so you'll listen to lots of other charges against other people." Her brown eyes summed me up while she spoke.

"Harper, honey, you're very wired up," she said after a moment or two. "You need to try to relax."

"You don't know how bogus this is!" I whispered. I was trying hard to keep my voice down, because we were in a public hallway and the people who went by were eyeing us curiously, but I was so anxious I thought my frayed nerves would snap. "Are you telling me that the Montana thing is just going to go away?"

She glanced down at her watch. "I think it just might. We have a while before they bring him in. Let's find a quiet place. I think you need to tell me the whole story."

I didn't think it would be possible to tell Phyllis Folliette everything that had happened in Sarne, but I did manage to arrange enough of it in a coherent narrative to bring it to a conclusion with Tolliver's arrest.

"It's definite that some force in this town is against you," she said, after a silence. "It's evident you're being hounded. No matter what I think of the way you make your living, Miss Connelly, what's being done to you is wrong. And your brother is apparently being held to reinforce the message that you're unwelcome here. I'll do my best to get him out. He was actually arrested in Montana last year, right?"

"Well, yes. This guy threw a rock at me. Tolliver got upset. Of course."

"Of course," she said, as if she routinely spoke to clients who'd been literally stoned. "Tolliver was upset enough to put the man in the hospital?"

"Hey, those charges were dismissed."

"Um-hm. I think you had some luck with the judge on that one."

"You have a sister?"

"Uh . . . yes."

"Someone throws a rock at her, you'd go after the rock-thrower, right?"

"I think I'd probably be taking care of my sister. I'd let the cops arrest the rock-thrower."

"Look at it from the guy point of view."

"Okay, I see your drift."

"You talked to Tolliver about this, right?"

"Yes, they let me see him this morning. He mentioned the incident, but didn't give any details."

I smiled. "That's Tolliver."

"You two are close," she observed. "Why the different names? You've been married?"

"No," I said. "His father married my mother when we were both in our teens." I didn't like explaining this.

She nodded, giving me a sideways look. She excused herself to go to the ladies' room, and I stared at my feet for a while. When Phyllis emerged, she did a lot of meeting and greeting on her way back to our bench, in particular with a man with graying hair, probably in his early fifties, who was wearing glasses and a nice suit.

After he went into the courtroom, Phyllis Folliette made her way back to me, giving me a brisk nod. "Time to go in or we won't get a seat," she said, and we joined a stream of people passing through massive double doors to the courtroom.

The ceiling was somewhere in the clouds over our heads. There was no telling how many words were buzzing around under that high ceiling, trapped there over the years. Phyllis and I sat quietly, and people began filing in. The jailers brought a line of prisoners in, and I got to see Tolliver.

I stood up, so he could see me right away, and he gave me a serious look. I sat down in the folding wooden seat. "He looks all right," I said to the lawyer, trying to reassure myself. "Don't you think he looks all right?"

"He does," she agreed. "I don't think orange is his color, though."

"No," I said. "No, it isn't."

As all the people in the courtroom seemed to be sorting themselves out, Phyllis said, "While we have a minute, I'm just curious. Are you any relation to the Cameron Connelly who was abducted in Texas a few years ago? I'm only asking because when Art Barfield called me, he said you had grown up in Texas and you and the girl who vanished both have what could be last names for your first name. If that makes sense."

"Yes, it makes sense," I said, though I can't say I was totally focused on the conversation. "I was named for my father's mother's family, Cameron for my mother's mother's family. She was my sister."

"I notice you use the past tense. Was she ever found? Once the media stopped covering it . . ."

"No. But someday I'll find her body."

"Ah . . . okay."

After a beat, I noticed the peculiar tone to the lawyer's voice. "You know," I said more directly, "that when people are gone that long, they're dead."

"There was that girl in Utah, Elizabeth Smart."

"Yes. There was that girl in Utah. She turned up alive. But mostly, when people have been gone for more than a couple of days, and no ransom's been asked, they're dead. Or they wanted to go. I know Cameron didn't want to leave. So she's dead."

"You hold no hope?" She sounded incredulous.

"I hold no false hope." I knew my business.

The bailiff told us the judge was coming in, and we rose. A spare gray-haired man (in a suit, instead of a robe) took his seat before us. I wasn't surprised to recognize the man with whom Phyllis had been chatting earlier. The city attorney (at least I guessed that was what he was) was already in his seat facing the judge, a huge pile of files in front of him, and the proceedings began.

I'd been in court before, for this or that, so it no longer surprised me that it wasn't like *Perry Mason* reruns or the more recent *Judge Judy*. People wandered in and out. Prisoners were removed and brought in. Between cases, there was a low buzz of conversation. There was no reverential air, and there were very few dramatics. Justice was conducted as business-as-usual.

When their name was called, people went up to the podium in front of the judge's bench. The judge read out the offense, asked if the plaintiff had anything to state, then (after discussion) told the plaintiff what his fine was.

"Isn't this more like traffic court, or something? This doesn't seem serious enough," I whispered to Phyllis. She'd been listening to the judge carefully, getting his measure.

"Those warrants were bullshit," she said, just as quietly. "He's just going up for the taillight. This is unbelievable."

It took an hour for the judge to work down the list to Tolliver. Tolliver looked tired. Every now and then he'd look toward me, and he tried to smile, but I could tell it was an effort.

Finally, the clerk called, "Tolliver Lang."

Tolliver wasn't handcuffed or shackled, thank God. He went up to the podium, with one of the jail guards accompanying him.

"Mr. Lang, I see here that you were initially charged with outstanding warrants from Montana, and that you had a problem with a rear taillight." The judge didn't seem to expect Tolliver to answer. The judge had a frown on his narrow face. "But the officer who gave you the ticket for the taillight—Officer Bledsoe? Is he here?"

"No, your honor," answered the clerk. "He's on patrol today."

"Amazing. He says now he made a mistake about the warrants?"

"Yes, your honor," said the city attorney. "He apologizes for the mistake."

"This is a very serious error," said the judge. He frowned at the papers some more. "And very strange. What about the taillight?"

"He stands by the taillight, your honor," said the attorney, with a straight face.

"How long was this man in jail?"

"Two nights."

"In jail two nights for a broken taillight."

"Uh, yes, sir."

"You didn't resist arrest?" For the first time, the judge addressed Tolliver directly. I could see Tolliver's back straighten.

"No, sir," Tolliver said.

"Have you ever been arrested in Montana?"

"Yes, sir, but the charges were dismissed."

"That's a matter of public record."

"Yes, sir. And it was over a year ago."

"Mr. Lang, do you want to bring charges against Officer Bledsoe?"

"No, sir. I just want out of the jail."

"And I can understand that. You'll be released, no bail, just pay the fine for the taillight. You don't contest that, I guess?"

Tolliver was silent. I was sure he was debating about telling the judge that Bledsoe had broken it with his nightstick.

"No, your honor."

"Okay, broken taillight, one hundred fifty dollar fine," the judge said, and that was that. The jailer led Tolliver back through the side door where he'd entered, I assumed to return him to the jail and start the release paperwork. "Someone here to pay the fine?"

I held up my hand.

The judge barely glanced at me. "Through the door behind the clerk," he said, inclining his head in the right direction. On shaky legs, I made my way to the back of the court and through the door, where I was faced by a phlegmatic woman in khakis and a T-shirt, and an armed Hollis in full uniform. The woman was sitting behind a small table holding a cash box. I guess she needed Hollis to guard the money and make sure someone angry about paying a fine didn't decide to take it out on her.

"It all came out all right, then?" Hollis asked, looking genuinely relieved.

"Yes," I said, handing over the papers the clerk had given me, along with one hundred fifty dollars in cash. She filed the money and stamped "PAID" on the papers, handing them right back to me. I wanted to say something else to Hollis, but I couldn't figure out what, and there was someone right behind me waiting to make her own payment. So I smiled at him, happy for the first time in days, and went back through the courtroom, which looked just as full as it had when the morning began. The lawyer was waiting for me outside in the cavernous hall.

"Thanks, Phyllis," I said, and I pumped her hand.

Phyllis smiled at me. "All I did was show up and let the court know I was here," she said. "If you were to ask me what happened, it sounds like someone told Bledsoe to back off, not to make an issue of what he'd done."

"Maybe he did it on impulse, thinking he'd please someone, and then found out he hadn't."

Maybe it was his cousin Paul. Maybe it was his boss, the sheriff. Maybe it was the lady who owned half the town, Sybil. Maybe . . .

"Let's go over to the jail," Phyllis said. "I saw the van leave. I'll wait with you until they process him out, just to make sure."

We went into the jail again, and I asked the woman behind the counter where to wait. She pointed at the chairs in the same reception area where I'd waited so nervously to see Tolliver the day before.

It took a long time to process out a prisoner, and Phyllis Folliette stayed with me faithfully. Of course, I knew she was billing me for her time, but most lawyers would have given me a pat on the back and sped on their way to their office. She pulled something out of her briefcase to study when I showed I'd rather be silent. I sat with my eyes closed, letting the world go by, and I thought about all the people I'd met in Sarne, how closely they all seemed connected, how the repugnant stereotype of uneducated, inbred, unsophisticated-but-surprisingly wise hillbilly was both mined for tourist money and denigrated by the people who lived here. What had begun as a way of life determined by geographic isolation and poverty had become simplified and mythologized and made fun of for the world's consumption. And all of the people we'd been dealing with had been living in this town for several generations, except Hollis.

I let the incidents of the past week flow through my mind, not trying to sort them out. I thought it might help to make a list. That would be our program for tonight, maybe.

Then I heard footsteps I knew, and I opened my eyes. Tolliver was coming toward me, and I jumped up. We hugged, hard and fast, before I introduced him to Phyllis, who was looking at him with some curiosity. Tolliver thanked her, and she again protested that she hadn't done anything at all other than show up.

"But you called the sheriff yesterday," Tolliver said. I was eyeing him anxiously, but he only looked tired and in need of a shower.

"Yes, I did that," she said, smiling slightly. "I figured it couldn't hurt for the sheriff's department to know that someone from out of town was keeping an eye on the situation, someone with a little legal clout. Don't worry, you'll be billed for it."

"It was worth the money," I said, and after shaking our hands, Phyllis got back into her BMW and left Sarne. Lucky Phyllis.

While we drove to the motel, I explained to Tolliver about his room, and he said, "I don't care. I'm going to have a shower and some decent food, and then I think I'll sleep for a few hours. Then I'll get up and shower again and eat more decent food and sleep again."

"And this, after being in jail all of thirty-six hours! What if you'd had to stay in all week?"

He made a big production of shuddering. "You wouldn't believe how bad that jail is. I think they're trying to feed the prisoners on a dime a day, or something."

"You've been in jail before," I said, a little puzzled by his violent reaction.

"I wasn't worried about you getting hurt then, and I wasn't worried the whole town was in on some kind of conspiracy."

"You feel that?"

"I would have felt better if the most prominent lawyer in town and the sheriff hadn't been big buddies, and both involved in the deal that brought us up here. I couldn't sleep in the jail; the guy in the cell with me was brought in extremely drunk, and he snored and stank. I lay awake so long I convinced myself that something would happen to me in there, and they'd say I'd slipped on a bar of soap and banged my head, or accidentally tripped with my head in a noose. And then they'd get you."

"Phyllis says we don't have to stay in Sarne."

"Then we're leaving in the morning."

"That's fine with me."

Tolliver rummaged around in his suitcase for clean clothes and stalked off to the bathroom. I went out to get him some food. I even went through the drive-through so I wouldn't have to get out of the car. My paranoia was running high; although I had to admit that I had gotten nothing but good treatment from the people of Sarne I'd run into in impersonal capacities. The drive-through girl was polite and cheerful, the woman who took my money at the gas station was civil, and the judge had been businesslike and brisk. No question but that I was getting a skewed picture of Sarne and its people.

*So be it,* I thought. *We're outta here.*

I ate the food I'd gotten for myself with a better appetite than I'd had in days. Then I lay down and snoozed. I distantly heard the water shut off and then Tolliver eating. The paper bags made rustling noises, no matter how quiet he tried to be. Just as I was really drifting away to sleep, I heard the creak of bedsprings as he lay down on the other bed. Then there was peaceful silence, underlined by the drone of the heating unit.

I didn't nap as long as my brother, because I'd had some sleep the night before. I parted the curtains to peer outside and looked at the sky, gray with impending rain. It was about four in the afternoon, but it would be full dark within an hour. I brushed my teeth and hair and put my shoes on, and then I sat at the little table with a sheet of motel paper and a pencil. I like to make lists, but there's seldom any need for me to do so; I don't go to the grocery store much, and most of our errands are undertaken on the road.

I decided to list all the facts I could recall and see what shook out.

1. Sybil and the sheriff were brother and sister.

2. Sybil and Paul Edwards were lovers.

3. Sybil's son had been murdered.

4. Sybil's son's girlfriend had been murdered at the same time.

5. The girlfriend, Teenie Hopkins, was sister to the murdered wife of Deputy Hollis Boxleitner.

6. Sally (murdered wife) had been killed after she cleaned the study of . . .

7. Sybil's husband, victim of an untimely heart attack, while he was examining . . .

8. Medical records of his son (at that time alive) and daughter and himself.

9. Also murdered—Helen Hopkins, mother of Teenie Hopkins and Hollis Boxleitner's wife.

10. Helen had been the cleaning woman for Sybil's family for years, until she began drinking heavily and had an episode of violence with her ex-husband, Jay Hopkins.

11. Her attorney in the case against her ex-husband, and her attorney in the much earlier divorce, was Paul Edwards, also Sybil's attorney and lover.

12. Terry Vale recommended my services to Sybil.

13. Hollis had wanted to know for sure what had happened to his wife.

14. Paul Edwards had been glad to pay us.

15. Someone inflamed teenager Scot to the point where he accepted money (or maybe just followed the suggestion) that he lie in wait for me and beat me up.

16. That same someone, or possibly someone different, took a shot at me in the Sarne cemetery.

17. My brother went to jail on trumped-up charges; possibly to leave a shooter free to make a try at me, possibly just to shake us up enough that we would leave no matter what the sheriff had told us.

Tolliver stretched and yawned and came to look over my shoulder.

"What's this for?" he asked.

"We've got to understand what's happening. That's the only way we can get out of here."

"We're leaving in the morning. I don't care if they put a roadblock across the highway, we're getting out of this town."

# Fourteen

I had to smile, even while I shook two Tylenol out of the bottle and swallowed them down.

He went to the windows to look outside. "Ah-oh," he said. "It's coming up a storm."

"*That's* why my head's beginning to hurt."

"Maybe, too, you're hungry?" he asked mildly.

"I ate a few hours ago."

"It has been a while."

"You ate half a sandwich. Let's drive to Mount Parnassus. We don't want to get into any more trouble."

"Sounds good. But you know, we could just pack up our stuff and start driving now," I said.

"Not with a storm coming on."

It was because of me we couldn't drive during storms, because sometimes I had a very bad reaction; another weakness on my part.

"We'll go to Mount Parnassus," he said. "It's just twelve miles north."

It was dark already, at least in part because of the oncoming storm. Tolliver was driving because of my headache, so I answered the cell phone when it rang. It was Tolliver's older brother, Mark.

"Hi," I said. "How are you?"

"Well, I been better," he said. "Tolliver there?"

I silently handed Tolliver the phone. He disliked driving and talking at the same time, so he pulled over to the side of the road. Mark Lang had been nearly old enough to leave home by the time my mother and his father started living together and eventually got married. He hadn't liked my mother, hadn't liked the situation in his home, and had gotten out as soon as possible. For Tolliver's sake, he'd checked in at the house about every two weeks. He'd also helped to feed and clothe us, and he'd gotten us medical help when we'd needed it and the adults had been too strung out to provide it. And Mark had been especially fond of Cameron, as Tolliver had been of me. The little girls just represented two more sets of needs and wants, to Mark. I could imagine how unhappy he was at being called about Mariella's disappearance, and I was sure that was his reason for calling Tolliver now.

"He found her," Tolliver told me now, leaning away from the phone briefly. "Took him an hour."

That wasn't bad. I had a few questions, of course, but I decided to let the conversation run itself to a halt before I asked them.

Tolliver hung up soon enough. "They were hiding in Craig's Sunday school building," he said briefly.

"What—where is she now?"

"She went home. Craig had run out of food, anyway, so there wasn't any more fun in it for her."

We fell silent. There wasn't any more to say about Mariella. Mariella had seen too much as a kid to ever be innocent, and she'd probably go down the same path as our mother as fast as could be, despite all the Sunday school lessons and hours in Iona's church, despite the moral teachings and the days of school. So their lives wouldn't be all work and no play, Tolliver and I had sent funds for extras for Mariella and Gracie: dance lessons, voice lessons, art lessons. All this was a familiar litany in my head, as I tried again to figure out what else we could have done. The court would never have left the girls' upbringing to Tolliver and me.

My head pounded harder, and I looked at the sky ahead of us anxiously. I knew soon I would see a flicker of lightning.

We turned on the radio to listen to the weather. Storms were predicted, with heavy downpour and thunder and lightning. What a surprise. Flash flood warnings—which you had to take seriously in a terrain that included roads that dipped so deeply before rising again—in an area where all the streams and ponds were already full from plentiful rainfall earlier in the season.

We reached a little chain restaurant within ten minutes and went in, taking our raincoats with us. Inside, there was an older couple sitting close to the kitchen door; there was a single guy reading a newspaper, a dirty plate shoved across the table. A young couple, in their early twenties, sat with their two children in a booth by the big window. They were pale and fat, both wearing sweats from Wal-Mart. He wore a gimme cap with his. Her hair was pulled back into a curly ponytail, and her eyelids were blue with makeup. The little boy, maybe six, was wearing camo and carrying a plastic gun. The little girl was a pretty thing, with lots of light brown hair like her mother's, and a sweet and vacant face. She was coloring.

A waitress in jeans and a blouse strolled over to take our order. Her hair was dressed in a formidable bleached bubble, and she was chewing gum. She told us she was pleased to help us, but I doubted her sincerity. After we'd looked at the menus for a minute, she took our orders and strolled over to the window to the kitchen to turn them in.

After she'd gotten our iced tea, she vanished.

The couple started arguing about whether or not to enter their daughter in the next beauty pageant. It cost quite a bit to enter a child in a pageant, I learned, and to rent a dress and take time off from work to do the girl's hair and makeup cost even more.

I raised my eyebrows at Tolliver, who suppressed a smile. My mother had tried to get Cameron to do the pageant circuit. At the very first one, Cameron had told the judges she thought the pageant system was very close to white slavery. She had accused the judges of many unpleasant perversions. Needless to say, that had ended Cameron's career as a beauty contestant. Of course, Cameron was fourteen at the time. The little girl across the room was maybe eight and didn't look like she'd say boo to a goose.

Our cell rang again, and this time Tolliver answered it.

"Hello?" He paused and listened for a moment. "Hey, Sascha. What's the word?" Ah. The hair samples. The DNA test.

He listened for a few moments, then turned to me.

"No match," he said. "The male is not the father. Female One is the mother of Female Two." That was the way I'd marked the samples.

"Thanks, Sascha. I owe you," he said.

He'd no sooner put down the phone than the phone rang again. We looked at each other, exasperated and I answered it.

"Harper Connelly," said a strained voice.

"Yes. Who is this?" I asked.

"Sybil."

I never would have known this was my former client. Her voice was so tense, her enunciation so jerky.

"What's wrong, Sybil?" I tried to keep my voice level.

"You need to come here, tonight."

"Why?"

"I need to see you."

"Why?"

"There's something I need to tell you."

"You don't need to talk to us," I said. "We've finished our transaction." I struggled to keep myself calm and firm. "I did what you paid me to do, and Tolliver and I are going to get out of town as soon as we can."

"No, I want to see you tonight."

"Then you'll just have to want."

There was a desperate pause. "It's about Mary Nell," Sybil said, abruptly. "It's about her obsession with your brother. I need to talk to both of you, and if you're leaving town tomorrow, it's got to be tonight. Mary Nell's talking about killing herself."

I held the phone away to stare at it for a minute. This

sounded wildly unlikely. In my limited experience of Mary Nell Teague, she'd be more apt to be thinking of taking Tolliver hostage and bombarding him with love until he yielded to her. "Okay, Sybil," I said warily. "We'll be there in about an hour."

"Sooner, if you can," she said, sounding almost breathless with relief.

The waitress brought our food as I was relaying the conversation to Tolliver, who'd been able to hear most of it, anyway.

He made a face.

I wrote SO MO DA NO on an extra napkin with a tine of my fork. I looked at it while I picked at my salad, which was about what you'd expect at a diner in the middle of nowhere. I tried to think myself into the scenario. Okay, Dick's been making notes to himself while he goes through the family's medical records for the year, getting ready for tax time. Four separate notations. Four members of the family.

S could be Sybil, M could be Mary Nell, D could be Dell, then N could be . . . who? I'd already gone over the fact that Dick Teague had called his daughter Nelly. But if that took care of the N, what about the M? I stared down at the napkin, thinking about making little notes about myself and my family . . .

Oh, for God's sake! The M was for Me!

I put the fork down.

"Harper?" Tolliver said.

"Blood types," I said. "Stupid, stupid, stupid me."

"Harper?"

"It's *blood types*, Tolliver. Dick Teague was saying, 'I have type O, Sybil has type O, Mary Nell has type O, but Dell has type A.' That was what Sally Boxleitner was looking up in her high school science textbook. She suspected right away when she found the note Dick left on the medical records right before his heart attack. Dick had discovered he could not have been Dell's dad. Two O's can't have an A."

"I can see where that might trigger a heart attack," Tolliver said slowly. He put down his own fork, patted his lips with his napkin. "But why would that lead to Dell and Teenie getting shot?"

"I'm thinking," I said.

The family of four had cleared out while we were eating, with the topic of the beauty pageant still unresolved. I would put money on the mother winning. The older couple ate in a leisurely way, and just as slowly paid and took their leave, exchanging pleasantries with the waitress. The single man was still reading the paper, and every now and then the waitress would top off his coffee cup. Tolliver paid our bill while I stared into space, trying to imagine what had happened next in the Teague family drama.

Okay, next Hollis's wife had been killed. Sally had figured out that Dell wasn't Dick's son. Who would she tell? She would be more likely to tell a woman.

I thought she would tell her mother. But there must be something else . . .

We were in the car going back toward Sarne when I told Tolliver what I was thinking. "Why wouldn't she tell Hollis?" he asked. "It would be natural to tell your husband."

"Hollis told me she didn't like to talk about her family troubles," I said. "I think to Sally, Dell's parentage would fall into that category. So, Sally told her mother. Her mother, rather than Teenie, because Sally was closer to her mother. Besides, the secret was about Dell, and Teenie would've told him."

"So what happened next?" Tolliver asked, as though I would surely know.

I did try to puzzle it out. "Helen," I muttered. "What would Helen do? Why would she care whose kid Dell was?"

Why, indeed?

Say Teenie and Dell don't know anything about this. And then Sally dies. Sally dies because . . . she told. Because she told her mother. But I remembered Helen's overwhelming grief, and I didn't think Helen had known why Sally died. Until I came along and told Hollis and Helen differently, they'd thought her death was an accident. As far as I knew, Helen had never questioned that. And she'd believed Dell shot Teenie. Why? Over Teenie's pregnancy, of course! And then, unable to face what he'd done, Helen believed that Dell had shot himself.

Only then, to clear his name, Sybil had hired me, and I'd told Helen that Dell hadn't shot Teenie. I'd told Helen that both her daughters had been murdered by someone else.

I didn't exactly feel like all these deaths were my fault, but I didn't feel good about them, either. I'd done what I'd been hired to do, with no idea what the consequences might be in a confused place like Sarne. I believed after she found out they'd been killed, Helen must have realized who would have wanted both her daughters to die. I believed she would have arranged to confront that person to verify her suspicions, and during that confrontation that person had killed her, watched by all those pictures of two dead girls, in the little box-like house.

"I don't believe Sybil," I said abruptly.

Tolliver looked over at me briefly before turning his attention back to the rain-slick road. There was a distant rumble. I shivered.

"Why?"

"I don't believe Mary Nell would ever threaten to kill herself," I said. "I don't believe she would resort to tactics like this to win your interest. I think she's too proud."

"She's sixteen."

"Yeah, but she's got her backbone in straight."

"So, why are we going?"

"Because Sybil wants us there badly enough to lie about it, and I want to know why."

"I don't know, maybe we should just go back to the motel. It's thundering, and you know there may be lightning."

"I got that." As a matter of fact, the Tylenol hadn't prevented the ferocious headache building behind my eyes. "But I think we should go to Sybil's." Something was pushing me, and I had a bad feeling it wasn't something smart.

I spotted a flash of lightning out of the corner of my eye and tried not to flinch. I was safe, in a car, and when I got out, I'd be very careful not to step into a downed electrical wire or hold a golf club or stand under a tree or do any of the myriad things people did that increased their chances of being electrocuted by lightning, either directly or indirectly. But I couldn't help ducking and hiding my face.

"You can't do this," Tolliver said. "We need to get inside."

"Go to the Teagues' house," I yelled. I was terrified, but I was driven.

He didn't say anything else, but turned in the right direction. I was ashamed of myself for yelling at my brother, but I was also strangely light-headed and focused on what lay ahead. A little part of my brain was still gnawing at the problem: Why would Dell and Teenie have to die, if Dell wasn't Dick Teague's son? What secret was so important that all those people had to die, the people who could reveal it?

The Teague house was mostly dark when we pulled up to it. I'd imagined it would be blazing with light, but only one window glowed through the darkness. None of the outside lights were on, which I thought was strange. If I'd been Sybil, I'd have turned on all the outside lights once I'd made sure company was coming, especially on an evening when bad weather was obviously imminent.

"This is bad," Tolliver said slowly. He didn't elaborate. He didn't need to. We parked at the front of the house. The rain drummed on the roof of the car. "I think you better call your cop buddy," he said to me. "I think we better stay out of that house until we have someone with authority here." He switched on the dome light.

"I can't count on him being the one on call," I said, but I dialed his home number on the chance that Hollis was snug and warm and dry in his little house. No answer. I tried the sheriff's office. The dispatcher answered. She sounded distracted. I could hear the radio squawking in the background. "Is Hollis on patrol?" I asked.

"No, he's answering a call about a tree being across the road on County Road 212," she snapped. "And I got a three-car accident on Marley Street." I could see that a personal call to a busy officer would not be priority.

"Tell him to come to the Teagues' house as soon as he can," I said. "Tell him it's very important. I think a crime's been committed there."

"Someone'll come as soon as they can get free from the ones we're sure about," she said, and she hung up the phone.

"Okay, we're on our own," I told Tolliver. He switched off the light, leaving us in a dark island of dry warmth. The cold rain was pelting down, drenching the lawn and rinsing off the car. The flashes of lightning were only occasional. I could stand it, I told myself. We'd parked at the end of the sidewalk that led directly to the main doors. The garage, with its door into the kitchen, was to our left on the west side of the house.

"I'll go in the front, you go in the garage door," I said. By the distant glow of the streetlights, I could see Tolliver open his mouth to protest, then close it again.

"All right," he said. "On the count of three. One, two, three!"

We leapt from our respective sides of the car and took off for our separate goals. I reached mine first, without being hit by anything except leaves and twigs snapped from a tree by the high winds.

The front door wasn't locked. That might not mean anything. I was pretty sure that in Sarne no one locked up until they turned in for the night. But the hair on my neck prickled. I pushed it open, but only a foot.

The door opened directly into the large formal living room, which was unlit and shadowy. The rain running down the big picture window and the streetlight shining through it made the room seem underwater in the glimpse I had before I crouched and rolled as I pushed the door wide open. A shot whistled past and above me. I scrambled to take cover behind a big chair. I'd never held a gun in my life, but I was regretting my lack of firepower at this instant.

There was a scream from somewhere else in the big house. I thought it came from the back, maybe from the family room.

Where was Tolliver? But he'd have heard the shot. He'd be careful.

For an unbearably long moment, nothing more happened. I wondered how many people were hiding from each other in these rooms, and I wondered if I'd survive to find out.

Gradually, my eyes became used to the faint and watery light. Though the drapes had been partially drawn, I could identify the furniture by shape.

There was another doorway directly opposite the front entrance, and I was pretty sure that was where the shot had come from. I took a deep breath and rolled from the armchair to a coffee table. Next step, the couch. That would put me within a few feet of the other doorway, which was the only way into the rest of the house, if I was remembering the layout correctly.

"Nell!" I yelled, hoping to distract the shooter from Tolliver's progress, wherever he was. "Sybil!"

There was an answering shriek from the second floor. I didn't know which one of them was yelling, and I didn't know the location or number of people in the house, but I did know all of them were alive. Not a buzz in my head.

I'd been feeling very determined, but now the storm

kicked up a notch. The rain began lashing harder at the window and soaking the carpet through the open front door. The rumble of thunder became almost continuous, and the crack of lightning followed right after. I felt as though I was pinned on a map and the lightning could see me, was tracking me, getting closer and closer until it could hit me again. Then I'd lose everything. The unimaginable pain would arc through me for the second time, and I'd lose my sight or my memory or the use of my leg, or something else irreplaceable. I moaned in fear, covering my eyes, and when I took my hands away, a man was standing over me with a gun in his hand.

In a desperate attempt to save my life, I dove at him, grabbing him around the knees and bringing him down. The gun went off; he'd had his finger on the trigger, oh God oh God. But if I was hit I didn't know it yet, and when he swung the gun at my head I grabbed his wrist with both hands and clung to it, literally for dear life.

Maybe my intense fear made me stronger than usual, because I was able to keep my hold on him though he hit at me with his other arm and thrashed around to shake me off. He was trying to bring the gun to bear on me, trying to force his arm into a straight line so he could fire at me, and as we rolled around in a snarling heap I saw my chance and sank my teeth into the fleshy heel of his hand and bit down with all my might. He gave a cry of pain—*yay!*—and let go of the gun. I would like to say that had been my intent, but if it was, I'd made the decision on a level I'd never tapped consciously.

Then the lights came on in the room, blinding me, and a shape I thought was Tolliver leaped forward. All three of us were in the melee on the floor, crashing into tables and sending heavy lamps toppling to the pale carpet.

"Stop!" screamed a new voice. "I've got a gun!"

We all froze. I still had my teeth in the man's hand, and Tolliver had raised a heavy glass ornament shaped like an apple to bash in his head. For the first time, I unclenched my teeth and looked up at the man's face. Paul Edwards. He was a far cry from the suave lawyer I'd met in the sheriff's office. He was wearing a flannel shirt and khakis and sneakers, and his hair was completely disheveled. He was panting heavily, and blood was streaming from his hand where I'd bitten him. Most striking of all was the absence of that calm assurance he'd had, the certainly that his little world was his to rule and order. He looked more like a raccoon that had been treed—bared teeth and glinting eyes and hissing noises.

"Oh my God, Paul," Sybil said, the gun wavering in her hand. Dammit, why does everyone have a gun? Sybil's was smaller, but looked just as lethal. "Oh, my God." She was as struck by the transformation as I was, probably more. "How could you do this?"

I hoped she was asking him, not us. At least the light had made the storm retreat in my forest of fears. Tolliver gently set the glass apple on a table by the kitchen doorway.

"Sybil, I couldn't let them know." He was trying to sound reasonable, but it just came out weak.

"That's what you said before, when you made me call them. I still don't understand."

Tolliver and I might as well not have been in the room.

I noticed for the first time that Sybil had a scarf tied to

one wrist, and the other wrist was deeply scored with a red line. He'd had her tied up.

"Where's Nell?" I croaked, but neither of them answered. They were so focused on each other, we weren't even on the same planet. I noticed that Tolliver silently bent to retrieve Paul's gun where it lay against the baseboard. The gun looked horribly functional in the expensive, feminine room, which right now was not looking its orderly best. Tolliver slid the gun under the skirt of the couch. Good.

"Sybil, we were together for so long," Paul said. "So long. You'd never divorce him. You'd never even agree to quit sleeping with him."

"He was my *husband,* for God's sake!" she said harshly.

"So when Helen divorced that bastard Jay, she . . ." Paul looked at the carpet as if it covered a secret he needed to know. "We got close."

"You had an affair with her," Sybil said, absolutely stunned. "With that low-class drunken slut. After you denied it to my face! Harvey was right."

I risked a look at Tolliver. He met my eyes and we exchanged looks.

"I knew Dell was really my son," Paul said. "But Teenie was mine, too."

"No," said Sybil, shaking her head from side to side. "No."

"Yes," he said. But his eyes were straying now and again to the gun. Sybil was holding it pretty steady, for now. Tolliver and I had edged away from Paul, naturally, not wanting to be in the line of fire, but now I wondered if we shouldn't have kept hold of him, and possibly Tolliver should have bashed him with the glass apple, just to be sure. The lawyer was getting his spirit back, the longer Sybil talked to him without shooting him.

"You could have just told them," she said. "You could have just told them."

"I did tell them," he said. "That day they died. I did tell them." His voice was unsteady, as shaky as Sybil's.

"You killed them? Why'd you kill your son, our son?" Tears were running down her cheeks, but she wasn't ready to crumple yet. I'd been right when I'd pegged her as stoic.

"Because Teenie was pregnant, you stupid cow," he said, retreating to a more comfortable emotion, anger. "Teenie was pregnant, and she wouldn't have an abortion! Said it was wrong! And your son, our son, wouldn't make her!"

"Pregnant! Oh! Oh, my God. How did you find out?"

"From me." A bedraggled Nell stood in the doorway. She had a letter opener in her hands, and her wrists held the same red marks that her mother's showed. "I'm the most stupid person in the world, Mama. I was so worried about Teenie being pregnant that when Dell told me, I thought I'd ask Paul to talk to her, tell her to give it up for adoption. Dell was too young to get married, Mama, and I just didn't want to be Teenie Hopkins' sister-in-law. So they died! He killed them, Mama, and it's all my fault!"

"Don't you ever think that, Mary Nell. It's *his* fault." Sybil gestured with the gun toward her longtime lover.

It seemed to me it was sort of Sybil's fault, too, but I wasn't going to raise any issues as long as she was holding the gun. While I was being ignored, I wanted to put a safer distance between me and Paul Edwards, so I was edging back to the far end of the couch. On Edwards's other side, Tolliver was shifting himself a little closer to the two women, but he was careful to keep the line of fire between Sybil and Paul free and clear.

"Yes, it's my fault," Paul gabbled. He was looking around the floor surreptitiously. He was looking for his gun. Paul Edwards was not down for the count.

"You need to tie him up," Tolliver suggested. "Call the police."

Nell began to move back through the doorway, presumably to go into the kitchen to call the police, but Paul made a sudden move and she stilled.

"No, don't call," Paul said. "Mary Nell, I'm your dad, too. Don't give me up."

Poor Nell couldn't have looked more horrified if he'd said he'd made an offer for her hand.

"No," Sybil hissed. "Don't listen, Mary Nell. It's not true."

"She's right," I said, very quietly. But no one paid attention. My brother and I were definitely the audience. The innocent bystanders. You know what happens to innocent bystanders.

"Did you kill my dad, somehow?" she asked Paul. "My real dad?"

"No," I said. "Your dad died of a heart attack, Nell. He really did." I didn't see any need to throw in the circumstances.

"You . . . you . . . asshole," she said to Paul Edwards.

Her mother opened her mouth to reprimand Mary Nell, then had the good sense to close it.

"You killed my son," Sybil said instead. "You killed my son. You killed his baby. You killed his girlfriend. You killed . . . who else did you kill? Helen, I guess. The mother of your *daughter*."

"You have yourself to blame for that," he said sullenly. "It was you hiring Helen, you having her around here cleaning that gave Dell and Teenie a chance to get to know each other."

"Gave you a chance to see Helen again, too, I guess," Sybil said in a very ugly voice. "Who else did you kill, Paul?"

"Sally Boxleitner?" I suggested.

Edwards gaped at me as if I'd sprouted another head. "Why do you . . . ?" he began, then trailed off, apparently at a loss.

"She figured it out, didn't she?" I asked. "Did she call you?"

"She called me," he admitted. "She said she, she . . ."

"What did my wife tell you?" Hollis asked from the open front door.

I wondered if Tolliver and I could just creep out through the kitchen and be gone. We could go back to the motel and grab our stuff, leave this town forever. I caught Tolliver's eye and tilted my head toward the doorway into the rest of the house. He shook his head slightly. We were just spectators at the showdown at the OK Corral, but that still meant some injudicious move might get us killed in the cross fire.

Hollis didn't look like the stoical cop I'd met when I'd come to Sarne, and he didn't look like the lover I'd joined in bed. His eyes were showing a lot of white. He was wearing a long shiny waterproof slicker, and his uniform hat had a plastic bag on it. His face was wet with rain, and his slicker dripped onto the carpet. He was wearing rubber boots over his heavy cop shoes, and he had a glove on his left hand. His right hand was bare, holding his own gun in a very businesslike way.

I wondered if Mary Nell had a firearm tucked in a pocket.

"I didn't kill her," Paul said. "She called me, told me she had some questions about blood types. I agreed to meet her, though at the time I didn't know what she was talking about."

"You killed Dell," Mary Nell said. "You killed Teenie, and the baby, and Miss Helen. How can we believe you didn't kill Sally, too?"

"Sybil," I whispered.

Only Tolliver heard me. His eyes widened.

"You can't pin that one on me," Paul Edwards said, beginning to pull himself to his knees. I thought it was strange that the charge would make him indignant enough to be defiant, with all that he'd admitted. "I think you can understand why I didn't want Teenie to bring a child into the world with a bloodline like that," and he half-smiled in a parody of a reasonable expression. "But I never laid a hand on Sally. Sally was a good girl. And definitely not mine, of course."

"Good," Hollis growled.

"But you know, since I thought she'd drowned in the tub by accident, like the coroner said, I'd never stopped to think. Sybil, I told you that Sally called me, said she had something to tell me about Dick's death. At the time, I thought Sally might be priming up to tell me a tale for some kind of blackmail. But when she died, too, it didn't seem to make any difference. Sybil, did you go talk to Sally?"

Mary Nell gave a choked laugh. "Don't you try to go blame that on her, you murderer! Mama, tell him . . ." The girl's voice trailed off when she saw her mother's face. "Mama?" She sounded lost. Gone for good.

"She said she'd looked up blood typing, and she knew Dell wasn't really a Teague," Sybil said dully. "She wanted me to ask Harvey to resign early. Sally wanted Hollis to have Harvey's job. She was scared Hollis would get restless without it, that he wasn't happy piecing together a living in a little town like this."

Hollis looked like someone had hit him in the head. His hand was wavering. He didn't know who he wanted to shoot most. I understood the feeling.

Sybil gulped. Her own gun was falling down to her side. "I couldn't do that. And I couldn't stand her lying like that. I made myself believe it was a lie. So I went by one afternoon. She'd left the door unlocked, which I figured, and I walked in with this gun, but she was in the tub, singing away."

Hollis looked sick.

"And I just stepped in the bathroom and I grabbed her heels and pulled," Sybil went on. "And after a minute, she stopped trying to get up." Sybil stood there, lost in the memory, the gun down by her side.

Mary Nell screamed in horror. Paul Edwards launched himself at Sybil's gun, and Tolliver leaped over to knock me down behind the couch, his arms wrapped around me. Of course, a bullet could pass through the couch like it could pass through butter, but at least we were out of sight and mind.

A gun fired, and there were more screams—I was pretty sure Mary Nell's was one of them. When there was a little period of silence, we stuck our heads around the end of the couch.

"You can get up," Hollis said, his voice heavy and about a million years old. Tolliver straightened first and helped me up. My bad leg refused to lock for a minute, leaving me wobbly.

Paul Edwards was on his knees, clutching his shoulder. Behind him there was a dent in the wall, and pieces of glass glinted on the carpet. Mary Nell was standing as if she'd been turned into stone, glaring at Paul. Sybil was looking at her daughter.

"You dislocated my shoulder," Paul wheezed, "you little bitch."

"I hit him," Mary Nell said in a disconcertingly childish voice. "I threw the glass apple and hit him."

"Were you trying to hit him in the head?" Hollis asked. "I wish you'd aimed higher."

Horribly, she laughed.

"Why don't you shoot me, Hollis?" Sybil's voice was deep and throbbing. "Come on, you know you want to. I'd rather you shot me now than go through a trial and sentencing."

"You're the selfish bitch," Hollis said. "Sure. I'm going to shoot you in front of your daughter. Hell of a way to give her another great memory, don't you think? Take a moment to think of someone besides yourself, why don't you?"

After a second, he said in a voice much closer to sane, "Tolliver, please call the sheriff's office." My brother patted his pocket. No cell. He slipped past the little group into the kitchen, and I could hear him punching buttons and speaking. The storm had stopped; the only traces of it were heard in the drip, drip, drip of water from the eaves.

I felt like I was looking at them through the wrong end of the telescope. These four miserable people. They looked far away, small, but clear-cut in their distress.

"Everything's lost, for you," I said to Paul Edwards. His eyes widened as he looked at me. "I'm not sorry. Besides all the other, more horrible things you've done, you had my brother thrown in jail—though you had a lot of help doing that. You shot at me in the cemetery, and I have to believe that was you all by yourself, right? Now, your life is over."

"What are you now, a seer?" Sybil said bitterly. "I wish I'd never asked you here, never tried to find out what happened to the girl."

"Then I'm glad you already paid me." It was all I could think of to say. She laughed, but not as if she really found it humorous. Her daughter was still looking from Sybil to Paul, from her mother to the man who'd been her mother's lover, and she looked sick and young and defenseless.

"You're going to be a great woman," I said to Mary Nell. She didn't look at me; I don't think she was any fonder of me at that moment than was her mother or Paul. Even as my brother came back in the room, we heard sirens approaching, and lights began to flash up and down the soaking suburban street.

"Why'd you do all that to me?" I asked Paul. "I don't understand."

"The baby," he said. "I never thought you'd find Teenie.

When you did, I was sure you knew about the baby. I thought if I kept you scared, you wouldn't figure it out."

But the baby had left no bones. If Paul had left us alone, we'd have departed Sarne without a second thought.

We didn't get away until perhaps three in the morning. We had to tell many, many people what we'd seen and heard. We were too wired to sleep for an hour after we got back to our room, but once we did, we slept until noon.

We had our bags in the car an hour later. We settled with the front desk, and the odious Vernon practically did the macarena when he found out we were really going. I felt empty, hollow; but I wanted to leave Sarne so badly I pushed myself to do all the right things toward that end. We got gas and swung by the police station as we'd been told.

Hollis was there again, or maybe was still there. Harvey Branscom's office was empty, the door wide open. I was sure he'd been having a terrible night and a bad day since his sister was in the pokey for murder. I studied Hollis's face. He looked somehow younger, as if the solving of his wife's death had erased a couple of years and some lines of tension.

"You all shoving off?" he asked.

"Yes," Tolliver said.

"We've got your numbers and your lawyer's address, just in case?"

"Yes," I said. I knew Hollis would never call my number.

"Okay, then. We appreciate all your help." He was trying to keep this as brisk and impersonal as possible. But I could see Tolliver bristling for my sake. I put my hand on his arm.

"No problem," I said. "No problem."

"Well, then."

We both nodded at him, and he gave us a curt nod back, and we went out the swinging glass doors for the last time, I hoped to God.

Tolliver was driving, and after we'd put on our seat belts and picked a radio station, he took the car through the streets of Sarne to the highway that would take us east.

"Think we could make Memphis before tonight?" I asked.

"I'm sure of it," he said. "Will you—are you okay with saying goodbye like that?"

"Yes. What's the point of a sentimental parting?"

He seemed to acknowledge this with a tilt of his head. "But you liked him."

"Yeah, sure. But, you know, it just wasn't meant to be."

"Someday . . ." he began, and let the idea trail off.

"You know what, Tolliver? You remember when we did *Romeo and Juliet* in high school?" We might have studied it years apart, but our high school stuck to its course of study religiously.

"Yeah. And?"

"There was that line that Mercutio says, when he gets killed in the feud between the Montagues and the Capulets. He says it in his dying speech. You remember?"

"No," he said. "Tell me."

"He says, 'A plague on both your houses.' And then he dies."

"'A plague on both your houses,'" Tolliver repeated. "That about sums it up."

I had a thought. "But of course, Paul Edwards had a foot in both houses—the Hopkins house and the Teague house."

"Somehow that seems like the right thing to say, anyway."

We were quiet for a minute. Then, as the last of Sarne fell behind us and we headed from the mountains to the delta, the flatlands that stretched on and on, I said, "You know, I keep thinking about Teenie, lying out there in the woods, all alone. No matter what happened, I did a good thing."

"Never doubt it. It was a good thing." He hesitated. "Do you think they know? When they've been found?"

"Oh, yes. They know," I said, and the miles to Memphis opened ahead of us.

Enjoyed this? Keep an eye out for more great
Gollancz Romancz titles:

*Dead as a Doornail* by Charlaine Harris
*Warprize* by Elizabeth Vaughan
*Rosa and the Veil of Gold* by Kim Wilkins